DEATHLESS

JEFF STRAND

Deathless © 2021 Jeff Strand

Cover art by Lynne Hansen
LynneHansenArt.com

For more information about the author, visit JeffStrand.com.

ISBN: 9798767029617

Dedicated to Tod Clark.
May the bodies buried under the Long Pig Saloon never be found.

PART I
BROKEN

CHAPTER ONE

I married the first girl I ever kissed. This left me ill-equipped to re-enter the dating scene as a damaged widower.

I'd met a beautiful, funny, and charming woman named Christine. I made it clear that I wasn't ready for a romantic relationship yet, and she said to take all the time I needed. What she actually meant was "you have six months to sort your shit out," at which point she told me it was time for us to go our separate ways.

I didn't want to lose her, so I put my arms around her and gave her a passionate kiss.

Then I started crying.

As you might guess, that pretty much ended it. I never saw Christine again, except outside of a movie theater a couple months later, where she was holding hands with a big burly guy who might as well have been wearing a shirt that said, "No Emotional Baggage."

On my thirty-second birthday, which was about three years

after I buried my family, my friend Jeremy insisted that it was time for me to start dating again. He was extremely persistent. And he had plenty of opportunities to be persistent, because he was living in the apartment next to mine.

At least he wasn't living with me anymore. He'd gone to California to pursue a career in acting. One year, a couple of minor roles, and a heroin addiction later, I'd received a distraught phone call in the middle of the night, and drove from Tucson to Los Angeles to pick him up. He'd stayed at my place for several months, but when the apartment next door became available, we both agreed that our friendship would benefit from seeing less of each other.

"I have zero interest in dating," I told him.

"Why?"

"Just not interested."

"That's not an answer."

"Who would want me?"

"Lots of women would want you," said Jeremy. "It's not like you're ugly."

"I never said I was ugly." I was long past the point of being self-conscious about the large purple birthmark on my chin.

"You're nice. You've got a stable job. Every once in a while you say something witty. Sure, there are dark things in your past that would cause most women to run away screaming, but they aren't *all* going to run away screaming. If I can get laid, you can get laid."

"When did you get laid?"

"I meant hypothetically."

I wasn't sure how dating would even work for a guy like me. Should I parse out the revelations over multiple dates, or just spill everything at once in an avalanche of romance-killing confessions?

First of all, I still wasn't ready to take off my wedding band. So I'd immediately have to explain that I was not some scumbag cheating on his wife. And if she asked how Melanie died, I couldn't say "car accident" or "terminal illness" or some other answer where we could both acknowledge that it was very sad and then move on with the fun part of the date. Nope, Melanie had been murdered. Horribly.

I hadn't actually seen it happen, because I was chained up in another room. I wouldn't tell my date what they looked like when I finally got free and found their bodies. That was something I would never—*will* never—talk about.

"Their bodies?" my date asks. "Plural?"

Yes. My five-year-old daughter, Tracy Anne, had also been murdered.

Did I handle it well?

Do you mean apart from shoving a revolver in my mouth?

So now I'm the guy whose wife and young daughter were savagely murdered. Maybe my date drops the subject and we discuss whether or not we want to start with crab rangoon as an appetizer, or maybe she wants to delve further, see what kind of scary issues I've got going on because of my experience.

Did I know the person who did it? Oh, hell yeah.

Darren Rust. I met him when I was twelve, when we were both at Branford Academy boarding school. That's also where I met Jeremy, and our other friend Peter. The four of us shared a room. Darren was a rotten little creep back then, but when our paths crossed again in college, he seemed to be a completely different person. We became friends.

And then…we very much *stopped* being friends.

Nobody is going to say, "Why, I'd never date a man whose wife and daughter died ghastly deaths!" Maybe they'd even think they could fix me. Bring some happiness and emotional stability into my life. But the next revelation is the big one.

I'd murdered an innocent woman. A mother.

I had to do it. Darren forced me. By doing it, I stopped him from killing a little girl, so, really, it was almost like I was a great big goddamn hero. Superman could stop a runaway train with his amazing strength; I could chop off a woman's head with a hatchet.

"I had no choice," I explain, as my date decides that she isn't hungry for crab rangoon anymore.

"It was at least quick, though, right?" my date asks, if she hasn't already fled. "One swing of the axe? No suffering?"

"Oh, sure, sure, her head popped off really quickly," I lie. "There was barely even any blood."

So, yeah, my reluctance to date wasn't about my birthmark.

Jeremy had fared much better with the whole Darren Rust thing. Yes, Darren had gotten him expelled from Branford Academy, but that was when we were twelve, and there was really no long-term trauma from that because Branford Academy sucked. Jeremy had helped me out when I decided that it was time to take the initiative in dealing with my Darren problem, so he basically got the feeling of satisfaction that came from assisting in the capture of a killer, without the dead family or the forced murder to taint the experience.

"That stuff is all a matter of public record," Jeremy told me. "They'd probably know about it anyway."

He made this point every time he urged me to be more social. But honestly, I was surprised how many people *didn't* know who I was. They knew of Darren but not his victims. I could go grocery shopping or see a movie quite easily without anybody saying, "Hey, aren't you that guy…?" And I was extremely relieved about that.

I had a very uninteresting desk job that involved studying numbers all day. In a previous life, this type of job had been a source of intense frustration. Now, honestly, I was happy for the lack of excitement. I could keep my head down—not literally, since

I had to stare at a computer screen—do my work, and have very little human contact except for weekly meetings, where I sat in the back and contributed nothing.

I was lucky to have a job at all. In addition to my wife and daughter, Darren had murdered my previous boss. It was the kind of thing that made the "So why did you leave your last place of employment?" question during a job interview quite awkward. I was more than qualified, but it took forever to find a place that would hire me.

"Anyway," said Jeremy, "when you *are* ready to go barhopping with me, let me know. I'll be your wingman."

"I'll definitely let you know. What are your plans for tonight?"

"Probably watch YouTube videos until I pass out."

"Sounds like an evening well-spent."

"Can you imagine how much easier it would've been if we had YouTube three years ago?"

"We did. It just wasn't popular yet."

"Can you imagine how much easier it would've been if YouTube was popular three years ago?"

Jeremy and I had made a video to attract Darren's attention, but instead of recording it on a cell phone and making it available to the entire world within seconds, we'd made copies and mailed them to news outlets, hoping they'd show it on the air. It had been a very inconvenient and uncertain way to lure a psychopath out of hiding, but it worked.

After taking a couple of beers out of my refrigerator, Jeremy went back to his own apartment. I checked my voice mail.

"*Hi, Alex, it's Tiffany Russo. Guess who's in town this weekend for a film festival? Any chance you'll let me take you out to dinner? Give me a call, thanks!*"

I sighed.

I considered simply ignoring her message, but Tiffany was extremely persistent and she'd be calling me every hour until she flew back to New York City. So I called her back.

"Alex! Hi!" she said. "I didn't think I'd hear from you!"

"The answer is no," I told her.

"What if I said it was just dinner?"

"Then you'd be lying."

"You're right, I would," Tiffany admitted. "But what if I took you someplace great? Anywhere you want. You get a free dinner, and all you have to do is listen to my pitch. I'll even set a timer, so it's five minutes of business, and the rest of the time we can talk about whatever you want."

"I'd be taking advantage of you. I have absolutely no intention of saying yes. I'd be using you to get a free meal."

"So use me."

"Let me be clear. Zero percent chance that I say yes to your pitch. *Zero* percent. And I'm going to pick someplace expensive. If you're cool with me scamming you, I'm in."

"I'm totally cool with that. Are you available tonight?"

Friday night with no advance notice? Yes, I was available. Just as I would be any other night of the week. "Sure."

"Seven o'clock?"

It was six o'clock now. Enough time to take my dog for a walk, change out of my work clothes, and drive across town for overpriced Mexican food. "Sounds good."

C——.

TIFFANY WAS ALREADY THERE when I arrived. She sat at a corner booth, a bowl of tortilla chips in front of her, looking at a menu. She was a stunning redhead, a few years older than me, wearing a fancy black dress that revealed nothing. I assumed she was dressed up for the film festival and not for me.

"This isn't all *that* expensive," she said, as I slid into the booth.

"I took mercy on you."

"Margarita?"

"Yes, please."

The server came over to take our drink orders, then left.

"What's your pitch?" I asked.

"Can I get you drunk first?"

"There's not enough alcohol in the world to make me say yes."

"I don't understand why you're so reluctant," she said. "Why wouldn't you want to tell your side of the story?"

Tiffany was a documentary filmmaker. Her first feature had been about a nine-year-old who'd gone missing three decades ago, making a very strong case that his teacher—who died of natural causes a few years after the disappearance—was the culprit. It won a crapload of awards and aired on HBO. Her latest project, which she'd started working on several months ago, was about Darren Rust.

I didn't want to be part of any documentary about him. She'd contacted me, Jeremy, and Peter, and the three of us had made a pact to decline to participate. My hope was that if she couldn't get the core interviews she needed, she'd move on to a different project. So far, she hadn't.

"I told my side of the story during the trial," I said.

"There were no cameras allowed in the courtroom."

"And I'm glad about that. I don't *want* people talking about what happened. I don't want your documentary to suddenly remind the world about the hell I went through. I want it all to go away."

"This could be your final word on it, though."

"No, it would be your final word. I can't control how you edit me."

9

JEFF STRAND

"I'll be fair."

"You had re-enactments in your other movie. It makes me sick to think of actors recreating that stuff."

"Well, they're going to be in there either way. I'm still making the film. I just feel like you'll be a lot happier with the final product if you and your friends agree to be interviewed."

I grabbed a chip from the bowl, dipped it in salsa, and took a bite. It was kind of stale. Surprising—this place was usually really good. "We've already had this discussion. More than once. This isn't why you wanted to buy me dinner, is it?"

Tiffany shook her head. "You have to promise not to make a scene."

"Define 'making a scene.'"

"You can't shout at me or knock anything off the table."

"I promise."

"Darren would like to apologize to you, on camera."

"Are you out of your fucking mind?" I asked, not shouting.

"Hear me out. He would be restrained on the other side of the table. Guards would be present the entire time. You would be completely safe."

"I'm not worried about my safety."

"It's the chance for you two to find resolution."

"No, no, no, I already found resolution. I found it when I shattered a bunch of his teeth, and cut off his middle finger, and decided not to shoot him in the face. I even gave a nice little speech. And now that asshole is in a maximum-security prison for the rest of his life and I don't ever have to see him again. That's all the resolution I need. If *he* needs resolution, he's not going to get it from me."

"I'm not asking you to forgive him. But how bad would it be to listen to his apology?"

I wanted to knock the bowl of chips off the table, but I'd

10

promised to behave. "If he tried to make up with me, I'd bash his face against the table until there was nothing left of his skull to hold onto. The guards wouldn't be able to pull me off of him."

"This doesn't have to be a moment of healing between you two. Obviously, nobody's going to let you kill him, but it could be your chance to reject his apology. Set yourself free by telling him to his face what you still think of him."

"What were you thinking?" I asked. "Seriously, Tiffany, what were you thinking?"

"I thought you might want to talk to him."

"I don't even know what to say. It's like…I don't know…it's like somebody saying they don't want to try sushi, so you…" I was so angry that I was having difficulty articulating the comparison I was trying to make. "You say, okay, since you don't want sushi, instead of going to a restaurant, let's grab a raw fish out of the ocean and take a bite. That's what it's like." Yeah, I really botched that analogy, but I was angry and flustered.

"That's fair," said Tiffany. "And I think our five minutes is up. We can talk about whatever else you want."

"Nah, I'm done."

"I promised you dinner. You kept up your end of the bargain, so let's enjoy a nice meal."

I shook my head. "Not interested."

"Alex—"

"Go to hell." I slid out of the booth and walked toward the exit. I almost wanted her to come after me, so that I could scream at her to leave me alone, but she let me go.

When I got to my car, I dropped my keys on the ground. My hands were quivering.

I got inside my car and dropped the keys again when I tried to start the ignition.

It wasn't safe for me to drive right now. I needed to calm down.

I got out of the car and walked away from the parking lot, looking around for what else was in the area.

After a moment of indecision, I went into a bar.

CHAPTER TWO

I didn't belong in a bar.

It's not that I was an alcoholic—even in my darkest moments, that sort of thing never became a regular part of my life. A twelve-pack of beer in my fridge could last a month, unless Jeremy swiped them. But when I was in a bad place, mentally, a bar was not someplace I went for merry fun with my friends. It was a place I went to try to pulverize my bad feelings into oblivion. And it never worked.

But I was sure that wouldn't happen this time. I just needed a few minutes to regain my composure. I'd have a beer or two, no hard liquor. I'd keep my blood alcohol content well below the legal limit, and then I'd go home. Maybe I'd grab some Taco Bell drive-thru on the way, just to pretend that I'd had Mexican food for dinner.

I showed my ID to the guy at the door and walked inside. The bar was small but crowded, with music blasting at an ear-disintegrating volume. I glanced around and saw that I was the oldest person in there. This wasn't really what I was looking for. I wanted a quiet, sad bar.

Screw it. I was already there.

I walked up to the counter, waited about ten minutes to get the bartender's attention, shouted my order at him, and waited another ten minutes for him to hand me the bottle. All of the stools and booths were taken, so I walked over and leaned against the wall.

This wasn't going to calm me down. If anything, my nerves were more frayed now than they had been when I stormed out of the restaurant. I took a couple of drinks of my beer and decided to throw the rest away and leave. Maybe I'd go get ice cream or something.

A woman approached me. She looked like she was in her mid-twenties, though it was kind of difficult to tell for sure. Her face was vampire-pale, with blood-red lipstick and that raccoon-eyes makeup thing. She had straight black hair that hung over her shoulders, and was wearing black jeans and a black lace blouse. This bar had more of a "rich college kids" vibe and she didn't really seem to fit in.

She said something to me that I couldn't hear.

I shook my head and pointed to my ear.

She leaned in close. "Hi!" she shouted.

"Hi!" I shouted back.

The woman said something else that I couldn't hear. I shrugged and shook my head again, admitting defeat in my ability to carry on a conversation in this environment.

She reached into her purse and took out her phone. It was, at the time, a top-of-the-line model where you could slide the screen forward and reveal the tiny keyboard underneath. She typed with her long, red fingernails and held the phone up for me to see.

I can't hear a fucking thing. Do u want 2 go someplace quieter?

I definitely did. I didn't really want to leave the bar with a strange woman, but I did want to get out of there. So I nodded and followed her outside, tossing my bottle in the garbage on the way.

"That place sucks," she said.

"Not a regular?" I asked, because when you're as suave with the ladies as I am, you respond to "That place sucks" with "Not a regular?"

"Hell no. Not my kind of music. I was trying to find my friend, but I guess she didn't show up."

"Sorry to hear that."

"I'm not. I like you more than her already."

"Thanks."

"What's your name?"

"Alex."

"Do you want to know my name?"

"Sure. What's your name?"

"I'm Luna." She extended her hand. "Pleased to meet you, Alex."

I shook her hand. I wasn't sure what to say. Strange women being friendly to me was not the natural order of things.

"You didn't look like you were having a very good time in there," she said.

"I wasn't."

"Then why were you there?"

"I needed a drink. It was a bad night."

"Do you want to talk about it?"

"Not really," I said.

"That's fine. I can respect that. You don't know me well enough to share your problems. Where are you off to now, Alex?"

"Home, I guess."

"To your wife?"

I nervously fiddled with my wedding ring. "No."

"Are you separated?"

"No."

"Divorced?"

"No. She's…gone."

"Oh." She looked at the ground for a moment. "I'm sorry. I didn't mean to pry."

"No, it's okay. It was a long time ago."

"How long?"

"About three years."

"I'm sure it still hurts, though, right?"

"Oh, yeah."

"Can I ask how she died?"

I didn't feel like getting into the truth right now. "She drowned."

Drowned? Why had I said that she drowned? Now I was either going to have to make up some elaborate story about Melanie's death, or admit that I was a liar.

"I can tell that you don't want to talk about it," said Luna. "Look, Alex, I'm not trying to bother you. I'm not a hooker, and I'm not some desperate chick who's going to try to lure you back to my place to bang your brains out. If you want to hang out a little longer, that's cool, and if not, that's cool, too. You looked miserable in there and I thought you could use a friend."

"Yeah, I could, actually," I said.

"See? You look less angry already. Still want to go home?"

"Nah."

"Want to find a better place to get a drink?"

"I was thinking of getting ice cream."

"Ice cream is awesome," said Luna. "But so is art. Do you like art?"

"Yeah, I like some art. I'm not an art critic or anything. I mean, I don't *hate* art."

"I know a great little gallery. It's not close, but it's open late. I promise it's not the kind of art that looks like a three-year-old scribbled it. It's really impressive and quirky, and you can appreciate it without thinking about themes and symbolism and stuff."

Going to an art gallery is not at all how I'd expected to spend my evening, but why not? "Count me in."

Luna smiled. "We have to drive separately, because it would be a pain for me to come all the way back here to get my car, and I don't know yet if you're a crazed killer. Do you think you can follow me without losing me, or should I give you the address?"

"You should probably give me the address," I admitted.

"Okay. Don't chicken out and go home instead. I promise it'll be worth it."

C—

WHAT THE HELL are you doing? I wondered.

I was going to an art gallery with a woman who seemed very friendly. No big deal. It wasn't like I was going back to her sex dungeon. This was how things worked. People met each other, hit it off, and decided to spend more time together. I met Melanie when she accidentally bashed me in the stomach with a bag of books.

This was safe. It was totally fine. I had to get over the idea that I was betraying Melanie's memory.

And it would get Jeremy off my back for a while.

Not to mention that art galleries were culture. Culture was good, right?

C—

THE ART GALLERY was extremely small, almost claustrophobic. Everything veered toward surrealism. Was that supposed to be an octopus? A crown? A crown made out of an octopus?

After we finished admiring the weirdness, we got to the "tell each other about ourselves" part of the conversation. Luna was relentlessly suggestive, and despite her earlier comment about not banging my brains out, I was almost positive that if I invited her to turn this into an overnight experience, she'd give me an enthusiastic yes. That wasn't going to happen, though. If I was going to move on with my romantic life, it wasn't going to start with a one-night stand.

Luna Booth was twenty-nine, a little older than she looked. She'd majored in elementary education in college, but discovered during her classroom visits that she didn't like young children as much as she'd thought. She'd then changed careers "pretty much every year," and was currently working as a receptionist at a large hair salon, a job that she expected to leave fairly soon.

We had very few common interests. I did not recognize a single one of her favorite musical groups, and though she recognized all of mine she did not approve of them. We didn't like any of the same movies or TV shows. We were both avid readers, but I read mostly novels and she read exclusively non-fiction.

I was truthful in everything I said. She didn't ask any further questions about Melanie, and when she asked if I had kids, I simply said "No." If I saw her again, I'd tell her the whole story, but for now I really didn't want to talk about the nightmares in my past.

Next to the art gallery was a doughnut shop, also open late.

Because I hadn't had dinner, one doughnut became two, and then three. I was starting to feel a little queasy.

"Damn, I'm a fat pig," Luna said, pulling up her shirt and patting her well-toned belly. Clearly, a three-doughnut dinner was a rare treat and not part of her usual dining habits.

"We're allowed to do this," I said. "We're grown-ups."

She looked me directly in the eye. "Yeah, we are. We're *adults*."

And in that moment, I wondered why I shouldn't just let this happen. I'd had some happy times over the past three years, but nothing that involved an attractive woman taking me back to her place for some adult activities. I was almost positive I could have sex with Luna without bawling before or during the act, and if I felt emotional distress afterward, I'd excuse myself and go home.

I felt weirdly fine with the idea.

Why not? Seriously, why not? It had been three years, for God's sake. It's not like I was flirting with somebody at the funeral reception.

I knew what Jeremy would tell me to do.

Melanie wouldn't want me to be alone forever.

Assuming that we practiced safe sex and didn't do anything that would get us arrested, there was absolutely no reason that I shouldn't—

No, I couldn't do it. Not tonight. Maybe if it was a one-nighter where we never saw each other again, I could get away with sleeping with her and not sharing any of my secrets, but if this turned into something more, I'd deeply regret having been intimate with her before I told her about that one time I chopped a woman's head off.

Maybe I was being ridiculous. Maybe I didn't owe her any revelations about my history. I didn't know how this all worked. I hadn't read any books about the etiquette in this situation. But I knew that I'd be wracked with guilt if I went home with her and later said, "Hey, have you heard of the psycho killer Darren Rust? We used to be besties."

I supposed I could tell her now, but I didn't want to ruin what had turned into a very pleasant evening.

"I'm not going to be able to eat a fourth one," I said.

"Me either. Look, Alex, I'm not exactly an introvert, as I think you've figured out, so I'm just going to come right out and say this. I like you and trust you. If you would like to continue this back at my place, I'm completely in favor of it."

It was a good thing I didn't have a bite of doughnut in my mouth, or I would've choked on it. "That's the best offer I've had in ages. I can't, though. Not this soon after we met. I need a little bit of time. Not a lot of time. Tomorrow might work. Just not tonight. It has nothing to do with you."

"Has there been anybody since your wife?" she asked.

"No."

"Then I completely understand. I don't want to scare you away. So we'll revisit this issue tomorrow?"

"Absolutely."

"Do you promise that you'll call me, even if it's to say that you're not interested? I'm a big girl and I can handle rejection, but don't ghost me."

"I won't ghost you."

"Okay, then. I'm at least going to make you hug me."

We stood up and hugged. God, she smelled great. Maybe I should—

No. This was the right thing to do.

We walked to our separate cars and I drove home. As I opened the door, Tucker, my beagle, came running over to greet me. Tucker's original name had been Killer Fang II, a tribute to my friend Peter's dog Killer Fang, but after a couple of weeks I'd decided that I was not the kind of person who would own a dog named Killer Fang II and formally changed it to Tucker. When I said that there'd been some happy times over the past three years, Tucker had been responsible for most of them.

Jeremy apparently heard me open the door to my apartment, because he knocked a minute later.

"So, what did she want?" he asked.

I told him about Tiffany's request and my reaction.

"And she actually thought you'd do that? For real?"

"Apparently so."

"She's deranged. Why are they letting deranged people make documentaries? How would Darren even phrase an apology? 'Hey, dude, sorry for the inconvenience.'"

"I don't give a shit how he'd phrase it."

"He'd probably just try to get inside your head."

"I don't want to talk about him."

"Where did you go after that?"

"What makes you think I went anywhere?" I asked.

"Ummm, I guess it's my knowledge of how time works."

"I have to take Tucker for a walk."

"I'll join you."

As I walked Tucker around the block, I gave Jeremy the full, unedited version of the evening's events. Not surprisingly, he expressed disapproval with my decision in the moral dilemma.

"You could've just called me. I would've walked your dog for you."

"It wasn't about that."

"You could be in her right now. I really don't understand you."

"I'm seeing her tomorrow. There's no rush."

"Well, I'm proud of you for not holding up a cross and trying to ward her off," said Jeremy. "At least you're one step in the right direction."

We waited for Tucker to do his business, then I scooped up after him like a responsible citizen. When I got back to my apartment, I still felt good about this evening. I wasn't necessarily envisioning Luna and I celebrating our fiftieth wedding anniversary, surrounded by a plethora of children and grandchildren, but why not pursue this and see what happened?

I'd forgotten to ask if she liked dogs. It would be a deal-breaker if she didn't.

I was going to call her tomorrow anyway, as promised, but it wouldn't be to tell her that I wasn't ready for a relationship. I'd invite her to lunch.

I took a shower and went to bed.

I woke up as my cell phone buzzed. It was 12:01 AM. I flipped open the case and saw a text message from Luna.

It's technically tomorrow. Just saying.

Screw it. I was going to go over there.

CHAPTER THREE

Her apartment was about twenty minutes away, during which time I spent fifteen seconds thinking this might be a mistake and the rest of the time almost giddy with excitement.

I did get a little nervous when I knocked. I heard footsteps inside, and as the door opened I half-expected her to be standing there in a bra and panties, or nothing at all, but she was wearing the same clothes from earlier.

I stepped inside and closed the door behind me.

There was very little ambiguity about what was going to happen next. She immediately put her arms around me and we kissed. I saw that her apartment had kind of a punk rock vibe, but she didn't give me a tour and there wasn't much time to take in my surroundings as she led me back to her bedroom.

"I need to tell you something," I said, as she took off her shirt.

"Do you have an STD?" she asked.

"No."

"Then I don't need to hear it."

"It's kind of important."

"Is it an actual emergency? Are we in physical danger right now?"

I shook my head. "Nothing like that."

"Then it can wait. Tell me later. I promise I won't hold it against you."

She kissed me and pulled off my shirt.

I wanted to offer a disclaimer, reminding her that I hadn't had sex in years and not to expect stunning endurance, but decided that this was a good time to shut the hell up.

Luna was not gentle. Slow lovemaking was not on the agenda here. This was wild animal stuff. I quickly realized that she was going to be the one to call the shots about positions and activities, so I happily let it happen.

We lay there afterward, me on my back with her snuggled up against me. I'd thought that this would be the part where guilt began to seep through me, but no, I was still pretty damn upbeat about the addition to this night's itinerary.

"I can't even explain how much I needed that," she said. "What'd you think?"

"That was unbelievable."

"Yeah?"

"Yeah."

She kissed my chest. "Just so you know, we can do whatever you want. Anything. Don't be embarrassed about asking. You won't be able to shock me. Nothing is off limits."

I wasn't sure how I should properly respond to this information. "I appreciate that."

"I know you think that means, hey, let's bring in another chick, and that's fine, but I'm dead serious about this. You can explore anything you want with me. No boundaries. No judgment."

"Well, that's, uh, very generous of you," I said, finding it difficult to talk because my mouth suddenly went dry. This was not the type of offer I'd ever received in the past. Right now I was still kind of in shock from the vigorous-but-vanilla sex I'd just had, and wasn't really thinking much further ahead.

"I expect you to take advantage of this," Luna said. "Don't disappoint me."

"I'll brainstorm some ideas."

"I'm sure you need some recovery time, so what is it you wanted to tell me?"

"It can wait."

"Why not tell me now? I'm not going anywhere."

"It'll spoil the mood."

"You won't be able to spoil the mood enough to stop me from attacking you again. It won't upset me. We all have skeletons in our closet. I swear to you, whatever it is, I won't get mad. I know you come with a history."

"I do. That's definitely true."

"Should I take a guess?" Luna asked.

"If you want."

"Is your wife still alive? Does she think you're pulling an all-nighter at work?"

"No, no, I'm not cheating on anyone."

"Then tell me."

"It's very dark."

"I'm totally into dark."

"I lied when I said that my wife had drowned. She was murdered. And my five-year-old daughter Tracy Anne was murdered, too. It wasn't during a robbery or anything like that. It was a psychopath named Darren. For a while, we were best friends. He thought he could turn me into somebody like him, and later he thought he saw the same potential in my daughter. He was wrong.

But he killed Melanie and Tracy and it was more horrible than you can imagine." That all came out in one breath.

"Oh my God," said Luna. "I'm so sorry you had to go through that."

This felt like a good place to stop, but no, I might as well tell her the part that had the highest risk of getting me kicked out of her bed. "Earlier than that, while we were still in college, he kidnapped me. Took me to this cabin. He had a woman and a little girl there. He made me play this game where I had to hunt down and murder the woman, or he'd torture the little girl to death."

Luna sucked in a deep breath. "What did you do?"

"I hunted down and murdered the woman."

"Jesus. Are we talking about Darren Rudd?"

I flinched. "Darren *Rust*. Yes. That's him."

"I remember hearing about it on the news. I didn't follow it that closely, but the details you mentioned stuck out. He's in prison now, right?"

"Yes."

"Think he'll ever get out?"

"Hell no. Life in prison with no chance of parole. He's there until he dies of natural causes, gets murdered, or kills himself. I'm fine with any of those."

"I completely understand why you didn't want to share this," said Luna. "But none of this was your fault. You saved that little girl's life, and I'm sure you sacrificed a lot of your sanity in the process. You could've gone to prison, too, even though you were forced to do it."

I nodded. "I lucked out. The little girl's dad was a very good lawyer."

"I promised you that I wouldn't get freaked out, and I meant that. I'm not gonna lie, it was a little more extreme than I was expecting, but it's over now. He's in prison and you're in bed with a naked woman. You win."

"That's a really good point."

"I think I'm going to be great for you, Alex. Other women might draw away from you after hearing this. I'm going to get closer. There is nothing you can't confess to me, all right? You can't scare me away."

"Thanks," I said. "But I'm fine."

"I don't believe you. You're not fine. I can tell from the way you told me the story that you're not fine. I'm not saying that I can fix you. Nobody can make you good as new. But I can make it a little better, I promise."

"You already did," I told her.

Luna smiled. "Here's what we're going to do. You're going to climb out of bed and get us each a bottle of water from my refrigerator. I need to hydrate. Then we're going to have sex again. And then you're going to tell me the whole story of you and Darren Rust, starting at the beginning."

"You don't want to hear that."

"I want to hear every last detail."

I liked the first two steps of her plan, so I got out of bed and retrieved the water. She gulped hers down, set the empty bottle on the nightstand, then immediately set to work getting me ready for our next session. It didn't require much effort.

I lasted quite a bit longer this time. Not in a way that would impress spectators, but not bad at all considering my sexual drought.

When we were done, I got her another bottle of water, and then she snuggled up against me again. "Tell me everything," she said. "I want the entire story. Start as early as you can."

"You mean, like, my birth?"

"If you want."

"I was kidding."

"I don't want the edited version. If I'm going to help you, I need to know it all. Everything."

"Are you sure you're not a psychiatrist?"

"I'm a friendly ear. I'm sure you've told this all before, to cops or lawyers or whatever, but I bet you've never told it to somebody as nice as me." She ran her tongue over the side of my neck.

"You're right about that."

"So let's hear it."

I didn't start from my birth. I started from when, on a dare, I tried to steal a box of condoms from a convenience store. That's why I got shipped off to boarding school. If that sounds like a pretty severe punishment for the infraction, especially considering that the shopkeeper didn't even press charges, I'm in total agreement. So was Luna. When she asked why my parents would do such a thing, I had to admit that they'd simply been looking for an excuse to get rid of me. Stolen condoms did the trick.

She asked a lot of questions as I told the story. What did the room I shared with Darren, Jeremy, and Peter look like? What kind of dog did Peter have? How did I feel when Darren told me that he wished he could kill a bird? Many of her questions were of the "How did you feel?" variety. And she seemed to want the full sensory experience.

I didn't think I was on the road to a clean bill of mental health, but honestly, it was refreshing to be able to share the story like this. No police or lawyers trying to find inconsistencies. No documentary filmmaker who'd try to give my nightmare as wide of an audience as possible. Just Luna, who hung on my every word. Maybe I was her little project, and she'd move on to another broken soul when she thought I was repaired.

Because of all the questions and requests for more detail, it took over two hours to tell her the entire story. If I excluded sleepless nights, this was the latest I'd stayed up in a very long time.

"Thank you for sharing all of that with me," said Luna. "Do you feel good about telling me?"

"Yes, I do, actually."

She gave me a deep kiss on the lips. "And now that we've gotten all of the unpleasantness out of the way, do you want to get back to the fun stuff?"

I'd kind of assumed that the sex part of the night was over, and that we'd just go to sleep at the end of my tale of misery. "I can't," I said.

"Technical difficulties? I'm very good at fixing those. *Very* talented."

"Oh, I completely believe you. It's just that, you know, I told you all about my wife and daughter being murdered. Not exactly pillow talk. It would feel wrong going straight from that to…the fun stuff."

"You're absolutely right," said Luna. "It's messed up that I didn't think of that. I may be a bad person."

"You're not a bad person."

"I know. That wasn't really me wallowing in self-loathing. But you're right and I apologize. That was extremely uncool. You're staying over, right?"

"If you'll let me."

"I insist. Do you have anywhere you need to be in the morning?"

"Nope. When we wake up, I'll call Jeremy to have him take my dog out."

"Then let's get some sleep and resume this in the morning."

⌒

On weekdays, I woke up when the alarm went off. On weekends, I woke up to Tucker's cold nose pressing against my face. On this fine Saturday morning, I woke up to Luna going down on me. I vastly preferred this new method and hoped to incorporate it into my routine going forward.

She pulled her mouth away. "Oh, good, you're up."

Luna climbed on top of me and we started the day off right.

"Here's what I propose we do," she said, when we were technically finished but she hadn't yet dismounted. "We order a pizza. Then we spend our whole day eating pizza, watching movies, and fucking."

"I approve of that plan," I said.

I didn't really want to keep Jeremy apprised of my whereabouts, but I also didn't want to return home to a dog who had no choice but to use the living room floor as his restroom, so I called and asked him to take Tucker for a walk, hoping he'd take the hint and not ask invasive questions.

Jeremy did not take the hint, but he was more mature about it than I would've expected. I didn't share any details, nor did I promise any in the future. He said that he would take Tucker out as many times as necessary, so I was welcome to spend the entire rest of the weekend in physical ecstasy.

Luna and I stuck to the plan. We watched bad movies, ate mediocre pizza, and had great sex. When we thought we were done with the lovemaking for a while, we took a shower together, but that led to shower sex.

I'd had worse days in my life.

"Staying over again?" she asked.

That sounded like a great idea. We weren't up as late this time, because we were both drained and exhausted, and we fell asleep in each other's arms, at least until I woke up with numb limbs and a desperate need to stretch.

Sunday was more of the same, except that we ordered Chinese food. And we actually made it through an entire movie without pausing it.

That evening, though, I knew I had to be a responsible adult and return home, since I had to go to work in the morning. There was the temptation to use up all of my vacation time and just spend the next two weeks here immersed in carnal activity. But I'd be dead by the end of it. And, in fact, one more day might send me to the hospital, so going home was also a wise safety precaution.

Before I left, Luna made me promise to call her, and also to introduce her to Jeremy very soon. I promised both.

Yes, that had been a delightful weekend. No complaints. Five stars out of five.

Was she my girlfriend? I wasn't sure. With Melanie, it had been a much more gradual courtship, and by the time we made love, there'd been no question of where we stood. With Luna, I kind of thought that I could find her with another guy and she'd say, "Oh, I'm sorry, is this a problem?"

When I got home, Tucker wasn't there. There was a flash of worry, but I'd save my concern for after I checked in with Jeremy. I knocked on his door. Tucker was on his couch, asleep.

"I didn't want you to be able to avoid me," Jeremy said.

"I wasn't going to avoid you."

"You might have, so I thought I should hold your dog hostage. How'd your date go? Since you were gone the entire weekend, I'm guessing that it went reasonably well."

"It did."

"And...?"

"And?"

"You're seriously going to hold out on me?"

"We got along really well. We ate a lot of doughnuts. Later,

31

there was some intercourse. I'm not sure what other details you need."

"So you didn't tell her about your history with Darren?"

"No, I did. I told her everything. Beginning to end."

Jeremy raised an eyebrow. "Really?"

"She wanted to know."

"Was this before or after the intercourse?"

"After the first time, before the next several."

"Wow. It didn't freak her out?"

"No," I said. "She was very understanding about it. She wants to help me try to work through it."

"I've tried to help you work through it."

"This is different."

"Well, yeah, I don't put out. So is this 'friends with benefits' territory, or do you think there's something there? Because it sounds like she's either a keeper, or you should be scared."

CHAPTER FOUR

My day at work was not nearly as enjoyable as my weekend in Luna's bed. We sent each other a ridiculous number of text messages, and since I was being charged thirty cents for each one, I was setting myself up for a very jarring experience when I opened my phone bill. My concern with fiscal responsibility was not enough to make me stop sending texts, though. If this continued, I'd have to switch to a service with an unlimited plan.

We decided that we didn't have to see each other *every* night, and that we'd reconnect on Tuesday. Then we changed our minds and after a quick shower I was on my way over to her place.

This time we didn't make it to her bedroom, using her living room sofa instead.

"Thank you," she said, when we were done.

"Thank *you*."

"I can't tell you how much these past few days have rejuvenated me. I thought my dry spell was going to kill me. I get that it wasn't anywhere near as long as yours, but I was seriously going to start humping people's legs if I didn't get some."

"How long was it?" I asked.

"Six months. Maybe seven. I had a bad breakup, so I swore off men, and then I un-swore off men, but then I couldn't find anybody. I trust my first instincts. With my ex, my initial impression was that he was kind of a jerk, but he managed to win me over, and then I finally realized that, yeah, he was a jerk. I saw you and could tell immediately that you had a kind heart, but also an emptiness. I thought you could use me in your life."

"You were absolutely right. In what way was your ex a jerk?"

Luna smiled. "I'm the one who's supposed to be asking the personal invasive questions."

"So it was really bad?"

She shook her head. "Nah. He didn't hit me or anything like that. Didn't even cheat on me, as far as I know. Just your standard issue asshole." She didn't seem to want to talk about it beyond that, and I decided not to push the subject. If an angry jealous boyfriend burst into her apartment with a shotgun...well, I'd faced worse threats.

We got dressed. Because Luna only ate junk food on weekends, we sat at her dining room table and enjoyed some sliced apples. We did not try to eat them erotically—we just ate them like regular apple slices.

We returned to the couch and snuggled while we watched a PBS documentary about radio in the 1940s.

Then she took off her shirt and bra and tossed them on the floor. "Is it all right if we get back to some personal questions?" she asked.

"You have more to say about your ex-boyfriend?"

"Nope. I'm the asker."

"Okay."

"I want to delve a little deeper into when you were in college. The night Darren invited you over to his dorm room and he had a girl there."

Ah, yes. He'd called and told me to come over as soon as possible. When I arrived, there was a barely dressed woman on his bed, drunk off her ass and stoned to the point where she didn't seem to even know where she was. Darren had offered me the opportunity to lose my virginity right then and there, explaining that though she'd expressed a willingness to do both of us at the same time, he would let me have her to myself if I wanted.

I had, of course, declined.

"What about that night?" I asked.

"Do you regret walking out of the room?"

Her question surprised me. This had not been a moment where I was frozen with indecision. I hadn't started to go through with it and then thought, *"No, wait, I can't do this—it's wrong!"* I had told Darren in no uncertain terms that there was no way in hell I was going to do that. I hadn't made up a lame excuse for why I needed to leave. I'd said no, absolutely not.

"No," I said. "Not at all."

"Not even a lingering speck of regret? Most guys don't turn down the opportunity to have sex for the very first time."

"Not even a lingering speck. Like I'd told you, I was already seeing Melanie then. I had a much better first-time experience not very long after that."

"Okay. So you never even thought about you and Darren sharing her?"

"Never."

"We're not talking anymore about whether or not you regretted it. I'm asking if you thought about what the experience would've been like. If you had a mental image of it happening."

"No."

"I call bullshit."

"Maybe I didn't set the scene well enough for you when I told you about it last time," I said. "She looked like he'd found her passed out on a bathroom floor and dragged her to his room. It basically would've been rape. My regret is that after I said no and left, I didn't call the police. He could've really hurt her. He could've killed her."

"How do you know he didn't?"

"I don't." Darren had apologized the next morning and told me that he sent her away without touching her. I'd taken him at his word. Since then, there'd been occasional moments where I wondered if he was lying, but since I was driven near to the brink of madness with guilt over bad things that I knew *for sure* had happened, I couldn't really worry about the fate of a girl who might have just woken up with a hangover. If anything, I didn't think Darren could have snuck a human corpse out of his dorm room and off campus.

"I'm not saying that you're kicking yourself for not having gone through with it," said Luna. "I'm saying that I don't believe that you didn't think about how it would have happened. How it would have played out with you and Darren both on the bed with her. It doesn't sound like she would've put up a fight over anything you wanted to do."

"Well, yeah, because she'd been drugged."

"Ignore that part. You didn't think at all, not for one second, about the two of you sharing her? Not a single flash of a mental image popped into your mind?"

"No," I said. "I was horrified."

"Again, I'm not saying that you were thinking about how hot it would've been. I'm asking, horrified or not, if you had a picture in your brain about it happening. I don't mean some detailed fantasy. I mean an image."

"No."

"I don't believe you."

"Sorry."

"Do you have one now?"

"Nope."

"We're talking about it. How can you not?"

"Because it's awful."

Luna sighed. "Alex, I can't help you if you don't work with me. You have to be completely honest. I promise you'll feel better."

"I don't know what you're hoping I'll say. I was repulsed by the whole thing. I wasn't wondering what it would be like; I was wondering what the hell Darren was thinking by even suggesting it. Which is the same thing I'm wondering about you right now. How is this going to make me feel better?"

"You have to trust me."

"I trust you. But I'm answering you truthfully. I didn't think about it."

For an instant—so quick that I thought I might have imagined it—Luna looked angry. Then she shrugged and smiled. "Okay, then. Would you do me a favor?"

"Of course."

"Will you think about it now?" This was accomplished by just the slightest twist of her torso, as if to emphasize that she was bare breasted.

"I guess."

"I'm going somewhere with this, I swear."

"I believe you," I said, though I wasn't sure that I really did.

"I want you to close your eyes. This isn't hypnosis or anything, but I want to take you back to that evening."

If Luna wasn't a beautiful topless woman with whom I'd been having outstandingly satisfying sex all weekend, I would have said no, that this was too messed up. Instead, I closed my eyes, though I wasn't going to let this get too weird.

"Imagine the hallway in his dorm."

"Okay."

"Are you picturing it?"

"Yes."

"Describe it."

"It was a regular dorm hallway. There would've been fliers all over the wall, printed on different colors of paper. It was an all-boys dorm, so it smelled bad."

"You're speaking in past tense," said Luna. "Speak in present tense."

"It smells bad."

"What color is the carpet?"

"I don't remember."

"What color do you think it was?"

"Probably tan. With a lot of stains."

"Knock on Darren's door."

I didn't actually envision myself knocking on Darren's door, but to play along I said, "Okay."

"The door swings open."

"All right."

"Darren is standing there."

"Okay."

"What's he wearing?"

"I don't remember."

"Think."

"I have no memory of that kind of thing. I couldn't even tell you what clothes I wore yesterday. It probably would have been jeans and a T-shirt."

"Walk into his room."

"Okay."

"There's a girl on his bed."

"Okay."

"It's the same girl, but she's not drunk. Her hair is neatly combed. Her makeup looks like she just finished applying it. She's alert. Completely aware of her surroundings. And she wants to be there. She's in black lace panties that don't cover much, and her bra is sliding off in the front. She smiles at you. Winks."

"So…not at all the way it really happened," I said.

"Right. This is a much better version. She's gorgeous. She does all the talking. She says that Darren told her all about you, and she's the one who asked him to call you over. She tells you that she likes what she sees."

I opened my eyes. "I hate to say it, but this is seriously cheesy."

Another flash of anger. "Do you want my help or not?"

"I don't see how this is going to help."

She folded her arms across her chest. "Could you at least respect me enough to trust that I know what I'm doing? Is it really that hard to go along with this?"

Were we having our first fight? Already?

The answer was: *yes, it really is that hard to go along with this, because although this particular incident was not as traumatizing as some of the others, it was one step along the path to pure horror.* I could not see any possible benefit to doing a revisionist history makeover where Darren and I double-teamed a hot chick in his dorm room.

"You get why I'd have a problem with this, right?" I asked.

"Yes. That's why I'm trying to solve that problem."

"Are you trying to give me new memories? So that when I think about what happened, I remember it as something out of a letter to *Penthouse*? *'Dear Penthouse, I never believed this sort of thing could ever happen to me, so imagine my surprise when my best buddy Darren called me over to his room that evening…'*"

"If you're going to be sarcastic, you're welcome to leave. Take this seriously. After all I've done for you, you can humor me with this one thing."

I was almost tempted to get up and walk out. But though her little experiment was kind of creeping me out, it was not creeping me out to the extent that I wanted to forfeit a night of sexual escapades. Maybe she really *was* going somewhere with this, though I couldn't imagine where.

"All right," I said. "I'll behave."

"Close your eyes."

I closed them. I felt her lean over me, and then her nipples brushed across my chest. One of them slid over my lips, and then she leaned back again.

"She tells you that she likes what she sees," Luna repeated. "And then she reaches out her hands, one to you, and one to Darren. She's almost glowing."

This detail actually conjured up a mental image of the woman glowing as if she'd fallen into a vat of nuclear waste, but I didn't share this with Luna and I forced myself not to smile.

"You both join her on the bed. Where do you kiss her first?"

Fine. I'd play along with this ridiculous game. "Her neck."

"Her neck. Perfect. Where does Darren kiss her?"

"I guess the other side of her neck."

"Don't say 'I guess.' Just give me an answer."

"The other side of her neck."

"I like that. Which of you two would be more likely to unfasten her bra strap?"

"Definitely Darren."

"Darren unfastens her bra strap. It falls away. You have never seen such perfect tits."

"Better than yours?"

"You wouldn't have met me yet."

I opened my eyes. "Still..."

"Keep your eyes closed until I tell you to open them."

"Sorry." I closed my eyes again.

"Darren takes your hand and puts it on her breast. How does it feel?"

"Good."

"Give me more than that."

"It's firm. Natural." I wanted to ask if Darren had removed his goddamn hand yet, but if I spoiled the mood again I was sure Luna would send me home.

Luna ran her finger across my forehead. "You're sweating a bit."

"Yeah." She must've thought it was the perspiration of somebody who was really getting into the experience, though it was really oh-God-this-is-so-uncomfortable sweat.

"She turns her head toward you. Asks you to kiss her."

"I kiss her."

Were we really going to talk our way through a hypothetical sex scene? By the time the imaginary three of us were naked, it was clear that yes, we certainly were. I got better at it as we went along, once I figured out that the trick was to not think of Darren or the actual girl who'd been in his dorm. I replaced them with stand-ins, whose faces I couldn't see in my mind, but who had the bodies of people who spent six hours a day at the gym.

When the girl got on all fours, Luna asked which end I took. I told her that I started in the front.

Luna unzipped my pants.

I kept my eyes closed, but it wasn't easy not to peek as she tugged them down. I raised up to make it easier for her, although I wasn't feeling the urge right now.

"Keep talking," she said, as she took me into her mouth.

I talked her through the process of enjoying what was happening up front for a while, and then trading ends. The imaginary Alex was rock-hard and thrusting into her like a porn star, while in real life absolutely nothing was working down there.

It was more difficult without Luna guiding the conversation.

After a couple of minutes she pulled away from me. "How close is Darren to coming?" she asked.

"Very close."

"Can he take it any longer?"

"No."

"What does he do? Tell me." She was breathing heavy.

"He...he grabs a handful of her hair, and finishes in her mouth."

I heard movement that seemed to be Luna taking her pants off.

"How much is there?" she asked.

From a purely logistical standpoint, from my perspective I would not be able to see how much there was, unless the girl had a transparent head. But we'd gone through this whole deranged scenario, so I might as well give her an answer she wanted to hear. "There's so much. It's actually dribbling out of the corners of her mouth."

"Yeah, it is," said Luna. "Open your eyes."

I did. She was completely naked.

"I need you to fuck me as hard as you can."

"I..." It simply wasn't going to happen. Not a chance. I was out of commission for the night.

"It's okay." Luna put her hand between her legs and went to work on herself. It didn't take long at all. Seconds. When she finished, her whole body arched, and she let out a cry that was louder than any release she'd experienced from my efforts.

She immediately went for a second one. That didn't take long, either.

Then she lay there, gasping for breath. I just watched her, unsure what I should be doing.

She closed her eyes, and I genuinely believed she might go to sleep. But she finally opened them again and sat up.

"That was nice," she said.

"It's not quite what I thought we'd be doing this evening."

"What I did is take a horrible memory and replace it with a much better one. Now when you think about it, you'll think about this, not what really happened."

I didn't argue, even though I wasn't at all convinced that this was true, and replacing it with a memory of me sitting there, limp and embarrassed, was not all that much of an improvement. This was some truly strange therapy.

And I wondered what would've happened if we covered the full story of what had happened that evening. Because Darren had also offered to let me hit the girl, if I wanted.

CHAPTER FIVE

I didn't really want to spend the night, but Luna knew I'd brought my work clothes for tomorrow and arranged for Jeremy to take care of Tucker. So unless I intended to actually break up with her, I either had to stay over or come up with an excuse about why I needed to head back home.

I decided that I'd stay.

If I was looking for warning signs to indicate that this might not be the healthiest relationship in human history, I'd just seen a great big shiny bright red flag. I wanted to give her the benefit of the doubt and agree that, yes, this had all been for my benefit. But unless her sexual arousal had been completely faked, it was hard to imagine that her intention had legitimately been to reimagine the previous experience as something more appealing. I couldn't imagine a professional psychologist signing off on this technique.

We'd gotten dressed and were eating hummus and pita chips. The easiest thing to do would've been to pretend that this hadn't bothered me very much. Tell her that I understood what she was trying to accomplish, and hey, maybe I'd find out later that it had actually worked!

If my plan was to enjoy a brief sexual relationship with her and then move on, that was the way to go. Lie and say everything was cool. If I intended for us to stay together for a while, we needed to work this out and make sure it never happened again.

I was no fan of confrontation, so I was tempted to wait until tomorrow, but, no, I'd talk to her now.

"I really didn't like that," I said. "Not at all."

"Sorry." Luna didn't sound sorry.

"I need more than an apology. I need you to swear that you won't repeat that kind of thing, no matter what. I understand your intention, and I know your heart was in the right place, but it was absolutely not okay. Not at all. It cannot happen again. All right?"

"I think you need to calm down," Luna said.

"I'm calm. I'm speaking calmly. I'm not yelling. I'm just trying to be as clear as I possibly can so that there's no misunderstanding."

"All right. I messed up. I thought it would be good for you. We'd start there and work through the whole long series of events. By the end, you'd have replaced every horrible memory with a better version. And then you could finally move on with your life and be happy."

"It doesn't work like that, though," I said. "Unless we're in some science fiction movie where you implant new memories directly into my brain, what you're trying to do has no basis in reality. Making up some sexual fantasy about Darren is *not* going to get me over this. It just adds a big blast of weirdness into my life when I'm trying to keep everything normal."

Luna bit her lip and looked like she might start to cry. I didn't get the sense that she cried very often.

"I'm really sorry, Alex," she said. "It all made sense to me when I planned it out, and I thought it was working great, but it looks like I was completely wrong, and I apologize." She reached out and put both of her hands on the side of my face, emphasizing that she was looking me directly in the eyes. "It will never happen again, I promise."

"Thank you."

She lowered her hands and smiled. "You know what we should do right now? We should have a serious, uncomfortable discussion about our relationship. How does that sound? It sounds like fun, right?"

"Oh, it sounds delightful."

"Unless you want to start, I'll go first."

"Go for it."

"I like you a lot, Alex. And I'm pretty sure you like me. But I don't get the sense that you hear angels singing when you look at me, or that you're envisioning us in the nursing home together."

She paused long enough that it became awkward. Was she waiting for me to speak? I wasn't sure where she was going with this.

"I'm totally fine with that," she finally said. "I'm not going to make you put a ring on my finger. I'm not going to make you write me love poems, or serenade me, or buy me flowers, or anything like that. I'm very happy with what we've got, where we're good friends who enjoy each other's company. We have somebody to hang out with, and we get laid a lot. I'm more than willing to let this continue for as long as we both want, and I won't ask you to take it any further."

I've had plenty of reason in my life to be paranoid, and I wondered if this was a test. Or maybe "trap" was a better word. As somebody who'd had exactly one prior relationship, the idea of a woman saying "Let's just continue to have a sexual relationship and I'm not going to ask for any kind of a commitment" felt more like a frat boy fantasy than something that would actually be proposed to me.

She was right, though. I liked her a lot, but I wasn't naming our grandkids.

As long as she didn't repeat tonight's insanity…well, we had a fun thing going, right?

"Maybe we'll just see where it all leads," I said.

Luna shook her head. "No. That sets expectations. I'm proposing that we agree that it *isn't* going anywhere, and just enjoy it for what it is. Ride it out for as long as we want. Nobody gets hurt."

I hated to admit it, but this sounded like a pretty good deal.

Would I be a jerk for going along with this? I had pretty traditional views about courtship. But she was right—if nobody got hurt, why not?

"Okay," I said. "I'm all for it if you are."

"Perfect." She gave me a quick kiss on the lips. "But I've got some rules."

"Let's hear them."

"You don't get to hide me away. I'm not saying that you have to take me home to meet Mom and Dad, but I still want to come over and meet Jeremy and Tucker."

"That can be arranged. Jeremy will embarrass me, but it can be arranged."

"Next rule. You can be with anybody you want, but you have to tell me about it. No secrets. If you meet some hot chick at a bowling alley and take her back to your place, I won't be jealous at all, but you can't sneak around. Full disclosure."

"That's fair," I said. "When would I let you know?"

"After the condom is on, right before you slide in, you have to send me a text message. No, I'm kidding. You can tell me after the fact, but you have to tell me. No secrets."

"No secrets. Got it. What else?"

"I think I've already said this one. Don't ghost me. If you're done with us being together, tell me. You don't have to do it in person or even call me, but you at least have to send me an e-mail. I don't think that's unreasonable."

"Not at all. I promise I won't be a coward and ghost you."

"Well, then, I think we've officially set the parameters for our ongoing relationship," said Luna. "Do you want to fuck?"

"I do, actually."

"Then let's get right to it."

⌒⟶

I GOT VERY LITTLE SLEEP, I was late to work the next morning, and I was so chafed that I was pretty sure I'd need a couple days of healing before I could perform again. Luna, who was even more chafed, agreed that we should give ourselves time to recover so that we didn't risk permanent injury.

We decided that she was going to come over to my apartment Friday night, and Jeremy would join us for dinner.

"Do you want me to cook?" Jeremy asked.

"Why would I want you to cook? What have you ever cooked that I would serve to a guest?"

Jeremy shrugged. "I was just trying to be nice."

"You're thirty-two years old and I've watched you have a big bowl of instant mashed potatoes for dinner."

"Are you going to cook?"

"Hell no. I never promised her a home-cooked meal. We'll order something. The point is that she wants to meet you."

"Why? I'm really mediocre."

"Behave yourself when she's here."

"I will. I swear the phrase 'fuck buddy' will never pass my lips."

I'd told Jeremy that part. I hadn't told him about her psychological experiment, because I didn't really want to hear his opinion. I wasn't sure how he'd feel about it. The options were "Don't give up this exquisite sex, but watch yourself," or "Run, Alex, run!" I didn't want to run, so I didn't want him to give me that advice. Ultimately, it was none of his business.

I was also a bit worried that if I told him the entire story he'd think that Luna was just really into the idea of having two guys at once, and that was *not* a scenario I wanted in his head when we were having dinner together.

When Luna showed up on Friday night, she looked positively radiant in a red dress, and I felt horrifically underdressed, having assured Jeremy that our regular slob clothes were fine. She laughed it off. I also felt like we should be dining upon something fancy, instead of lasagna and garlic bread sticks.

Credit where it's due: Jeremy was indeed on his best behavior. He was polite, charming, witty, and his table manners were much better than usual. (I'm not saying that he was the kind of person who would eat lasagna with his bare hands, but he didn't belch even once.) He and Luna got along great, laughing at each other's jokes and seeming to genuinely enjoy each other's company, though not so much that I thought she might try to invite herself over to his apartment when we were done.

After dinner, we just sat around and talked for a couple of hours. Jeremy told the tale of his ill-fated time in Los Angeles, and Luna told some stories I hadn't yet heard about her childhood in Portland. The subject of Darren Rust never came up.

Luna loved Tucker, and Tucker loved Luna. Admittedly, Tucker loved everybody.

Finally, Jeremy yawned (Real yawn? Fake yawn? I didn't know) and said it was time for him to head off and that it had been wonderful to get to finally meet Luna. Luna said it had been equally wonderful to finally meet him. They hugged, and Jeremy left.

"He's great," Luna said. "You're lucky to have a friend like that."

"You were seeing him at his best, but yeah, I really am."

"I really enjoyed this. Hopefully we'll do it again sometime."

"You're welcome here whenever you want, and he's right next door, so I'm pretty sure we will."

"How thin are your walls?" she asked.

"Not too bad."

"Do we need to be quiet? I don't want it to be weird for him to hear us."

"We should maybe keep the volume down, yeah."

"Do you want to do dishes first, or get naked?"

"Maybe we should do the dishes naked."

Luna smiled. "Do you really want to be naked while I'm washing knives?"

"Was that a 'cut my dick off' joke?"

"It was. Just a joke, though. I prefer it attached."

"Let's get naked. The dishes can wait."

ONCE AGAIN I was late to work. This time my boss called me into his office and asked if there was something going on that he needed to know about. We did not have the kind of boss/employee relationship where I could admit that I was late because my fuck buddy refused to remove the handcuffs in a timely manner, so I simply apologized and assured him that I'd be on time from now on.

For a couple of weeks, my life was honestly pretty damn good.

After our third dinner with Jeremy, he'd gone back to his apartment. Luna accompanied me while I took Tucker on his evening walk, and then we went back inside and sat down on the couch. She offered me a foot rub, which I gratefully accepted. Melanie had what she called "an anti-foot fetish," so foot rubs had never been part of my life until now.

"Feel good?" she asked, rubbing the lotion into the bottom of my left foot.

"God, yes."

"So how bad would it be if we talked about Darren again?"

"Why would we want to do that?"

"I swore to you that what happened the last time would never happen again, and I'm keeping that promise. I still think you have very definite unresolved issues about him, and I believe we can make it a little better."

This had no appeal whatsoever, but I'd give her a chance. "What did you have in mind?"

"Just talk about him. Nothing intense."

"He's basically my least favorite subject in the world. Tell me what you're thinking."

"What was he like?"

"We already covered this."

"No," Luna said. "We talked about what happened. We didn't talk about what he was *like*."

"He was like a criminally insane piece of shit."

"But he had charisma, right?"

"I guess."

"Tell me about that."

"When do you mean? When he was twelve? He actually had no charisma back then. He was just a creepy little kid."

"When he was eighteen."

"He could be very likable when he wasn't being a manipulative psychopath."

"Tell me more about that. What made him likable? What made him charismatic?"

"No," I said. "I'm not going to do this. I'm not at all interested in analyzing his good qualities."

"All right, okay, I completely get it and I won't push any further. We won't talk about him any more tonight. I haven't earned your trust yet. Maybe I will someday, or maybe I won't. But the subject of Darren Rust is off the table."

"It's not about trust," I said.

"It's totally about trust. You don't trust that I know what I'm doing and that it'll be worth it in the end. That's fine. We haven't known each other that long. No more needs to be said. Kiss me."

I kissed her. "I don't want to talk about him with you anymore. Not ever."

Luna nodded. "So be it."

CHAPTER SIX

I hadn't spent Friday night with her, but I came over Saturday afternoon. As I walked into the lobby, past the mailboxes, an elderly man I'd seen a couple of times called out to me. "Hey, you're Luna's friend, right?"

"Yep."

He held out a couple of envelopes. "They put her mail in my box."

"Thanks. I'll give it to her." I took the envelopes from him. They were both pieces of junk mail that she'd almost certainly throw away, but that wasn't my call to make. I went up the stairs to her apartment and knocked on the door.

"Come in!" Luna said.

I walked inside. Whatever she was cooking smelled delicious. She stood in her kitchenette, stirring something in a pot. "Hi, sexy!"

"Hi." I held up the envelopes. "I have your mail."

There was a flash of anger, just like the one when I'd said she was being cheesy.

"You got my mail?"

"Yeah. I mean, I didn't *check* your mail. I don't have a key. It got put in the wrong box and your neighbor asked me to give it to you."

She smiled. "Oh, okay. That was nice of him." She was trying a little too hard to course-correct.

"It's just junk." I walked into the kitchenette and handed it to her.

She glanced at the envelopes. "Ooooh, twenty percent off an oil change! Yeah, nothing I want." She tossed them into the garbage bin.

"Is everything okay?" I asked.

"Sure. Why wouldn't it be?"

"You seemed a little upset."

"Sorry. I used to have a roommate who would steal my mail. I'd get past-due notices on bills and stuff because she was swiping them. It was just some weird kleptomania thing she had going on. So I get kind of twitchy about my mail."

"Gotcha," I said. "I didn't know."

"Of course you didn't. Why would you? No big deal. Maybe you should try some kind of psychological experiment on me. I hope you're hungry."

And with that, I officially knew we were over.

Maybe she did indeed have a former roommate who stole her mail and created an aversion to anybody touching her letters. Maybe. Seemed very unlikely. And if she *was* telling the truth, why the flash of anger? Why was she so upset that I'd brought in her mail? What didn't she want me to see? There's a point where you have to look at the red flags and say, "There's something wrong here."

I'd screwed up in the past. When Darren came back into my life in college, I should've told him to go to hell. If I'd said, nope, sorry, not interested in trying to reconcile, kindly fuck off now, I'd still have a wife and a daughter.

Without her whole "Let's revisit the evening in Darren's dorm room" game, I would have thought that perhaps she was just mortified to think that I might have seen an envelope with "*Past Due – Final Notice*" on the front.

Maybe I was being paranoid, but at this moment I was pretty sure that I needed to take a serious look at the clues and not blunder into another devastatingly toxic relationship.

I'd respect her wishes. I wouldn't ghost her.

I should break up with her now. Or whatever the term was when you were officially parting ways with somebody who wasn't technically your girlfriend.

No.

Not yet.

I needed to find out what the hell was going on.

AFTER A DELICIOUS DINNER, Luna suggested that we head back to her bedroom. This idea held great appeal, obviously, but though my penis said "Yes, please!" my conscience was less enthusiastic. Barring a miracle where her ex-roomie showed up and offered profound apologies for inflicting the mail trauma upon her, we were done. And I was planning to violate her privacy in a big way. Having sex with her now, knowing that I was going to betray her trust, was something that a complete scumbag would do. And I liked to think that I wasn't a complete scumbag.

"I hate to say it," I said, "but I'm not really in the mood right now. I think I'm just tired. I'd rather just watch a movie or something."

"Sure, okay." Luna didn't seem upset. "Popcorn and a movie

sounds good to me."

We watched a politically incorrect 1980's comedy that didn't hold up very well, and then I browsed her DVD collection looking for the second movie in our double feature. She had *Threads of the Noose,* a terrible drama that Melanie and I had seen on our first date. We obviously wouldn't be watching that one. I decided to stick with the theme and put in an '80s action flick.

About halfway through, we turned it off and went to bed. Luna made a mild effort to initiate some sex, but didn't make an issue out of it when I declined. Apparently it was okay to not be having hot wild sex every single time we were together.

I woke up first and kissed her shoulder.

"Good morning," I said.

She groaned. Luna was not a morning person.

"I'm going to get us some bagels. Sound good?"

"Sounds great."

I climbed out of bed and got dressed. I gave her a kiss, then left the bedroom. On my way out the door, I grabbed her keys from the kitchen counter.

I drove to the nearest hardware store. I didn't even have to speak to anybody—they had an automated key duplication machine. I put the key to Luna's apartment into the slot, let the machine do its work, and a couple of minutes later I had a copy.

Then I went and got us some bagels.

I'd hoped that she'd still be in bed when I returned, or at least in the shower, but she was seated on the living room couch. Not a big deal. She wasn't likely to notice that her keys were missing unless she needed them.

As I recited the selection of bagels and flavors of cream cheese I'd obtained, Luna got up and walked into the kitchen. She selected a raisin bagel with blueberry cream cheese. When she opened the refrigerator door to get the jug of orange juice, momentarily blocking me from her view, I quickly put the keys back where they belonged.

We enjoyed a nice breakfast. Then I said that I had a lot to do today and needed to head off, but asked if we could get together tomorrow night. She said of course.

At the door, our goodbye kiss turned into a brief makeout session. I felt guilty about this, but I didn't want her to be suspicious.

Then I left.

When I got back to my apartment, I sent my boss an e-mail, telling him that I needed to take a personal day tomorrow.

C.

THE HAIR SALON opened at ten. Luna was supposed to be there by nine-thirty, so if I arrived at her apartment at ten-fifteen, there was no chance that she'd be home unless she too had taken the day off work.

Her car wasn't parked in its designated spot.

I drove around the apartment complex to make sure it wasn't there, just in case.

I had some very intense second thoughts as I parked and got out of my car, but I needed to know what was going on. There was an excellent chance that searching her apartment wouldn't give me any answers, especially since I didn't even know what I was looking for. If this turned out to be a waste of time maybe I'd reconsider breaking up with her.

But I was very sure that something strange was going on.

I unlocked her door and went inside.

I didn't have a cover story for if I got busted. I shouldn't have my own key to her place—we'd never even discussed such an arrangement—so no excuse could suffice. I'd simply have to fess up to what I'd done. But there was no reason to think she wouldn't be at work.

Where to start?

There wasn't much to her apartment. Living room, bedroom, kitchenette, and bathroom. I was unlikely to find any shocking evidence in her kitchenette or bathroom, and I'd thoroughly perused the shelves of her living room as part of the natural process of being a frequent houseguest, so the bedroom seemed like the only logical choice.

I had, of course, spent a great deal of time in here. But I'd never been invited to look in her closet, or under her bed, or go through her dresser drawers.

I started with the closet. I knew that it was neatly organized because I'd seen her pull clothes out of it, and as I peered inside I realized just how easy this part of the search was going to be. There were small cardboard boxes neatly arranged on a shelf above her clothes, and an opaque plastic box on the floor in the back.

I pulled out the plastic box and took off the lid.

It was filled with sex toys. I mean, a *lot* of sex toys. I knew she had a wide selection, because two drawers in her nightstand were jam-packed with them, but those must have been the ones in heavy rotation. There was nothing truly frightening in the box, although there were a few items that I would prefer not to use or have used upon me.

No mysteries there. Luna was extremely unashamed of her fondness for toys. The mailman could've wheeled in a huge wooden crate of them and she wouldn't have minded that I saw. I put the box back where I'd found it.

I took down the closest cardboard box. This didn't have an actual lid, just flaps folded in, so I was careful when I opened it so as not to rip anything. Inside were three pairs of shoes. I closed it again, replaced it on the shelf, and moved on to the next one.

More shoes.

The third box was filled with random cords and chargers.

The fourth box, smaller than the others, was filled with cash. Not stacks of large bills, like she'd get from a bank heist, but a lot of change and mostly one-dollar bills, with a couple of fives in there. It looked like it had just been randomly thrown in there. Perhaps at the end of each day she'd emptied her pockets and tossed the cash in here, then closed it up when it got full. I couldn't tell how much was in here, but it certainly wasn't "flee town" money.

I searched the remaining boxes. Nothing scandalous.

I surveyed the closet. Everything looked just as it had before I started searching.

Next I opened the drawers in her nightstand. I'd watched her open the top two. The third was more of the same—just more toys we hadn't gotten to yet.

I looked under the bed. More boxes. And a scrapbook.

I pulled it out and examined it. It was bound in red cloth and was held closed by a leather strap and a small silver lock, like a diary.

Cutting the strap would be very easy. I was pretty sure that any pair of scissors would do the trick. But my suspicions weren't strong enough for me to start destroying Luna's private property, and I definitely didn't want her to know that I'd been digging around through her things.

Reading her diary would be going too far, but I was pretty sure this was a scrapbook. I wanted to see what was inside.

It had been on top of the boxes, easily accessible, and there was no dust on it. I wasn't exactly Sherlock Holmes, but my deduction was that this wasn't some long-forgotten artifact.

So…where was the key?

It wasn't on her key ring. That only had her apartment key, her car key, and what I assumed was the key to her mailbox. Nothing tiny enough to open this lock.

Luna lived by herself. As far as she knew, nobody would have any reason to go snooping underneath her bed. I was no stranger to this bed, and the idea of peering underneath it had never occurred to me. The lock was just a token security precaution, something designed to keep younger siblings away from your private musings, so the key was unlikely to be in a fiendishly clever hiding spot.

I opened the top drawer of her nightstand and started rummaging through the contents. Less than a minute later, I found a tiny silver key. It wasn't the key to the handcuffs—I already knew what that one looked like.

What the hell was I doing?

I'd stolen the key to Luna's apartment, made a duplicate (which was illegal, of course), snuck in here while she was at work, gone through her private belongings, and now I was going to open a locked scrapbook. Why? Because she got horny over the fantasy of Darren and me sharing a girl in college? Because for a split-second she was pissed that I got her mail? Was that really enough for me to be doing this?

I sat on the bed for a moment, and then I decided that, yes, it was.

If the contents of the scrapbook were none of my business, I'd lock it back up, return it to its spot under the bed, and leave.

I unlocked the book and opened it.

On the first page, slipped into a clear plastic page protector, was a regular sized white envelope. Addressed to Luna Booth. Return address: Fitzpatrick Federal Prison.

I was so desperate for this not to be true that my first thought was, *well, this could be a total coincidence. Maybe she knows somebody else in that maximum-security prison. Darren's not the only prisoner in there, right?*

I turned the page. This had the letter that had presumably been inside the envelope. I recognized the handwriting.

I flipped through the pages. There were six more envelopes and letters from Darren.

And then a bunch of pictures of him. Some were taken from newspaper clippings and magazine articles, and others appeared to have been printed from the Internet.

I managed to set the scrapbook down and sprint to the bathroom before I threw up.

I couldn't believe this. Absolutely could not believe this.

Was that the sound of the doorknob?

Nope. I was imagining things. But even though Luna wouldn't be home for several hours, I decided not to take the risk that she'd come home early. I flushed the toilet and returned to her bedroom to collect the scrapbook. Then I took it with me.

C—

I JUST STARED AT IT, resting on my dining room table.

I was desperate to learn what the letters said, but I dreaded knowing. It couldn't be anything good. I wasn't going to read these letters to Luna from Darren and think, oh, goodness, what a silly misunderstanding! Everything is peachy between us now!

I delayed by taking Tucker for a walk.

A few minutes after I got back, I received a text message from Luna.

Hi, sexxxy guy! Thinking of u!

I texted back: *Thinking of you too! J*

Still on 4 tonite???

You bet!!!

Okay, no more delays. I had to read this.

63

CHAPTER SEVEN

Dear *Luna,* Darren wrote. *Thanks for the compliment! I'm blushing!*

As you might guess, things in here aren't super-duper great. I suppose that's sort of the point. A comfy prison where you lie in a hammock while half-naked ladies feed you grapes wouldn't be a deterrent for criminal behavior, now would it? I did manage to get past the rule that you have to kick somebody's ass or become somebody's bitch to survive. I've kicked nary an ass, and I'm certainly nobody's bitch. I'm just good at talking. I wouldn't necessarily say that I've got friends in here, but I do okay.

And thank you for the pictures. That was very generous of you. If you sent more graphic ones, they took them away when they screened my mail, but these will keep me happy for quite a while! If I was allowed conjugal visits, you'd better believe that we'd be conjugaling (no way is that a real word, but you know what I mean) non-stop.

Your fan too,

D.R.

That bitch.

She was sleeping with me because she was into Darren. I resisted the urge to fling the scrapbook against the wall, or to tear it apart with my bare hands, or to let out a bellow of pure rage. Trashing my own apartment wouldn't make me feel better.

I just needed to read the rest of the letters.

The next three were the type of flirting that would typically make me want to stick a finger down my throat. I didn't have copies of Luna's letters, but I got the basic gist of what she'd said to Darren from his reply. As far as I could tell, it was the kind of exchange between a celebrity and a fan where there was no expectation that they'd actually get together. No plans to visit him in prison. But her infatuation was obvious.

I stopped reading and paced around my apartment for a few minutes to calm myself down. No reason to have a stroke over this. Luna was one of those deranged women who fell in love with convicted killers, and she was using me to feel like she was closer to Darren. No big deal. I mean, it *was* a big deal. It was a huge fucking deal. But I could just tell her to leave me the hell alone—maybe I'd get a restraining order, to be safe—and then never see her again. I was horrified at the thought of her using me like this, but ultimately, being used wasn't the worst personal relationship I'd ever had.

I felt calm enough to continue reading.

That's an interesting question, isn't it? First of all, I didn't do any of this, of course. I'm innocent and I hope the real killer is brought to justice. So anything I'm about to say is completely hypothetical and for entertainment purposes only.

And I know this isn't the answer you want to hear, so I apologize in advance. But I have to admit it: I took no pleasure in killing his wife and daughter. None. I'm not saying that I regret doing it. I'm just saying that it wasn't fun. It wasn't fulfilling. I didn't feel better afterward.

I can tell that you were hoping it was this AMAZING rush, better than drugs, better than sex, better than anything, but it wasn't and it's never been like that for me. I did it because he deserved to lose his family. I didn't rub their blood on my face and cackle with glee. I felt nauseous while I was doing it and for a long time afterward. And I didn't enjoy the thought of his reaction when he found them. I could have taken him to see their bodies, but I didn't.

Yes, I could've just made something up, told you it was the greatest thrill of my entire life, but I don't want to lie to you, in case I get off in sixty years for good behavior and you're still waiting for me.

But if it makes you horny to imagine it happening in a completely different way, I'm all for it. Fantasize about it however you want. Imagine me painting exquisite works of art in their blood. The real event was no fun, but you can make it as fun as you want!

XOXOXO

D.R.

I wanted to kill her.

I knew that I wasn't literally going to kill her, but as I sat at my dining room table, hands trembling with rage, I sure *wanted* to murder her. Choke her to death. Break her goddamn neck. Twist her head until it tore off.

I would not confront her in person about this. Because if I did, though I was ninety-nine percent sure that I could stop myself from physically attacking her, I was not one hundred percent sure. And even if Jeremy was there to keep things from getting out of control, I wasn't sure he could hold me back.

I didn't want to destroy my own possessions or get evicted from my apartment or have somebody call in a noise complaint, so my recourse at the moment was to beat the absolute living shit out of the mattress on my bed and hope that I felt a little better afterward.

That's what I did for about ten minutes. I was surprised to discover that you can hurt your fists pretty badly by repeatedly pounding them against a mattress as hard as you possibly can. I didn't draw blood, but my hands were swollen and were going to be extremely sore for a while.

I left my bedroom and got an ice pack out of the freezer.

I didn't feel any better.

Well, so what? Why should I feel better? Why would I even *want* to feel better right now? The proper response to reading those letters was absolute fury, and there'd be something wrong with me if I quickly got over it.

Of course, I was going to destroy that scrapbook.

I wished I lived in a house with a fireplace. Though I could safely burn it in my sink, that still might set off the smoke detector. I had a shredder, but there'd be no satisfaction in that—it would be like destroying confidential business documents. I wanted to grab an axe and chop away at it until it was nothing but bits of paper, but I did not own an axe, and the idea of purchasing an axe and then finding a secluded spot where I could furiously chop up a scrapbook without witnesses reporting the insane man to the authorities didn't seem like the best way to go about this.

I decided to keep it simple and settled for tearing it to pieces.

The plastic page protectors wouldn't rip, so I removed the letters, thankful that nobody had seen my first inept effort. I ripped the letters apart until a forensic scientist couldn't piece them back together, then I tossed them into the sink, ran hot water, and crushed them into pulp. I removed the pulp so it wouldn't clog the drain and threw it into the trash. After that, I took a knife out of the silverware drawer and slashed the cloth binding of the scrapbook until it had been completely torn off, while muttering a constant stream of profanity. Then I tossed it into the trash with the pulp.

I felt a little better. Still trembling with rage, but I could probably look at myself in the mirror and not flinch in horror at the madman in the reflection.

I picked up my phone and realized that I'd missed three texts and a phone call from Luna. *What time r u coming over?*

And then: *Come up with something naughty u want 2 do that we haven't done yet. Don't make me choose. If I choose, u lose veto power. J*

And then: *Hellooooooooo? Sexxxy man?*

I texted her back: *Not coming over.*

Why not?

Sick.

In the head? J

I didn't respond.

Sorry, she texted a moment later. *My bedside manner is lacking!!! Want me 2 come over tonight and take care of u?*

No.

K.

A moment later: *What's wrong?*

Just sick.

All right. Hope u feel better. I'll keep myself company. Good thing I have toys!

I wasn't sure what to do. There was nothing illegal about writing letters to Darren in prison, and there was nothing illegal about keeping it a secret from me. So if I called the cops, they'd want to know if she'd made any threats or given me any reason to believe I was in danger, and I'd have to say no. Luna writing creepy letters asking what it felt like to murder my wife and daughter would help me get a restraining order if it came to that, but at the moment, there really wasn't anything the police could do.

I still had my whole day ahead of me. I considered just going into work, but if my boss or any of my co-workers gave me a hard time about anything, no matter how good-natured they were about it, it was very possible that I'd snap.

A better plan was to take Tucker for a very, very long walk.

When we returned, hours later, I had calmed down significantly. There was only so long I could sustain that level of rage and hatred. Oh, there was still plenty of rage and hatred, but I was no longer trembling.

I sat on the couch, with Tucker snuggled against me, and watched a bunch of my favorite silent comedy shorts. None of them made me laugh, but at least they were soothing.

Eventually it was six o'clock. I'd forgotten to eat lunch. Luna would be home now.

A text: *Feeling any better?*

No.

Sorry. Please let me know if I can help. I can bring chicken soup! Yummy!

I should probably eat something, but I wasn't the least bit hungry.

I kept watching movies. Charlie Chaplin. Buster Keaton. Harold Lloyd.

Around seven forty-five, my phone rang. Luna. I didn't want to talk to her, but I couldn't put it off forever. "Hello?"

"Where is it?" she demanded. She sounded panicked and furious.

"I don't know what you're talking about."

"Don't play dumb with me, Alex. Where is it? What did you do with it?"

"Oh, you mean your love letters from Darren Rust?"

"*Yes!* Where are they?"

"Go to hell."

"I'm coming over."

"No, you are not coming over. Stay the fuck away from me."

"I'm heading to my car right now."

"I mean it."

"You can't stop me."

"I'll call the police."

"I'm reclaiming my property that you stole from me. I have every right to come over there and take back what's mine. Or I'll call the cops myself and have them get it back from you. Your choice, Alex."

This wasn't how I'd imagined the conversation. I'd thought she'd at least start with "I can explain." I supposed she deserved credit for not trying to talk her way out of it.

"Call the cops," I said. "That's perfectly fine with me."

"Give me back my letters. They're not yours. They don't belong to you. They're mine. Give them back. I want them back. I want them back, Alex. I want them back now." Her voice was becoming hysterical.

I wasn't sure if I should tell her that I'd destroyed them. That might send her completely over the edge. Maybe it was better to give her an opportunity to calm down first.

"You don't get them back," I said.

"Neutral ground," she said. "How about that? Neutral territory. You drop them off somewhere. I'll come get them. We don't have to see each other. You'll never have to see me again. You can forget that I exist. I'll completely disappear from your world. That works, right? Neutral ground. You choose the place. Any place. I don't care where."

"I don't have your scrapbook anymore," I told her. "It's gone and you're not getting it back. If you come over here I'll have you arrested. Good-bye."

I hung up. Hopefully she'd think I'd turned it over to the

authorities. I didn't regret destroying the letters—they were Darren's responses to fan mail about slaughtering my family. Giving them back to Luna, letting her use them like an aphrodisiac, simply wasn't an option.

Somebody knocked on my door.

Holy shit. Had she been outside my apartment the whole time?

I walked over and looked through the peephole. It was Jeremy.

"Hey," he said, after I let him in. "You were being kind of loud."

"Not as loud as I wanted to be."

"I got the basic gist. Do you want to fill me in?"

I gave Jeremy a summary of my terrible day. My earlier efforts to calm myself down were completely undone as I described what was in the letters. Jeremy stared at me in disbelief, though he also looked a bit frightened of me, as if he thought I might lose control and just start throwing punches at the nearest person.

"So is she on her way?" he asked.

"She'd better not be. But I don't know."

"What if she does? What are you going to do?"

"Lock the door and not stand anywhere that I could get hit if she starts shooting through the wall." The last part was kind of, but not entirely, a joke.

"Do you think you should call the police, just in case?"

"She hasn't threatened me yet. And if they asked questions, I'd have to explain how I got the scrapbook."

"Does she know how you got it?"

"I don't think so. She probably assumes that I took it while she was in the shower or something. Still, I did steal and destroy her property. Unless she shows up and refuses to leave, I'm not sure the police can do anything."

"Well, clearly it wasn't a coincidence that she found you at that bar. She had to have been stalking you. Who knows how long she was doing it?"

I'd thought about that a lot during my walk. The odds of her walking into that bar, seeing me, and thinking "Wow, that's the former best friend of my prison crush!" were almost non-existent. And I rarely ventured out to that part of town, so she would've had to put some effort into following me.

"That'll help when I try to get a restraining order," I said. "It's a little too convoluted to explain if I'm calling 911."

Jeremy nodded. "I guess I'll hang out with you here and try to keep you safe from the crazy lady."

"Thank you. I appreciate that."

"Y'know, I knew Darren too. I get that if you have the chance to sleep with a band member, you go for the lead singer and not the bass player, but it still stings a little. Do you have any beer?"

A minute later, Jeremy and I stood in the kitchen, drinking beer and hoping that Luna didn't show up.

"Does it help that you got really well laid before this all fell apart?" he asked.

"Not at all."

"It would help for me, but I'm way more superficial."

"I should've known better," I said.

"Why?"

"Because her instant attraction to me was weird. That kind of thing doesn't happen."

"Nah, you're a good catch. I didn't think it was weird at all. If you keep hanging out in bars it'll happen again." He finished off his can of beer and set it on the counter. "I feel like we should stay sober until this situation gets resolved, but after that, let's get blackout drunk."

Somebody knocked at the door.

"Do we pretend we're not home?" Jeremy whispered.

I put my finger to my lips to indicate that he should shut the fuck up.

We waited.

The knocking intensified. As a puppy, Tucker had barked like crazy whenever there was a knock at the door, but I'd successfully trained him out of that.

"Alex?" Luna called out, ending my fantasy that maybe Jeremy had ordered a pizza for us before he came over.

Jeremy and I continued to stand in the kitchen.

"Alex? I know you're home. I saw your car out there. I saw Jeremy's car, too."

Jeremy looked confused. The question of how she knew which car belonged to Jeremy did not need to be asked out loud.

Now she was pounding on the door. "Talk to me," she said. "You owe me that much."

I didn't owe her shit. But I wondered how long she'd pound on my door before she gave up. I could imagine a scenario where each knock left a spatter of blood from her mangled knuckles.

She kept knocking. "I'm not leaving," she announced.

I walked out of the kitchen. If this continued, one of my neighbors would call the police, and if we had to take it that far, I'd rather be the one to contact them myself.

"Luna, go away," I said.

"Let me in. We can discuss this like adults."

"There's nothing to discuss."

"Give it back."

"I don't have it."

"Where is it?"

I decided that there was no advantage to letting her think that she could ever get the scrapbook back. "Gone. I tore up everything that was in there."

Silence.

I stood there, listening carefully. I took a couple of steps to the left, just in case she was taking out a gun and preparing to shoot me through the door.

It took about twenty seconds for her to speak again. "Please tell me you're lying."

"I'm not. What did you think I was going to do with them?"

"They didn't belong to you." I could barely hear her through the door.

"Are you trying to make me feel guilty?" I asked. "Seriously?"

More silence.

"Go home, Luna. Don't make this any worse." I felt really stupid doing it, but I moved again just in case she was pointing a gun toward the sound of my voice.

"I liked you a lot," she said. "None of that was fake."

"I don't care."

"I know you don't care. I just need to say it."

"You have to leave now," I told her. "If you go away, we don't have to involve anybody else. We can pretend this whole thing never happened."

This was the longest silence yet. I almost thought she'd left without me hearing her footsteps, but finally she spoke: "Goodbye, Alex." She sounded defeated. "I had fun. Sorry it didn't last."

I couldn't hear clearly through the door, but it sounded like she was walking away.

I waited for several moments.

"Did she leave?" asked Jeremy.

"As far as I can tell."

"Are you going to look?"

"Not for a while."

"I'll just hang out here until you decide you don't want my company anymore."

"Thanks."

"Do you think she'll leave you alone?"

"I really don't know." I wanted to believe that this was over. But she was infatuated with Darren, and I knew exactly what he would do in this situation.

Darren was very, very patient.

He would wait as long as it took for me to let my guard down.

CHAPTER EIGHT

Jeremy and I weren't certain when it would become ridiculous to keep hiding in my apartment. It had been a couple of hours. Surely Luna wasn't sitting at the end of the hallway with a revolver in her lap. I didn't even know if she was violent. Being obsessed with a serial killer didn't mean you had homicidal impulses yourself.

"Want me to spend the night?" Jeremy asked.

"Yes, but not to avoid going outside. Tucker needs to go for a walk."

"Can't he just poop on the floor?"

"I'm not going to let my dog poop on the floor because I'm scared of my ex-girlfriend."

"Then I'll take him. I didn't tear up her letters, so she probably won't try to stab me."

"We'll both go."

"Okay. But I'm checking first," said Jeremy. "No arguments."

He walked over to the door and carefully opened it. He peeked outside, looking to the left and the right, then turned back and gave me a thumbs-up.

I attached Tucker's leash to his collar and the three of us left my apartment.

The walk was completely uneventful.

I honestly had no idea how worried I should be about Luna returning. She had very definite mental issues, but after she had a chance to calm down, she couldn't fault me for destroying the letters unless she was flat-out batshit bugfuck crazy. She was far from sane, but would she actually seek *revenge* against me?

I had no idea what she might do. What was her endgame? Would she have eventually confessed to me? Did she even have a plan, or was she just getting off on my relationship with Darren for as long as she could?

I'd have to be vigilant.

Aside from my own unstable mental state, the next day was a normal day. I went in to work, though I didn't get a lot done. Luna didn't try to contact me.

The next day was also uneventful.

I refused to relax.

Of course, I couldn't live the rest of my life like this. At some point, I'd have to pretend that Luna had moved on. But not yet.

A week passed.

Darren had waited far longer than a week to resurface—he'd waited *years*—but again, I had absolutely no reason to believe that Luna was anything like him. She'd pounded on my door, talked for a bit, and then left. She hadn't threatened me. I couldn't rule out the idea that she had something else planned, but I also couldn't spend every waking moment worrying about it.

She waited exactly one month, as if she'd marked it on her calendar.

THE PHONE CALL came from a number I didn't recognize, so I didn't answer. They called back immediately, and I ignored that one too, figuring it was a telemarketer.

I got a text from the same number. *Answer.*

The phone rang again. This time I answered. "Hello?"

"Hey, Alex," said Luna.

"What do you want?"

"I just wanted to let you know that Jeremy is a loyal friend."

"What did he do?"

"It's what he didn't do. I tried to seduce him and it didn't work at all. And you know how persuasive I can be. I did get the hypodermic needle into him, though."

Oh, God no.

"Where is he?" I demanded.

"I'm looking at him right now."

"Where are you?"

"Relax. I didn't call you up to *not* tell you anything. It's not like I called just to make you listen to me cut up your friend."

"What do you want?"

"What I want is for you to stop asking questions. Obviously I'm going to tell you everything you need to know. I'm going to text you where to meet me, and you're going to show up there alone. I don't think I need to explain what happens if you break that rule, do I? Actually, I might as well. I want you to picture what Melanie looked like when you found her, and then superimpose Jeremy's face over her. I don't know what Melanie looked like after Darren was done with her, but I have a pretty good imagination and I'll make my best guess. Now are you going to make some empty threats, or do you want me to continue?"

I was clutching my phone so tightly that I thought it might shatter in my hand. "You can continue."

"I think I've covered it, actually. Go there alone. It'll take a couple of hours to get there. You can call the police if you want, but if you do, they'll just find a mess."

"Let me talk to him," I said.

"He's still asleep."

"Then how do I know you really have him?"

"Well, if you think that I would call you up like this without actually having Jeremy with me, I guess you're welcome to ignore this. Just hang up and go about your day. Sorry to have bothered you."

"I need a picture or something," I said. "I'm not going to walk into a trap without proof."

"I'm pretty sure I won't be able to wake him up yet. I guess I could kick him. Would you recognize the way he sounds if somebody kicks him? Here, let me hold the phone down and see if this works."

I heard a thump. Then another. And, yes, a groan that sounded very much like it could come from Jeremy.

"Did you hear that?" she asked.

"Fine. I believe you."

"That was the one and only time you get to demand something from me. From now on, you do exactly what I tell you to do, no questions asked. Do you understand?"

"Sure."

"How about you answer me without the sarcasm?"

"I understand," I said.

"I expect you to get right on the road. Trust me, you don't want me to get bored waiting for you."

She hung up.

I couldn't believe this. For a moment, I was in such a state of shock that I couldn't even move. How had I gotten myself back into a situation where I had to take orders from a psychopath?

She'd said to arrive alone, yet she hadn't said to be unarmed. I couldn't imagine that she'd let me have a gun handy during our encounter, but I owned one, and I'd bring it along.

Her text message arrived: *Meet me where the rope burned his neck.*

Of course.

Of *course* that's where she wanted to meet.

When we were twelve years old, as students at Branford Academy, we staged a mock trial and phony hanging for Darren out in the woods. The intent was to put a good scare into him, after I discovered him cutting up our other roommate Peter's dog. Darren claimed the dog was dead when he found it, and he may have been telling the truth, but he was definitely mutilating its body. That was enough for Jeremy, Peter and I to decide that we needed to set him straight.

It went awry. Darren got a serious rope burn on his neck.

As adults, when we tried to lure him out of hiding, that's the code phrase I used in the video: *Meet me where the rope burned your neck.* (Technically, it was phrased as "*I'm gonna rip his fucking guts out where the rope burned your neck,*" which made perfect sense in context and was bleeped out of most newscasts.)

So I had to go back to the woods near Branford Academy. Wonderful.

I retrieved the gun case from my closet. I considered bringing Tucker along, but I didn't want to put my beagle in harm's way. I poured a couple of extra bowls of food for him. Rent was due tomorrow and my landlord was a real hardass about being paid on time, so if I never came home, he'd enter the apartment and find my dog.

Then I began the road trip.

C⟶

I BLASTED rock music at top volume in an attempt to distract myself from my thoughts. Many of them still managed to get through, as I wondered what I could have done differently. Not gone to that bar, obviously, though I supposed that Luna would have met me someplace else instead. Dump her immediately after her weird "revise the memory" session? Would that have changed anything, or would she simply have kidnapped Jeremy sooner?

I wanted to blame myself, but except for banning all new relationships, which is basically what I'd been doing before I met Luna, I wasn't sure what I could've done. Taken it slower, maybe. Recognized that it was too good to be true. Refused to tell her anything at all about Darren.

A couple of hours and countless dark thoughts later, I parked along the side of the road closest to where I needed to be. I took my pistol out of its case and stuck it in the back of my pants. Then I went for a walk in the woods.

I was surprised how easy it was to find the tree. I walked right to it.

Now what? Luna hadn't given me any instructions about what to do when I got there. I sent her a text message. *I'm here.*

No ur not.

I could immediately see this turning into a confusing and frustrating text message exchange, so I called her instead.

"I'm right here," I said when she answered.

"So am I."

"The place where the rope burned his neck. Unless there was some other rope incident that nobody told me about, I'm in the right place. I'm looking at the tree right now. I don't know what else to tell you."

82

"Okay," said Luna. "Shit. Jeremy must have taken me to the wrong spot."

"Let me talk to him."

"I told you that you don't get to demand anything else from me. Anyway, he's not quite awake yet. I had to give him another shot."

"Then what now?"

"I'm thinking."

"This is already crashing and burning," I said. "Why not pull the plug? Let him go. I won't say anything to anybody."

"Of course you will. I would. Don't treat me like I'm stupid."

"I just want to go back to keeping my head down and going on with a quiet life. I don't want any drama. If you let him go, Jeremy and I will pretend this never happened."

"Would Darren have let him go?"

"If he realized he was in a no-win situation, yeah, I think he would."

Luna laughed. "Jeremy lying about the spot is nowhere close to putting me in a no-win situation. You're treating me like I'm stupid again."

"He didn't necessarily lie. He may have been confused. You said you'd injected him with something."

"True. That's not really relevant to what we're talking about right now, though."

"So back to my original question. What now?"

"I said I was thinking, but you won't shut up long enough for me to do that. Will you do that for me, Alex? After all the good times we've shared together, will you be a sweetie and shut up?"

"Sure."

She was quiet for a moment. "Shout something."

"What?"

"Anything."

83

I called out "Hello!" as loud as I could. "Did you hear me?"

"Yeah, I heard you. You're pretty far away. Goddamn it."

"Do you think you can find me from my voice?"

"I'm not dragging Jeremy all the way over there. Do you know your directions?"

"What do you mean?"

"North, south, east, west."

"I know what directions are."

"Then why did you ask what I meant? Are you trying to get Jeremy killed?"

"Just tell me what to do, Luna."

"Walk northeast for a couple of minutes, then call out again."

"Do you want me to stay on the phone?"

"Yes."

I moved forward until I could see the sun, did some calculations, and walked in what I was relatively sure was a northeastern direction. Luna didn't speak to me until I called out "Hello!" again.

"That's working," she said. "Keep doing that."

I walked for another couple of minutes and called out. This time she told me to walk north instead of northeast. The next time she told me to switch back to northeast.

"You're close," she told me. "So let's talk about the rules."

"I'm here alone."

"Good. I didn't think I even needed to ask about that. Anyway, the rules are simple. Do exactly what I say, and don't try anything that makes me mad. If you brought a gun or a knife or whatever, now is the time to throw it away. If you have any kind of weapon when you get here, I'm going to kill you, immediately, no questions asked. Do you understand?"

"Yes."

"I mean it. I will shoot you in the head and that will be the end of it. Get rid of your weapons now."

I removed the pistol from the back of my pants and set it next to a tree.

"Are they gone?" she asked.

"I didn't bring any."

"Start walking again. I'll let you know when I see you."

I walked for a couple more minutes.

"There you are," she said. "Keep walking in that direction. Keep going. Do you see me?"

I did. I saw her up ahead, but there was no sign of Jeremy.

As I got closer, I saw him. He was lying on the ground next to her. As I got even closer, I saw that there was a lot of blood.

Luna disconnected the call and shoved the phone into her pocket. She was appropriately dressed for the environment—jeans and a white T-shirt. She hadn't fixed her hair or put on makeup. She pointed a gun at me.

"Keep walking," she said.

I walked until we were about twenty feet apart.

"That's enough."

I couldn't tell if Jeremy was breathing or not. He was on his side, and his hands were tied behind his back. His shoes were drenched in blood. Much of the fabric of his pants had been cut away, and Luna had used that and some sticks to make tourniquets on each foot. "What did you do to him?"

"Cut his Achilles tendons. I didn't want him to run away."

"Look how bad he's bleeding."

Luna glanced down and nodded. "I might have cut too deep. It was my first time. I did what I could to stop it."

"We have to get him to a hospital."

"Oh, sure, Alex. That's what's going to happen. I'm going to politely step aside and let you take him to the hospital. Do you ever think before you speak, or do you just blurt out whatever stupid thoughts run through your head?"

"If he dies, there's no coming back from this."

"Just stop. All you're doing is distracting me, and since he's bleeding out, you're going to want to keep things focused."

I nodded. "What do you want me to do?"

"Take off all your clothes."

CHAPTER NINE

"E xcuse me?" I asked.

"Relax," said Luna. "This isn't a sex thing. I'm making sure you aren't hiding a weapon."

"Just frisk me or something."

"What's wrong? Are you worried about me seeing your dick? This will go much smoother if I don't have to worry about you pulling a gun on me, and the only way for me to be comfortable about that is if you're bare-ass naked. So take off your clothes before Jeremy bleeds to death."

I quickly took off all of my clothes and tossed them aside. I stood naked in front of her. "Satisfied?"

"Turn around."

I turned in a circle.

"Just making sure you didn't have anything taped to your back. To keep things moving, we'll skip the prison search. And now we're—"

"You need to let me check him," I said.

"Did you seriously just interrupt me?"

"I don't think Jeremy's breathing."

It wasn't a trick. It legitimately did not look like Jeremy was breathing.

Luna kept her gun pointed at me and crouched down next to him. She placed her hand on his chest. "No, he's breathing." She pressed two fingers to his wrist. "We're good." She stood back up. "May I continue?"

"Okay."

"And now we're getting to the ironic part. Take three steps to your left."

I took three steps to my left.

"Your other left."

"So, take three steps to my right."

"Yes! Take three fucking steps to your right! Six steps, now!"

I took six steps to my right.

"Look down by the tree," Luna said.

There was a knife resting there.

"Do you get the irony?" she asked.

"Maybe…?"

"I'm letting you have a weapon."

"I get it. You told me to get rid of any weapons I might have brought, and now you're giving me one. Great big mind-blowing irony. What do you want me to do with this?"

"You're going to use it to slash Jeremy's throat."

"Not a chance in hell."

"It is, though. If you don't, I'll have to shoot you, and you're out of your mind if you think I'm going to drag Jeremy out of the woods by myself. I'll leave him here to die. If he's going to die either way, why not choose the option where you don't have to join him?"

"Let me be very clear about this," I said. "I'm not going to do it."

"Really? Your life is so empty that you're happy to let me shoot you? Who's going to take care of Tucker? Are you going to let him starve to death in your apartment?"

"He'll be fine. What exactly are you trying to accomplish with this?"

"It's not that hard to figure out. Take a guess."

"You're trying to impress Darren, right?"

"Ding ding ding!"

"He won't be impressed at all."

"I think you're wrong," said Luna. She smiled. "Making you murder your best friend? I think he'll be *very* impressed, thank you very much."

"If you actually believe that, you don't know him at all. You're trying to make me do it at gunpoint. Anybody could do that. You get a gun, point it at them, and tell them what to do. When Darren made me murder that woman, he didn't tell me that he'd shoot me if I disobeyed him. There's no sense of victory in that. You don't understand how his mind works."

Luna's smile faltered.

"I told you the entire story, beginning to end," I said. "What part of any of it made you think this was a good plan? He's going to laugh at you."

Now her smile was completely gone. "He won't laugh at me."

"Maybe he won't write 'ha ha ha' in a letter, but if you think you're going to get a positive reaction out of Darren Rust for making me kill Jeremy at gunpoint—Jeremy, who I might add, is unconscious and probably close to death anyway—you are more deluded than I ever thought possible. It's not the way he does things. Your problem is that you focused entirely on the location. You thought that bringing me here, the spot with all this history between us, would be enough. It's not enough. And it's not even the right fucking spot."

Luna kept the gun pointed at me. "You don't know what you're talking about."

"You do understand that pretty much my entire life has been defined by him, right? It sounds sad and pathetic when I say it out loud, but it's true. That's what'll be on my tombstone. *Alex Fletcher, Ex-Friend Of Darren Rust.* So trust me, I know what I'm talking about when it comes to that asshole."

Luna didn't say anything.

"I'll admit it, I'm trying to save Jeremy's life," I said. "But what I'm indirectly doing is saving you the heartbreak of having Darren reject your accomplishment. Because that's what he'll do. He'll tell you that you should have made this into some kind of demented game, or that you should have made me *want* to kill him. I'll make you a deal. Just let me drag Jeremy away from here. I can't get away from you while I'm trying to drag him through the woods, right? If you change your mind, you can shoot me any time you want."

"You're acting like I've already decided to end this."

"No, I'm acting like you're thinking about ending it. So keep thinking about it while I try to get Jeremy out of here. Because if he dies, and you kill me, Darren will be absolutely furious. He doesn't want somebody to murder me. He wants to get his own revenge."

I didn't know if that part was true. I hadn't spoken to Darren since I spared his life, and I didn't know what thoughts of revenge he might have for me. But I believed I was telling the truth. And I knew that he'd be disgusted by the "slash Jeremy's throat or I'll shoot you" approach.

"You hid a weapon somewhere," said Luna.

"I didn't. But if you believe that I did, we'll go back a different way." It wasn't out of the question that I could enact some clever scheme where I was reunited with the pistol I'd abandoned, but it really wasn't something I was considering. Way too risky. I just wanted to get Jeremy to a hospital.

I couldn't tell what Luna was thinking. It seemed equally likely that she'd go along with my suggestion or that she'd let out a shriek of rage and frustration and then put a bullet in my brain.

"Please," I said. "Just let me move him away from here."

"No."

"Luna—"

"No. I'll help you carry him."

She walked over to a tree and picked up a small purse that I hadn't seen behind it. She put her gun in the purse, put the strap over her shoulder, then crouched down next to Jeremy's head.

"Can I get dressed?" I hated to ask this when Jeremy might not have much time left, but it was crucial.

"Getting modest all of a sudden?"

"I'll walk a lot slower in my bare feet. And I'm going to get his blood all over me. If I need somebody else's help, being bloody and naked will make that a lot harder to get."

"All right. Get dressed. Do it however fast you want. You're the one who's concerned about him bleeding to death."

I got dressed so quickly that I put my shirt on inside-out. I took Jeremy by the legs and we picked him up. His hands were still tied behind his back, so Luna held him under the shoulders.

"Turn around," she said. "You're going to take the lead, and we won't make good time if you're walking backwards."

I turned around. We began walking, with my back to Luna, which was more than a little unnerving but better than twisting my ankle because I couldn't see where I was going. I walked as fast as I could, and Luna kept up with me.

I still had no plans to try to retrieve my gun. Even if we walked right past that particular spot, which was very unlikely, I'd have to drop Jeremy and grab the gun before Luna shot me. Not worth the risk.

We didn't speak until we reached the edge of the woods, right where I'd come in.

"I promise I won't tell anybody what happened," I said, lying but trying to stay on her good side as much as possible until Jeremy was in my car.

"Yeah, right. I'm pretty sure the people in the emergency room will ask what happened to him. It's okay. I had no intention of coming back from this."

"What do you mean? You were going to kill yourself?"

Luna let out a snort of laughter. "You wish. Nah, I've got a place to go. You don't need to worry about me. I'll be fine."

She gave me a kiss on the lips.

"It was fun," she said. "Maybe we'll do it again sometime."

She walked away. I hurriedly dragged Jeremy, whose breathing was faint but still happening, to my car. I managed to get him into the back seat, then sped off.

I didn't remember the area perfectly, but there was a hospital not too far from Branford Academy, and if I stayed on this road I'd see the sign.

I sped through a red light. If a cop was watching, I'd have a police escort.

Lesson learned. I should have stuck with the idea that trying to move on with my life after Melanie was a terrible mistake. Hell, I shouldn't have even agreed to meet with Tiffany about her documentary, free meal or not. The life of a hermit was perfect for me. Find myself a nice little cabin deep in the woods, go completely off the grid, and survive off of the contents of my own garden. Maybe let Jeremy build a cabin next to mine, if he wanted to join me. I felt like he'd probably want to swear off the rest of the human population along with me.

"You're going to be fine," I told him, as I saw the sign with an "H" on it. "Almost there."

I thought he groaned a response, though I might have imagined it. Most likely he was saying something unkind about Luna.

I should have asked her what she'd injected him with so I could report that to the hospital staff.

It might not matter. The important thing was to stop the bleeding. Luna's makeshift tourniquets were probably the reason he hadn't bled to death already, but the blood all over my clothes was proof that they weren't doing a perfect job.

I arrived at the hospital too late.

PART II
MARKED

CHAPTER TEN

The girl who walked into the convenience store looked vaguely familiar, but I couldn't quite place her.

I was not a customer. I worked here, thirty-nine hours a week, for just over minimum wage. But I got a discount on snacks and beverages, and my manager didn't care if I brought home hot food that had reached the age where we were instructed to discard it…which was quite a while after a health inspector would make the same recommendation.

After Jeremy's funeral three years ago, I'd vowed that I would not completely fall apart, and to my own credit, I hadn't. But I did give notice at work, break my apartment lease (forfeiting my last month's rent and security deposit), and, yes, move to a cabin in the woods. I now lived near the extremely small town of Moray, California, which had very little to offer beyond the convenience store where I worked.

What I did not do is go completely off the grid and live in my own self-contained ecosystem. Yes, I had a garden. No, it was not a high-quality garden. In the event of a global catastrophe, I'd have enough vegetables for a week's worth of side dishes. I didn't have much space in my one-bedroom cabin but I had running water, a working toilet, and electricity. No Internet. No neighbors.

I had let my hair grow out. Not for the whole three years, but my beard was at "old-timey prospector" level. There was a hell of a lot of gray in it; far more than should've been in the beard of a thirty-five-year-old man. I did keep the beard neatly groomed, since customers weren't supposed to think that some wild mountain man had murdered the convenience store clerk and taken his place, and on the days that I went into work I practiced good personal hygiene.

Was I happier? Kind of.

I had a lot of free time for reading, and had decided to embark on a quest to read as many of the classics of literature as I could. Basically, if it was something I would've hated in school, I read it now. Right now I was slowly working my way through *The Count of Monte Cristo*.

I went for a lot of walks, fished and canoed in a nearby lake, and lived a very quiet, peaceful life.

Last year Peter had come out to visit me. He was a minister and had given the eulogy at Jeremy's funeral. He'd left his wife and five kids at home in Oregon because there was still the unresolved situation with Luna, and I'd told him not to come to the funeral at all, but he'd insisted upon paying his respects to our friend and being there for me. When he visited the cabin for a weekend, we had a great time, and as I drove him to the airport he admitted that he'd expected to feel sorry for me, but that it seemed like I actually had a pretty decent life going on here.

I thanked him, then made one last joke about the fact that he was a minister whose wife wrote erotic novels, because that's what friends do. Did I own every single one of these books, even though she was amazingly prolific? Yes, I did. Had I, a fully grown adult,

98

highlighted key sections to read aloud in Peter's presence? Yes, I had.

Working at the convenience store wasn't *wonderful*, obviously, but it wasn't too bad. I didn't give a shit about the idea that I should be aspiring to greater things. This was perfectly fine. My expenses were low, and yes, I did eat the occasional expired taquito, but overall I was completely content to work behind the counter.

The girl looked like she was in her early twenties. She wore dark blue shorts and a light blue T-shirt. Her long brown hair looked like she'd been driving with the windows rolled down. She glanced over, saw me, smiled, and then hurried into the restroom.

She emerged a couple of minutes later. A man was at the counter, checking each individual Snickers bar until selecting the one that best suited his needs and purchasing it. The girl waited until he left the store before walking up to me.

She smiled. "Hi, Mr. Fletcher."

"Hi." I hadn't been able to place her, and there was no reason to try to buy myself a few more seconds. "Do I know you?"

"I'm April Gatheren."

"April? Oh my God! How are you?"

"I'm good, I'm good," she said. "And you?"

I shrugged. "It's not a glamorous life, but I'm happy."

On that horrible day when I was forced to kill Andrea Keener, Darren had set it up as a game. Andrea had a head start; I had a hatchet. My task was to catch her, decapitate her, and bring back proof within ten minutes, or Darren would murder the six-year-old girl he'd tied to a bed.

I hadn't seen April since her seventh birthday party.

"Well, happiness is important, right?" she asked.

"Yep." I was glad to see her, but I knew this wasn't a chance encounter, and I was ready for the small talk to end. "So what brings you here?"

"What, you don't think I just happened to be in town and stopped in here to buy a beef stick?"

"We have an excellent selection of beef sticks, but no."

"You do have a good selection. I saw it while I was waiting for the other guy to leave. It's an almost scarily vast selection of beef sticks. Who decided that we needed that many varieties of processed meat in stick form?"

"I feel like you're stalling," I said.

"I am," April admitted. "Is there somewhere we can talk?"

"We can talk right here. We're doing it right now."

"Somewhere better?"

"My shift ends in five-and-a-half hours."

"We can do it here, I guess. I missed you at the documentary premiere."

"Yeah, I would've been there, but I remembered that I'd rather pour bleach into my eyeballs instead. It took her forever to finish that thing. Was it any good?"

April shrugged. "It wasn't bad. She spent half a day interviewing me and then used about a minute of it, if that."

"That sucks."

"You and your friends not participating kind of hurt it, I think. It would've been interesting to hear your insight. It ended up being pretty much all about Darren."

"Well, he *is* the star attraction."

"He was—"

"I don't want to be rude," I said, "but I honestly don't care at all. I got the invite and I told Tiffany to fuck off. I haven't seen it, I didn't look up online reviews, and I'm perfectly happy to pretend that it doesn't exist."

"At the Q&A she said you weren't very cooperative."

"I wasn't. Telling her to fuck off was good for the soul. I highly recommend it. So if you're here on Tiffany's behalf, that's the message I want you to pass on to her. Two words. Easy to remember."

"I'm not here for Tiffany. I'm here to ask a favor, just for me."

"It must be a big one, if you're here in person."

"I didn't have your phone number. I e-mailed you a couple of times, but you didn't respond."

"Oh. I don't check my e-mail very often, and you probably had an old address."

"So I did a sixteen-hour road trip to come talk to you. Got a flat tire four hours into it. Every guy who stopped to ask if I needed help looked like a rapist. And my A/C doesn't work. It really wasn't that great of a drive."

"Did you have good music, though?" I asked.

April nodded. "Yes. I did have good music. Thank you for asking."

"I'm sympathetic to your plight. I've had some bad road trips myself." One of them involved being tied up in the back of a van, on my way to meet April for the first time. "What's the favor?"

"So…I'm in college. It's really expensive."

"I'm sure. Don't you have a rich dad?"

"No," April said. "He died a couple of years after the trial."

"Oh, shit. I'm sorry."

It was my trial. Andrea Keener's family wanted me to go to prison for what I'd done. April's father, who was a very good attorney, hadn't been my actual counsel, but one of his associates had represented me, and he'd been a *spectacular* witness on my behalf. The jury had been convinced of the truth—that I had absolutely no choice. I had to kill Andrea to save the adorable little girl that the jury kept seeing up in the front row.

So it was kind of a convoluted "Who owes who a favor?" scenario. I saved April's life. April's father kept me out of prison. But April wouldn't have been kidnapped in the first place if Darren weren't trying to force me into a situation where I had to murder an innocent woman to save a little girl's life. That last part is what made me think that I should at least hear her out, even though I could already tell that I wasn't going to like this favor she was asking.

"It's okay," she said. "When it started, he went quickly."

"How's your mom."

April frowned. "She didn't go as quickly."

"I'm sorry."

"Don't be. It's been a long time. I'm trying to make you feel guilty about the problems I had driving here, not my parents' deaths. Let's focus on that. A flat tire and no A/C for sixteen hours. Also, I'm a broke college student."

"How can I help?"

"I've been asked to speak at a small gathering. True crime enthusiasts. They want me to talk about my experience, and then answer questions. It pays really well."

"How much?"

"Fifteen thousand dollars."

"For one speech?"

"Plus a Q&A, yes."

"Okay, yes, I'd agree that it pays really well. Damn."

"And a trip up to Michigan. I've never been there before. Have you?"

"I've been to Grand Rapids once."

"This is near Detroit."

"Ah, Detroit. The most beautiful, picturesque town in America. Norman Rockwell was all over that place."

"Who?"

"What's the favor?"

"They want both of us."

"Not gonna happen."

"I phrased that wrong," said April. "They *need* both of us. It's both of us or neither. If you don't come it's no deal."

"Well, that bites."

"We wouldn't be sharing the fee. It would be fifteen thousand dollars each."

"I don't need the money."

"Mr. Fletcher, I would never criticize anybody who works an honest job. But you're working at a convenience store in—does this town even have a name?"

"Moray."

"You're working at a convenience store in Moray. There's no shame in that, but you can't tell me you're rolling in cash."

"I'm not," I said. "I'm dirt poor. I eat expired burritos. But I have everything I need."

"Well, I need a degree. I know you don't owe me anything and I have no right to ask you for a favor, but I can solve a lot of my problems with one day's work."

"Why didn't they come to me directly?"

"They say they did."

"Okay, they might have," I admitted. "I either didn't get it or I deleted it without reading it. But I'm really not interested. There has to be some way to convince them to do it without me."

"What if I gave you five thousand from my fee?" April asked. "You'd get twenty thousand dollars for a short speech and answering some questions. Please, Mr. Fletcher. It's either this or doing porn. I'm kidding. I'm not thinking about doing porn. But this would make my life so much easier."

I sighed. "What do you know about them?"

"It's a group that meets once a month to discuss a true crime case. Kind of like a book club, I guess.

"How can they afford thirty thousand dollars plus expenses?"

"It sounds like they're a bunch of rich assholes who split the cost amongst themselves. Also, they started a lot lower, but I'm a very good negotiator. I apologize for putting you in this position. I know it's not fair. I was hoping that you'd say 'Fifteen thousand dollars? Holy cow! Sign me up!'"

I sighed again.

"When you sigh like that, it makes me think you're considering it," said April. "What do I need to do to push you over the top?"

"What are you majoring in?"

"Business."

"Getting good grades?"

"Three-point-nine GPA."

I truly did not want to do this, but I also didn't want to screw up this opportunity for April. Not over a quick speech and a question-and-answer session.

"Maybe I'll donate my fee to charity," I said.

"Sure, sure, that's a great idea. And they won't make you shave your beard."

"What's wrong with my beard?"

"Nothing's wrong with your beard. I specifically said that they won't make you shave it."

"But you brought it up."

"Your beard is totally fine."

"I'm just messing with you," I told her. "I'll ditch the beard so I don't look like you found me in a cave."

"Your choice. I would never ask you for a huge favor and then criticize your facial hair."

"They're not allowed to record the speech."

"I'm sure that won't be a problem," said April. "I'm not actually the one setting any of this up, but we'll let them know that they can't record it. The guy I talked to seemed pretty easygoing, so I think they'll go with pretty much whatever you want."

"All right," I said.

"All right, meaning you'll do it?"

"Yeah."

April grinned. "Thank you so much! I can't tell you how much this means to me. Don't worry, I won't hug you."

"Why wouldn't I want you to hug me?"

"You flinched a bit, like you thought I was going to come around the counter and give you a hug. You don't look like somebody who likes being hugged."

"I have no problem with hugs." I was starting to think that my social skills had eroded since moving out to Moray. Did I look like some grouchy old codger who cringed at the thought of physical contact?

April didn't walk around the counter, but she did lean over it and give me a hug. And in that moment, I was able to convince myself that maybe this wouldn't be so bad.

CHAPTER ELEVEN

Six days later, with the first half of my speaker's fee in my bank account, I was on a flight to Detroit. First class, which was a brand-new experience for me. Legroom!

I'd considered trimming the beard way down to "dignified college professor" level, but then made an impulse decision to get rid of the whole thing. So I was now clean shaven. I'd also gotten a very short haircut, though I didn't try to cover the gray. I hadn't gone so far as to get a mani/pedi.

Since Moray didn't have any place where you could board a pet, I'd taken Tucker to a nearby town. This was only going to be an overnight trip, so hopefully he wouldn't miss me *too* much. The owner of the "doggie hotel" was an older woman with two-toned hair that was pitch-black and snow-white. It seemed like a questionable choice for somebody in her line of business to have Cruella De Vil hair, but since Tucker was a beagle and not a dalmatian I was sure he'd be fine.

At baggage claim, where my small suitcase was the first one to emerge on the conveyer belt, I saw a man holding up a sign that said "Alex Fletcher." He looked more like a stockbroker than a scary demented freak, so we were off to a promising start. I walked over to him and introduced myself.

"Very pleased to meet you," he said. "I'm Ian. I'm so looking forward to your speech."

"I didn't prepare much of a speech. The guy I talked to on the phone said it was okay to just go to questions pretty quickly."

"I'm looking forward to whatever you have to say."

He spoke very little as he drove me to the hotel (in a very nice car, though not a limousine). Though when he did a wide turn his sleeve slipped down, revealing the edge of a skull tattoo. A stockbroker with a wild side.

He got me checked in, and let me know that he'd be back to pick me up at six o'clock, so I had a couple of hours to take a nap or do whatever I wanted.

The room wasn't huge, but it had a Jacuzzi in it, and a plate of freshly cut fruit and some chocolates. I texted April to let her know I was there, then proceeded to enjoy the luxuries of modern life.

I finally got out of the Jacuzzi and got dressed in my professional speaker attire, which was slacks, a dress shirt, and an actual tie. They had not insisted on any kind of dress code, but for fifteen thousand dollars that was going to charity, I'd wear a tie. A few minutes before six, I went down to the lobby, where April was waiting.

"You're looking sharp!" she said.

"Thanks. So do you." Although "sharp" probably wasn't the right word. She was barely recognizable as the sweaty and tired girl who'd come into the convenience store. "Stunning" was a better word, with her dark purple dress, expertly applied makeup, and newly curled hair. I still thought of her as the terrified six-year-old and certainly had no romantic interest in her, but I recognized Hollywood-style glamour when I saw it.

Less than a minute later, Ian walked into the lobby. After he complimented us on our appearance, we followed him out to the car. He held the front door open for April while I climbed into the back, and then we were off.

"Are you nervous?" April asked, glancing back at me.

"Gastrointestinal agony," I said. "How about you?"

"Not quite that bad. I practiced my speech about three hundred times, so I should be okay."

"I didn't write one."

"Really?"

"I'm just going to wing it for a couple of minutes." If this were any other kind of public speaking engagement, I'd have obsessively prepared to make sure my mind didn't go blank and turn me into a babbling idiot while the audience stared at me. But I didn't care that much how this one went.

That said, I'd promised myself that I wouldn't let my disdain for the event show through. I would be cheerful and answer their questions, and fulfill my contractual obligation to talk for an hour. Mingling afterward was "strongly encouraged" but not mandatory. I might do that, depending on how it went.

It took about forty-five minutes to get to our destination. The event was at a country club, the kind where the driver had to show his ID to a security guard before he could drive us onto the premises. The building itself wasn't all that big, by country club standards—not that I had any real baseline for the size of a typical country club—but the front lawn was immense.

Ian pulled up in front, then got out to open the door for April. He probably would've opened the door for me, too, but I didn't wait for that to happen.

A man emerged from the building, a huge grin on his face. He was extremely tall, heavyset, and I suspected that his friends described him as "a great big teddy bear." He walked over to me and extended his hand. "A pleasure to meet you, man. A real pleasure."

"Thank you," I said, shaking his hand. He had one of those painfully tight grips that seemed designed to send the message that they could pop your hand like a water balloon if they felt like it. He let go of my hand and clapped me on the shoulder. "I'm Jax. We spoke on the phone."

"Right, right, thanks for inviting me."

"Thanks for coming. I know you were hesitant, but I think you'll have a good time. We're a fun little group."

Jax led us inside. Though the outside of the building had a "rich people playing golf" vibe, the inside was more like a hunting lodge. There were rifles and animal heads mounted on the walls. There was a bar, currently unattended, and a long table covered with snacks and beverages.

"Help yourself to whatever you want," Jax said. "We've got bottled water, soda, beer, wine—" He glanced at April. "You're old enough to drink, right?"

"Yes, but water is fine."

"And then we've got homemade cookies, these little sausage things, veggies and hummus, and other treats. But don't fill up too much, because we're going to have a great dinner during the break." He pointed to the left. "Restrooms are that way, around the corner. And if you keep going down that hallway, you'll see the door to the meeting room just past that. Any questions? Anything I can get for you?"

"No, this all looks great, thanks," said April. I nodded my agreement.

"Well then I'll give you two a few moments to grab some refreshments and decompress, and we'll get started in the auditorium right at seven. Thanks again for coming." He smiled at us and walked off.

April grabbed a small plate and put three cookies on it. "Are you glad you're here?" she asked.

"I'm glad to be here, right now, in this moment," I said. "I'm not looking forward to the next couple of hours."

"Are you going to watch my speech?"

"Of course." I picked up a beer, set it back down, and picked up a bottle of water.

"It might be fun."

"It won't be fun."

"It might not be a complete nightmare."

"That I will concede," I said, opening the bottle and taking a big drink.

I tried one of the little sausage things, and it was absolutely delicious—a reminder that sausage is much better when it contains a trace of moisture. April took a bite of one of her cookies, declared it scrumptious, but then decided that she was too nervous to eat any more.

A couple of minutes before seven, we walked down the hallway and into the meeting room. It had about a hundred seats, metal folding chairs, but only seven people. Six men, counting Jax and Ian, and a woman.

Jax walked over to us. "I just want to say again how excited we are about this."

"Is everybody here?" I asked.

He nodded. "I told you on the phone we were an intimate group."

I'd been uncomfortable since arriving here, but this crossed into "unnerving" territory. My feelings weren't hurt at the poor turnout —as far as I was concerned, the fewer people, the better—but at the same time, paying thirty-thousand dollars plus expenses to bring us in to speak to seven people seemed extremely strange.

Not that I knew much about speaking fees. Maybe you could

pay a lot more to have a musical superstar perform in your living room. Still…

"How can you afford this?" I asked. "It works out to, what, forty-five hundred a person? That's crazy."

"I think it's tacky to brag about wealth," said Jax. "But let me ask you a question. If you order an ice cream sundae, and it's an extra fifty cents for whipped cream and a cherry, and you *really* want that whipped cream and cherry, is the fifty cents a dealbreaker?"

"No."

"To our members, asking for forty-five hundred dollars to hear you speak is about the same as asking for fifty cents to make your ice cream sundae even more delicious. I promise you, they'll all be able to pay their electric bill this month."

"Gotcha," I said. "I was just wondering."

"It's a fair question. Now if you'll have a seat, I think it's time to begin." He clapped his hands together, twice. "Everybody, it's time for our presentations!"

The six other people all sat in the front row, side by side. To be perfectly honest, they didn't all *look* like rich assholes. The woman, who was maybe in her forties, looked like an executive who got called a bitch a lot behind her back. But the men, all white guys, didn't really convey an aura of vast wealth and privilege. One of them looked like a gas station attendant. As a convenience store clerk, I wasn't ridiculing his profession—I also did not convey the aura of somebody who could drop a few thousand bucks to hear a speech.

Jax gestured for April and me to take a seat as well. We sat in the third row, off to the side.

He walked up to the podium and tapped on the microphone to be sure it was on. A microphone didn't seem necessary to speak to a tiny group of people in the front row, but I guess he wanted a professional vibe.

"Thank you all for coming," he said. "We have a great lineup of speakers for you today. As you know, tonight we'll be discussing the Darren Rust case. And we're all thrilled beyond measure to have the man most tragically caught up in Darren Rust's orbit, Alex Fletcher."

The small audience applauded.

"Before that, we'll hear from a woman who encountered Darren Rust when she was only six years old. She shared her memories in the documentary *Rust*, but this evening she's here live to answer whatever questions you may have. Please welcome April Gatheren."

April smiled and waved as they applauded.

"But first," said Jax, "a few words from one of our own. Ian, come on up here."

Ian walked up to the podium while Jax stepped off to the side. Ian cleared his throat, coughed a couple of times, and then began to speak.

"Hi," he said. "You all know me. I made some mistakes. Did some bad things. Nobody's writing books or making documentaries about me, and nobody's meeting once a month to talk about somebody like me..." He held for laughter, and got a couple of chuckles. "But I was punished for my crimes, and I did six years in Fitzpatrick Federal Prison."

I was not happy to hear that little revelation.

"I got out early for good behavior, but in my last year we got a brand-new inmate. Young man by the name of Darren Rust. Nine fingers. Mismatched teeth—he had a bunch of them knocked out, and the prison dentist did a terrible job of putting his smile back together. A good-looking guy apart from that. Not that I'm queer or anything, just stating a fact." He held for laughter again, but nobody chuckled this time.

"He was kind of withdrawn at first. Which made sense. Most people aren't gregarious when they first get locked away for the rest of their lives. But one day at lunch he asked if the seat across from me was free, and I said that it was, and we struck up a conversation over our meatloaf and applesauce. The grossest meatloaf you ever did taste, by the way." This time he didn't bother to hold for laughter. "He's an interesting guy. A *very* interesting guy. He's the kind of guy who when he talks, you want to hear more. Oh, he did some monstrous things, and he'll answer for all of that when he finds himself at the gates of hell, but he also has a lot to say. And I'm not the only one who thought so. He asked permission to sit with me that first time, but it didn't take long before people were asking to sit at *his* table."

I wanted to stand up and tell Ian to shut the hell up. I wasn't here to listen to some ex-con give a speech about how enthralling it was to spend time with Darren. But, no, I could make it through this. I didn't want to embarrass April or make her forfeit the second half of her fee.

"On the day that I got to walk out of there a free man, we weren't friends," Ian said. "He told me that he doesn't have friends anymore. But I had an *understanding*. I understand why our guest speaker went along with him so long."

Fuck you, fuck you, fuck you, I thought.

"Is Darren Rust a terrible human being? Of course he is. But as somebody who spent time around him—and in prison, all you *have* is time—he's a lot more than just the guy who killed those innocent people. A lot more."

He coughed again.

"Anyway, you're not here for me, so I'm gonna sit back down. Thank you."

The other six people applauded. April clapped politely, though she gave me an uncomfortable look and mouthed "*I'm sorry*" while she did it. I restrained myself enough to settle for not clapping rather than booing.

If not for April, I would've stormed right out of there. Screw the fee. I was donating it anyway.

"Thank you very much, Ian," said Jax, returning to the podium. "That was very insightful. And now that our opening act is out of the way, let's give a very warm welcome to April Gatheren."

April took a deep breath, glanced down at her notes one last time, and walked up to the podium. Jax adjusted the microphone for her, then sat down in the front row next to the others.

She looked absolutely petrified. So much so that I worried that she might pass out, or at the very minimum vomit all over the podium. But after a few moments she regained her composure and began to speak.

CHAPTER TWELVE

"When I was six years old, I was tied to a bed by a madman," said April, in what I had to admit was a pretty gripping opening. "I don't remember everything about it. For example, memories of actually being kidnapped no longer exist for me. The rest of my memories are in flashes. Some are extremely sharp and clear. Some are vague and blurry, like they might have been a dream, or a story told to me by somebody else. But I'm not here to talk about the graphic details of that day. I'm here to tell you how it impacted the rest of my life."

She went on to talk about a childhood filled with nightmares and psychological counselling, followed by the loss of her father, and then her mother. But she overcame the fear. She still had some physical scars from Darren's knife, but the emotional scars no longer controlled her. She was, for better or worse, a normal college student.

April wasn't a fantastic speaker. She read directly from her notes, rarely looking up to make eye contact with her audience, and spoke in a nervous monotone. Also, sitting behind the seven people watching her, I could tell from their body language that they weren't there to hear about a young woman's inspirational journey. They were getting fidgety. I couldn't see Ian's face when he turned to look at Jax, but I definitely saw Jax's mild shrug.

We were each supposed to speak for an hour, with the opportunity to switch to Q&A whenever we wanted. April's prepared speech went on for almost forty-five minutes, and it was not at all the angle this audience wanted on the material. I truly wished that I'd been sitting beside the podium, facing them, able to see their faces as they endured this "be the best person you can be" talk. I loved their misery. Maybe I'd try the same tactic and improvise a speech about my journey from working a desk job to discovering true bliss as a convenience store clerk.

"Thank you," she finally said. "I will now take questions from the audience." She had clearly written "*I will now take questions from the audience,*" as the end of the speech itself, but now she looked up. "Anybody?"

Everybody's hand except mine and Jax's went up.

April looked momentarily confused. To Jax, she said, "Do I call on them? Do you call on them? How does it work?"

"You can call on them if you want."

April pointed to Ian. "You."

Ian cleared his throat, then stood up. "What Darren Rust did to you was horrible. There's absolutely no argument there. But my question is, on some level, perhaps even subconsciously, do you *admire* him?"

"No."

"Fair enough. But what I'm saying is, this isn't a man who had vast resources at his disposal. He was barely even a man—he was a college freshman, he couldn't even drink. He was working alone. There were a lot of moving parts in this plan, including abducting a six-year-old girl without getting caught, and I was just wondering if, on some level, you recognize the accomplishment."

I wanted to tell Ian to sit his ass down before I knocked out his teeth like I'd knocked out Darren's. But April wasn't six years old anymore. She didn't need me to rescue her from this guy. If I did anything that cut her speech short, they might withhold the second half of her fee, and then she'd be pissed at me. So I just sat there, fuming.

"I do not recognize the accomplishment," said April. She pointed to the man next to him. "You had your hand up."

Ian sat down while the man, the one who looked like a gas station attendant, stood up. "I had a different question, but I'd like to build off of what Ian was asking, if that's all right."

April shrugged.

"Rust's plan involved *three* abductions, all of which were successful. Again, he did this entirely by himself. Kidnappers usually work as a team for a reason—it's not that easy!"

Everybody except April and me chuckled.

"So he had to steal a little girl from her parents without getting caught. On its own, that's an accomplishment. Morally wrong? Of course. But impressive. Then he had to abduct Alex Fletcher." The man turned around and gestured to me. "They were no longer friends at this point. Mr. Fletcher would never have gotten into that van with him of his own free will. Again, another accomplishment."

I clenched my fists as the man turned his attention back to April.

"And then a third abduction. Andrea Keener. An adult who had no idea who he was. He did all three of these without getting caught. Moving on to the cabin—"

"I'm sorry, did you have a question?" April asked.

"The cabin belonged to a relative, but he needed to make sure

119

nobody escaped, so he had to have a fence installed all around it. He didn't do it himself, but still, the fence wasn't originally there."

"Right," said April. "He hired somebody to build a fence. I don't have a lot of time left, so I was wondering if you could get to your question?"

"I get that he hired somebody do it, but what I'm saying is that—"

"Mark," said Jax, "you're being rude to our guest."

"I apologize. Ms. Gatheren, I apologize. I'll let somebody else speak." Mark sat down.

"Anybody else?" April asked. She pointed to the woman. "You."

"What did he smell like?" she asked.

"Who?"

"Darren Rust."

"I don't remember."

"Was it a musky scent? Was it a woodsy scent? Did he smell bad? Did he smell good? Did he smell like blood?"

April gave her a twitchy smile. "I didn't know blood had a smell. You always read about it having a coppery *taste*, but I've never heard of it having a coppery smell. I honestly don't remember what he smelled like. It was a long time ago. I'm sorry."

This had been a terrible mistake. Why the hell were none of the others calling out the woman for her depraved question? What did Darren *smell* like? What kind of creepy-ass thing was that to ask somebody who'd been abducted as a child? I thought I'd be speaking to a group of true crime enthusiasts, but these people were starting to sound as messed up as Luna.

I was going to let April finish without intervening, but then we were out of there. I was done with this shit. They could keep the second half of my fee.

"Any—any other questions?" April asked, looking like she might start to cry.

A man in a nice suit raised his hand. April pointed to him. "What's your favorite color?" he asked.

"My favorite color?"

"Yes."

"I don't know. I don't really have one. Green, I guess."

"Thank you. Just trying to relieve the tension."

"Well, I think I'm about out of time," said April. "Thank you all for listening."

"No, it's okay, you still have another ten minutes," Jax told her. "There's time for some more questions. Anybody else?"

All of the hands went up.

April pointed to another man. "Go ahead."

"You've talked at length about how you were able to turn your life around. It sounds like you're a young lady with a very promising future ahead of you. In fact, my understanding is that you're using the money you've earned from this talk to finance your higher education. So my question is, is it possible that Darren Rust helped you? As traumatic as the experience was, do you think you could be worse off, right now, without it?"

"Are you out of your fucking mind?" April asked. "I'm sorry, no disrespect, but seriously, are you out of your fucking mind?"

"Hear me out," said the man. "You wouldn't command a speaking fee like this without the incident. You got to be in a documentary by a respected filmmaker. These opportunities were a direct result of your encounter with Darren Rust. I'm not saying that you owe him a debt of gratitude. Nobody here is saying that. That would be absurd. What I'm asking, and what I think others have been trying to get at, is whether Darren Rust might have *improved* your life?"

"I'm sorry, what's your name, sir?"

"Harvey."

"Harvey, that is a load of bullshit. First of all, I was barely in the documentary. They had that camera on me for a few hours but used, what, maybe a minute of it? Second of all, it's not like I'm getting flooded with offers for speaking engagements. This is the first one, and I'm standing here listening to you telling me I should be grateful."

Harvey shook his head. "No, no, I specifically said that nobody expected you to be grateful."

Ian spoke up. "All we want is for you to acknowledge that this could have been a positive thing in your life. That's all. We're not saying that you should have a Darren Rust poster on your bedroom wall or that you should send him Christmas cards. We're asking you to admit that Darren Rust brought some good into your life."

"Your name is Ian, right?"

"Yes."

"Did I call on you, Ian?"

"No."

"This is not an open discussion," said April. "This is a question-and-answer session. If you have a legitimate question, please raise your hand and I will call on you. Are you okay with that process, Ian?"

"I will consider myself properly chastised."

"Thank you. You know, I hate the phrase 'We're going to have to agree to disagree,' but I think that's where we are. If you all want to suck Darren's shriveled little dick, that's fine, but if you expect me to say that being kidnapped, tied to a bed, and worked over with a knife while I screamed for my mom and dad was a good thing, then fuck each and every one of you. Fuck you, Ian. Fuck you, Harvey. Ma'am, I don't know your name, but fuck you. I'm not going to go down the whole row, but if I didn't call you out you can assume that you can also go fuck yourself."

Suddenly this event wasn't so bad.

"All right, all right," said Jax, standing up. "We all enjoy a lively discussion, but this is becoming hostile. That was never our intention. I would like to apologize to our guest for the unpleasant vibe. We do very much appreciate you being here."

The woman raised her hand but didn't wait for April to call on her. "Did you see his dick?"

"Are you asking me if he was a pedophile? It wouldn't surprise me, but no, I didn't see his dick. Sorry to disappoint you."

"I'm asking because, whatever you think about Darren Rust, you can't deny that he projects a big-dick energy. There's not a chance in hell that it's shriveled and little."

"Not even when he gets out of the pool," said Ian. Everybody laughed.

April looked over at Jax. "Are we done yet?"

"I think it's okay to cut this off early, all things considered." He walked over to the podium as April stepped away from it. "I would like to thank Ms. Gatheren for being with us this evening and sharing her insight. Let's all give her a big round of applause."

Everybody applauded as April walked back and slammed herself down into the seat next to me. I tried to give her a sympathetic look, but she turned away.

"All right, well, it's now time for our dinner break," said Jax. "We've got a great spread for you—vegan for you, Mark—so let's all head over to the dining room!"

The members of the audience stood up and walked toward the exit. April and I remained sitting.

"Do you want to skip dinner?" I asked her.

April shook her head. "We have to endure another hour of this. We might as well get a nice meal out of it."

"Oh, no, screw that. I'm not giving my talk. If you're ready to leave, I'm all for it."

"You won't get the second half of your fee."

"I don't want it. If they try to take back the first half, they're more than welcome to send an attorney after me. Nobody warned us that we'd be speaking to a bunch of drooling perverts."

April wiped a tear from her eye and smiled. "I didn't actually see any drool."

"I'm sure it was there, glistening in the fluorescent lights. Seriously, to hell with these people. Let's go."

"Sounds good to me."

We stood up. Everybody had left the room except Jax.

"I'm sorry about that," he said. "We're a very passionate group, and we can occasionally get a bit enthusiastic about the subject matter."

"We're leaving," I told him.

"Excuse me?"

"We're done. We're going home."

Jax frowned. "That seems kind of extreme, don't you think?"

"That lady asked April how Darren smelled. That, to me, is a perfectly good reason to call it a night."

"I completely understand why that would have made April uncomfortable," said Jax. "I thought it crossed the line myself. But let's also not forget that you're both receiving a *very* generous speaking fee. I'm not saying that their questions were appropriate, but I do believe that you're being paid well enough to deal with some inappropriate ones."

"That's what you believe, huh?" I asked.

"Yes."

"Well, Jax, I hate to say it, but I'm not a prostitute. It's not a case where I'll do the really disgusting stuff if you pay me enough. We were brought here under false pretenses, and I'm not going to stand up there and talk to people while they whack off to thoughts about Darren. I've been through this before. Not doing it again. We're leaving now."

"What false pretenses?" asked Jax. "I never made any promises about how your audience would behave. If it offended you, I apologize, but I'm deeply insulted by the suggestion that you were misled."

"Then I'm so very sorry that I deeply insulted you. I hope you can find it somewhere in your heart to forgive me for my thoughtless comment. What I'm saying, and if you need me to say it louder I'll be more than happy to do so, is that we're done with this bullshit. We're leaving. Good-bye."

"All right. I can't keep you here against your will. I'll have Ian give you a ride back to your hotel."

"Nah, we're fine. I'll call a cab."

"We're not reimbursing you for the cab."

"I think we'll be okay."

"What did you mean when you said you've been through this before?"

"I mean that I had an ex-girlfriend who was infatuated with him. As you might guess, it didn't end well."

"I heard it was more like a fuck buddy."

I just stared at him. The circumstances of Jeremy's death were a matter of public record, but I *really* didn't like the way he said that.

Jax smiled, as if my expression gave away exactly how stressed-out I'd suddenly become. "What's the matter, Alex? Feeling nervous all of a sudden?"

CHAPTER THIRTEEN

For a moment, I couldn't breathe.

And then I realized that I needed to take action *now*. Run? Attack him? Waiting around for him to reveal his master plan wasn't an option. He was a big guy, but he might expect me to go with "stunned silence" over "immediate violence."

The Alex Fletcher who just passively let bad things happen to him was gone.

I sucker punched him in the gut. April's gasp was louder than Jax's grunt. As he clutched his belly, I grabbed the closest folding chair, and like a professional wrestler I bashed it into him. He stumbled away from me. Without hesitation, I swung it again, as hard as I could. He held up his arm to block it, which was a terrible mistake on his part, because his arm was no match for the chair. He cried out in pain.

I bashed him again, hitting him in the back, and he dropped to his knees.

There was a tricky balance here. I needed him to be dazed enough that I could use him as a hostage—or at least a shield—but not so badly injured that he couldn't walk. But we also needed to get out of this building as soon as possible, so I couldn't squander valuable time beating the shit out of him.

"Get up or I'll shatter your skull," I told him.

He didn't get up. I didn't swing the chair at his head, but kind of jabbed him with it, hard enough that it hurt but not enough to further incapacitate him.

"I mean it," I said. "I'll beat you to death."

He held up his good arm. I couldn't tell how badly his other arm was injured, but he certainly wasn't doing anything with it at the moment. "All right, all right."

"Now!"

Jax got up. Blood trickled from the corner of his mouth.

"We're getting out of here," I said, giving him a violent shove toward the door. "Move!"

April picked up a chair of her own. Threatening to beat a hostage to death with metal folding chairs unless we were allowed to leave was about as bad as escape plans got, but I didn't have anything better right now.

Jax spun around and grabbed for the chair.

I bashed him in the head. He dropped to the tile floor, landing badly.

The door opened and Ian walked in. "What the hell is—?" He saw Jax on the floor and gaped at me in horror. "What did you do to him?"

Ian stepped into the meeting room. "Stay back," I told him.

He held up his hands, palms out, in an "I mean you no harm" gesture. "Be cool," he said. "Be cool. Nobody's going to hurt you."

The others all filed back into the room. They all looked appropriately shocked at what they saw.

"Let me check him out," said Ian. "I'm not going to do anything to you. I just want to make sure he's okay."

I took several steps back, as did April. Ian hurried forward and crouched beside Jax, who wasn't moving and who was bleeding badly from his left ear.

The woman took out her cell phone and tapped at the screen.

Had I seriously messed up? In the moment, Jax sneering and asking if I was feeling nervous all of a sudden sounded like a cue for Luna to step out and reveal that she'd been the mastermind behind this all along. I'd felt like I needed to act without hesitation.

Now, with everybody looking genuinely surprised and distraught, the excuse of "He taunted me about Luna!" seemed woefully insufficient to justify the unmoving bleeding man on the floor.

The woman gave the address and explained that there was a man with a severe head injury who needed help. In response to an apparent question, she said it was blunt force trauma. "They're sending an ambulance," she informed everybody.

"Jax?" asked Ian. "Jax? Can you hear me?" He gently tapped Jax's cheek, but he was unresponsive. Blood from his ear was beginning to pool under his head.

"What the hell happened?" Harvey asked me.

"He—he—" He hadn't attacked me, really. He'd tried to take the chair away. I could lie, but April had seen the whole thing, and I didn't know if she would back me up or not. I noticed that she'd taken a couple of extra steps away, possibly to not be so close to me. "He threatened me."

"What do you mean he threatened you? What did he say?"

I tried to think of how to explain this. Saying it out loud, I was starting to worry that I'd sound like a paranoid psychopath.

"I heard it was more like a fuck buddy."

"What's the matter, Alex? Feeling nervous all of a sudden?"

After the way these freaks had behaved in April's Q&A, Jax's question had sounded incredibly sinister. I'd had to defend myself.

I'd had to act immediately to figure out a way to get April and me safely out of there.

It was all completely logical in that split second when I had to make a decision. Much less so in the aftermath.

"Let's worry about him for now," I said. I realized that I was still holding the chair and set it on the floor.

"Look at his arm," said Harvey. "What did you *do* to him?"

I was feeling serious panic, but maybe my instincts hadn't been wrong. Maybe we were still in danger. Maybe Luna was standing next to the food table, enjoying a cookie.

But I doubted I could get April to try to push past all six of them with me, and trying to flee the scene of a serious assault could work out very badly for me later.

"How's he doing?" the woman asked Ian.

"He's not breathing." Ian pressed his fingers to Jax's wrist. "I can't feel a pulse. I think he's gone."

Some of them stared at Jax. Some of them stared at me.

"Are you sure?" asked Mark.

"I'm not a doctor," said Ian. He gestured to the ever-expanding pool of blood. "If anybody wants to take over, be my guest."

Mark crouched down next to Jax. He pressed his fingers against Jax's neck. "Shit."

Maybe this was all fake. Maybe they'd set me up.

And maybe I was completely losing it. This wasn't a setup. Jax hadn't tricked me into bashing his skull in with a metal chair, and that wasn't karo syrup with red food coloring all over the floor.

"Anybody else want to check?" asked Ian. "Alex? April?"

I shook my head. I didn't look back at April, but presumably she shook her head as well. I could hear her softly crying.

"All right," said Ian. "There's an ambulance on the way, so we don't have very long to work this out. I think Jax is dead, but best-case scenario, he's going to be a vegetable. He wouldn't want to spend the rest of his life in a hospital bed, getting his meals through a feeding tube. Does anybody disagree with that?"

Nobody did.

"So we're all in agreement that letting the paramedics work on him and take him away isn't going to give Jax's story a happy ending. With that in mind, let's focus on the people who are still living. We have the resources to make Jax simply disappear. Nobody has to know what Alex did."

Wait…was Ian trying to *help* me?

"But the ambulance has given us a ticking clock, and we don't have time to discuss the pros and cons. We're going to take a vote, and it has to be unanimous. Who here agrees that we should bury the evidence of this crime?"

Ian raised his hand. A moment later, so did Mark, Harvey, and one of the other men whose name I didn't know. The second man whose name I didn't know looked at the others, then raised his hand as well.

"Wanda?" Ian asked.

Wanda sighed and raised her hand.

"Alex? You get a vote, too."

I raised my hand.

I looked back at April. She had her hand over her mouth.

"April?" asked Ian. "We need your vote. Nobody is being forced to go along with this. If you don't want to protect him, I completely understand, and we'll all tell the truth about what happened. Vote your conscience."

April let out a sob, then raised her hand.

"It's unanimous," said Ian. "Good. Right now our pressing concern is that we need to send the paramedics away. But it's a crime to make a phony 911 call, so we can't just tell them it was a joke. Wanda, what exactly did you tell them?"

"We had somebody with a severe head injury," Wanda said. "I

told them it was blunt force trauma."

Ian nodded. "If you didn't actually see it happen, you could've been wrong about the blunt force trauma. You watch a lot of crime shows but you're not a doctor, so if there's a lot of blood, you wouldn't know how severe a head injury is, right?"

"Right."

"So when the paramedics get here, we just need to present them with somebody who has a bleeding head injury. Any volunteers?"

Not surprisingly, nobody volunteered.

"Then the obvious candidate is Alex, right? He's the one we're trying to save. Alex, are you willing to slash open your forehead to stay out of prison?"

I was in such a state of shock at this point that it took me a moment to answer. "Yes."

"I'll do it," said April. "It's my fault he was here in the first place. He never wanted to do this."

"No," I said. "I'll do it."

"We don't have time for a full debate," said Ian. "I think that Alex is more likely than April to be able to convince them that he doesn't need to go to the emergency room, so Alex wins. Mark, David, Cliff—you guys drag Jax out of the way and clean this up the best you can. There's no reason the paramedics would come in here, but we might as well prepare for every possibility."

Mark, and the other two guys who were apparently named David and Cliff nodded.

"Everybody else come with me to the main room."

It felt like my legs were moving on their own as we filed out of the meeting room and walked down the hallway. I was dizzy but didn't think I was going to fall over. It didn't surprise me that this event had gone poorly, but I'd never really imagined that I'd be walking away from a bloody corpse.

We walked into the main room. "Should somebody warn the

security guard that an ambulance is going to show up?" Harvey asked.

"No," said Ian. "He'll let them through, but even if there's a ten-second conversation, that's ten more seconds we have instead of him already having the gate lifted for them." He looked at the table with all of the food. "We can make one of these knives work, I guess, but does anybody have a pocketknife?"

"I do," said Harvey. He took out a very large pocketknife and snapped out the blade.

"Do you want me to cut you, or do you want to cut yourself?" Ian asked me.

I didn't trust anybody else to do it. "I'll cut myself."

"You sure? You can't hesitate. And it has to be a real cut, not just a little scratch."

"I'll do it."

Ian shrugged, took the knife from Harvey, and handed it to me.

Wanda walked over to the front door, opened it, and peered outside. "The ambulance is at the front gate."

"Make yourself bleed," Ian told me. "You're the one who's screwed if this plan doesn't work, so don't be shy."

I didn't even think about it. Didn't think about the best way to go about this, or what germs might have been on the blade, or whether there was another solution to this problem. I simply slashed the blade across my forehead.

A searing pain shot across my skin, and the blood immediately began to flow.

"Yep, that'll do it," said Ian. He picked up a handful of napkins. "Let it gush until the ambulance pulls up in front of the building."

"How are we explaining this?" Wanda asked.

"I don't know," Ian admitted. "He tripped while he was carrying it?"

"That's more like something where he'd jab it into his eyeball," said Wanda.

"A drunken dare," said April. "Guys are stupid. One of you dared him to do it and he did."

"What do you think, Alex?" asked Ian. "Can you sell that?"

"It's the best we've got," I said.

"Then let's get this man some beer breath." Ian picked up a bottle of beer, popped off the cap, and handed it to me. I took a huge swig, swished it around, and swallowed. Ian took the bottle back from me as I blinked some blood out of my eyes. "You really went deep there," he said, looking at my forehead. "I think it's time to start mopping it up."

I pressed the napkins to my forehead as there was a knock at the door.

Wanda opened it. Two paramedics stood outside.

"Wow, that was really fast," she said. "Thank you so much. I apologize—it's not as bad as I thought, and he's an absolute dumbass. You don't even want to know how this happened."

She stepped out of the way and the paramedics came inside. I walked over to them.

"Sir, go ahead and have a seat," one of the paramedics told me. Ian slid a chair over to me and I sat down. I pulled the napkins away from my forehead. "Looks like you cut yourself good, but head wounds tend to bleed a lot, so they look more serious than they are."

I nodded my understanding.

"It's just a laceration?" he asked.

"He had fallen and I thought he hit his head," said Wanda. "But I guess he didn't."

"Is that true?" the paramedic asked me. "You didn't hit your head?"

"No."

"Any blurred vision?"

"No, nothing like that."

As he cleaned out the wound, he asked me some basic questions, which I assumed were to check if I had a concussion or not. I considered giving him a fake name, but he might need to see my ID for some reason, and in my flustered state I might blurt out something ridiculous.

"How did this happen?" he asked, tightly pressing some gauze against my forehead.

"We were just being stupid," I said.

"Being stupid how?"

"Stupid dares. You know how it is."

"Enlighten me."

"I'd had too much to drink," I said. Surely they wouldn't do a blood alcohol test to prove that I *wasn't* drunk, right? "We were playing this game, and it got out of control, and he said I was too scared to cut myself, and I said I wasn't, and he dared me, and I was just goofing around and I thought I had the dull end of the blade touching me. Obviously, I didn't. It was a really stupid way for this to happen."

"You'll get no argument from me," said the paramedic. He pulled the gauze away. "You were lucky. Looks like you'll only need a stitch or two."

"Is that something you can do here?" asked Ian.

The paramedic shook his head. "No, this isn't life-threatening at all. We'll get you patched up, and then you'll need to go to the emergency room." He didn't sound very sympathetic to my plight, probably because he thought I was a complete moron.

"Okay, thank you," I said.

"Yes, thanks," said Ian. "We'll take him right in."

"Oh, hey, I was wondering where I recognized you from," said the other paramedic. "You were friends with that guy Darren Rust, right? From that new movie?"

CHAPTER FOURTEEN

S hould I lie?

I wasn't sure what to do here. The idea that the dude who Darren Rust forced to decapitate a woman slashed open his own forehead on a drunken dare could be newsworthy. If that brought attention to this event, it might be more difficult for Ian and the others to make Jax disappear.

"Nope," I said. "Not me."

"Have you seen the movie?" Ian asked.

"No, but I read about it. I heard it wasn't that good." The paramedic went to work getting my forehead patched up without asking any further questions.

If he bothered to research it later, he'd pull up the name Alex Fletcher and see that I was indeed the guy. But that would only happen if he had lingering curiosity, and he seemed to have accepted my "Nope, not me," and moved on.

When he finished, he told me to have one of my buddies drive me to the hospital and get the stitch or two, and to be a little more careful in the future. Trying to lighten the mood, I asked if mine was the dumbest injury they'd seen lately, and he said no, but that I shouldn't be too proud of that.

The paramedics left.

We all stood in silence for a moment.

"All right," said Ian. "That went about as well as we could have hoped. Let's go back to the meeting room. Everybody, please feel free to help yourself to a snack to bring along."

April and I did not help ourselves to any snacks. We walked as a group back to the meeting room. When we went inside, I saw that Jax and the pool of blood was gone. Mark, David, and Cliff were seated, waiting for us.

"Nice work," said Ian.

"It wouldn't hold up to a forensics team, but if anybody came snooping around it would've been fine," said Mark. "How'd it go?"

"Great," said Ian. "Alex here did a lovely job of mangling his forehead, and they left. So now all we need to do is have a serious discussion about what happens next. Let's move some chairs into a circle."

Mark, David, and Cliff arranged nine chairs into a small circle, as if this was a Parent Teacher Association meeting. Actually, I didn't know how they arranged the chairs in a PTA meeting, since my daughter hadn't lived long enough for me to attend one.

We all sat down.

"First of all, congratulations to everybody for quick thinking and quick action in a very stressful, time-sensitive situation. Let's give ourselves a round of applause."

I thought he was kidding, but no, everybody except April and me offered up some light applause for their handling of this crisis.

"So, Alex, I guess the question on everybody's mind is, why did you do it?"

"I felt threatened."

"The ticking clock is gone," Ian told me. "You can give a full answer."

"Three years ago I was in a relationship with a woman named Luna Booth. I'm sure you all know about this. She was never interested in me. She was obsessed with Darren and basically exchanging love letters with him in prison. She ended up murdering my friend Jeremy and then disappearing to who the hell knows where?"

"Right, we know about her," said Ian.

"After you guys got all creepy during April's question and answer session, I mentioned to Jax that it wasn't that different from how Luna had behaved. I called her my ex-girlfriend. Jax said that he heard it was more like a fuck buddy. He said it in this weird, suspicious way. I'm sure I looked shocked, and then he smiled and asked if I was feeling nervous all of a sudden."

"And then...?"

"And then I picked up a chair and bashed him with it."

"Okay. So you understand why we have a problem with that, right?"

"I understand," I said. "And here's what you need to understand. You know my whole history. You know everything I went through because of Darren Rust and Luna Booth. I lost my friends, I lost my family, and I almost lost my life. So, yes, when Jax implied that I had walked into his trap, I took measures to defend myself."

"Extreme measures."

"Extreme measures were called for. I get how it sounds, but if you'd been through the same thing as me, you wouldn't have just stood there and waited for Jax to explain what he meant. And if you think it's ridiculous that Luna might have stepped out and said that the whole thing was a trap, you haven't been paying attention to my life."

Ian nodded. "That's reasonable. Is there anything else you want to add?"

"No."

"April?"

"I can't say how I would have behaved if I were Alex," said April. "But I agree that Jax sounded…I guess *sinister* is the best way to describe it. He sounded sinister. I also thought he might say that Luna was here."

"All right," said Ian. "Would anybody else like to speak?"

Wanda raised her hand.

"Go ahead."

"Clearly, you didn't kill him in cold blood," Wanda told me. "It wasn't premeditated. You reacted quickly to what you thought was a life-threatening danger. At the same time, our friend Jax is dead. He's not unconscious or incapacitated, he's dead. I believe you when you say you thought Luna might have been involved in this whole thing, and that you thought it might be a trap. What I don't understand is why Jax is dead. Why did you kill him?"

"I was trying to use him as a hostage. The chair was my only weapon. I tried to keep him dazed and injured so that April and I could force our way out of here if we needed to. When he attacked and tried to get the chair away from me, I had to bash him in the head."

"You *had* to bash him in the head?"

"I wasn't going to just try to fend him off like a lion tamer."

"Okay," said Wanda. "I guess what I'd like from you, to make me feel better about the way this all went down, is an acknowledgment that maybe Darren wasn't completely wrong about you."

"What?" I asked.

"You've laid out how everything happened and you've made a reasonably convincing argument for your behavior. To me, the missing element is the idea that, on some level, you wanted this to happen."

"You've got to be kidding me."

"Darren thought the two of you would make a great team. I don't believe that you have the soul of a serial killer, and I think it's safe enough to speak for everybody else and say that they don't believe it, either. But Darren saw *something* in you, and the cold, hard facts of the matter are that there was no trap, and that you brutally murdered Jax. I would just like to hear from you that he wasn't *entirely* wrong."

"What do you think is more likely?" I asked. "That Darren was partially right when he saw this magical aura of a psycho killer in me, or that my experience with him and Luna turned me into the kind of person who would take immediate action when he's threatened?"

"Quite honestly, I think it's a little of both."

I wanted to tell her that she was completely full of shit. But the stomach-churning fact was that I needed these people. "Jax was behaving in a sinister manner" wouldn't hold up in court. If they turned against me, I was screwed. As much as the idea sickened me, I was going to have to tell them what they wanted to hear.

"I don't know," I said. "Maybe."

"Darren's a pretty perceptive guy," said Ian. "He's not a good man but he's a good judge of character. I would trust his intuition over just about anybody else in the world. He noticed things about me that I hadn't even noticed about myself, and when he pointed them out it was life changing. So I'm not buying the idea that he got you completely wrong, especially after what happened tonight."

The other assholes murmured their agreement.

"Fine," I said. "I believe that, based on my past experiences and the way Jax was behaving, that my actions were justified. If you want me to admit that there's a tiny little chance that Darren was right, then okay, I'll admit that it's not one hundred percent out of the realm of possibility that he was right."

"You don't sound very sincere," said Ian.

"What do you want me to do, burst into tears and say that he was right all along? If any of you are a certified notary and you want me to sign a paper saying that, yes, there's a point zero zero zero one percent chance that Darren was right about me, I'll do it."

"No need," said Ian. "I'd like you and April to step away for a minute. Don't leave the room—just go over to the far corner while we have a quick discussion."

April and I stood up and walked away from the others. Their chairs squeaked on the tile as they tightened the circle.

"I'm sorry," I told April.

"I'm sorry, too. I should never have forced you to do this."

"You didn't *force* me."

"I made it hard for you to say no."

"You did, that's true. But don't go thinking you're so unbelievably charming that I had no choice."

April smiled, but it only lasted for an instant. "Do you think they'll let us leave?"

"Yeah." I was pretty sure they would. This could all still be some elaborate setup, but I was relatively confident that their plan was for us to come to terms so we could part ways. I didn't say this to April, but if I felt like we were in danger, I wouldn't hesitate to beat another one of them to death with a metal folding chair.

"I wish I'd brought a gun," said April.

"You'll know better the next time a group of psychopaths asks you to be their guest speaker."

This earned another very brief smile. Then we just stood there, not speaking.

"We're done," Ian called out.

April and I returned to our seats. The others kept their chairs in place, so it was a very tight circle, with our knees practically touching.

"We came to a quick decision," Ian informed me. "If you and April agree to these terms, we can all leave without tonight being even more unpleasant."

I nodded. "We're listening."

"First of all, you have both forfeited the second half of your payments."

"All right."

"The first half, you can keep. Not because we think you deserve it, but because we don't want the wire transfers to raise suspicion. If this were a joking matter, I'd say that you could keep it as a kill fee. But it's not, so don't laugh."

"I'm not laughing."

"We are all putting ourselves at risk to cover up your crime. It's not like you strangled a crack whore that we can fling into a Dumpster and call it a night. Making Jax disappear without it all crashing down on you is going to be difficult. We can make it happen, I promise, but you'll each owe us a favor in return."

"What kind of favor?" I asked.

"That will be determined at a later date."

"Fuck that."

"You don't have a lot of negotiating room here," Ian said.

"All of you incriminated yourselves as soon as we sent those paramedics away. You're all in this now. I'm not going to promise to grant you some mystery favor."

"Is that so? If we called the police right now, do you really think we'd all go to jail? We might have some explaining to do, but do *not* make the mistake of pretending that we're all negotiating from equal positions of power. *You* are the one who is in deep shit, Alex. And if we offer to help you out of this mess in exchange for a mystery favor, then you'd damn well better take our deal and thank us for it."

"What kind of favor?"

"We don't know yet."

"I don't want to have this hanging over my head."

"Do you think we care?" asked Ian, raising his voice. "Do you seriously believe that we care that you might have a sleepless night or two over this? You murdered our friend. You should be in handcuffs right now. You should be wondering if your eyes will explode in your head when they pull the lever on the electric chair. I think every one of us would be perfectly happy to watch you leave in the back of a police car. *We* are protecting *you*, not vice-versa."

"Well, I'm sorry, but I need to have some idea of what I'm agreeing to. Are you going to ask me to come over and help one of you guys move? Am I going to have to assassinate the president? What?"

"I said, we don't know yet. It will be appropriate."

"I don't know what an appropriate favor is."

"Neither do we," said Ian. "Look, we don't want to pressure you into taking this deal, but our involvement in this shitstorm gets deeper the longer we wait. So take the deal or we call the cops. Your choice."

"We'll take it," said April.

"No," I said. "She doesn't speak for both of us."

"We'll take it," April repeated. "We'll do the favor."

"It sounds like one of you is smarter than the other," said Ian. "Or at least more practical. Again, I'm not trying to rush you, but Wanda, please call the police and tell them that a man named Alex Fletcher just murdered somebody here."

Wanda took out her cell phone.

"All right, you win," I said.

"So you're saying we have a deal?"

"Yeah." If they upheld their end of the bargain, then they *would* be screwed if the police got involved, and I could tell them to shove their favor up their asses if it was something awful.

"Then let's shake on it." Ian stood up and offered his hand.

I stood up and shook it. He turned to April, who also stood up and shook his hand.

"This has definitely been our most interesting meeting," he said with a chuckle. "I guess it's officially adjourned now, except for the obvious matter of hiding a dead body and cleaning up every trace of a crime scene. Thank you for coming, everybody."

The others pushed back their chairs and stood up.

"Harvey, would you like to drive them back to their hotel?" Ian asked.

"We'll get a cab," I said.

"No, you won't. If you do that, then there's a record of a taxi showing up here to pick you up. That's one extra detail that could sink our effort to keep you out of jail. Harvey will give you a ride. Again, help yourself to some cookies and snacks on your way out."

NOBODY SPOKE as we rode back to the hotel. I kept expecting Harvey to pull off onto a desolate road, where April and I would meet our doom, even though if they wanted to kill us they could've done it just as easily before we left. If they had the means to hide one corpse, why not three?

We pulled up in front of the hotel. "You two have a good night now," said Harvey as we got out of the car. "Sleep tight."

April and I walked into the hotel lobby.

"What now?" she asked.

I shrugged. "I guess we fly back home and wait."

"I'm so, so—"

"No more apologies. I'm a big boy. I made my own terrible decision."

April gave me a hug, and then she began sobbing. I stood there, holding her, as she sobbed into my chest and the front desk clerk awkwardly pretended nothing was happening.

Finally, she stopped crying. "Let's promise to stay in touch," she said.

"Definitely."

"I know it's early, but I'm going to bed."

"Yeah, me too."

We hugged again, then walked to the elevators. She got off on her floor, then I returned to my room. I didn't feel like making use of the Jacuzzi. I flopped onto the bed, fully clothed, and lay there for a completely sleepless night.

CHAPTER FIFTEEN

April's flight was earlier than mine, so she was gone by the time I checked out of the hotel and took a shuttle to the airport. And then I flew home.

I was sick to my stomach, but feelings of guilt had very little to do with it. Yes, I'd taken a human life. Possibly one that meant me no harm. Yet nobody was going to convince me that I should have simply brushed off Jax's "Feeling nervous?" question and waited to see how things played out. If those people were going to have great big creepy boners for Darren, it was Jax's own fault that I'd took the initiative to defend myself.

No, the guilt was only a tiny part of my nausea. Mostly, I didn't know if I could actually count on them to protect me. Was Jax married? Did he have kids? A boss at a day job who'd wonder why he didn't show up for work? I hadn't asked for details of their plan, and quite honestly I didn't want to know, but did they really have the means to keep the authorities from discovering what had really happened to him?

Had they sawed up his body and put the parts into individual garbage bags, to be deposited around the city? Was he buried in a shallow grave in the forest somewhere? Were they going to hire a taxidermist to stuff him, so they could gather around and look at the man who was murdered by the man who'd killed for Darren Rust?

I also wasn't entirely convinced that Luna wasn't involved somehow. Maybe she *was* going to do a big dramatic reveal, and I'd messed it up.

And, of course, the favor. What the hell would it be?

I picked up Tucker and returned to my cabin, where I tried to return to the simple life that had made me perfectly content.

I got back to reading, even though it was much more difficult to focus on the words. I ditched *The Count of Monte Cristo* and switched to *The Adventures of Huckleberry Finn*, which was still classic literature but easier to follow.

I returned to work, thankful that working at a small-town convenience store did not require much in the way of brain power or physical energy.

We hadn't made any actual arrangements for how I could be contacted about this favor. Would Ian e-mail me? Call? Send a raven at the stroke of midnight? I figured that was his problem, not mine, but every day began with the worry that this could be the one.

Days passed.

Then weeks.

April and I spoke on the phone about once a week, though we had very little to say to each other besides "Have you heard anything yet?" I'd offered to give her the money I'd earned for a speech I never delivered, and she refused to take it.

Each day ended with relief that Ian hadn't yet contacted me, but also the maddening desire to just get it over with.

And then three months had passed since I killed Jax. No police officers showed up at my cabin to interrogate me. I was happier basked in ignorance, so I only followed the case at a very high level. Jax's wife had reported that he never came home from his true crime club meeting. The others at the meeting had reported that he seemed "troubled" and had perhaps drank more than usual but certainly not enough that he shouldn't have been able to drive home. They were all praying for his safe return.

Six months after the murder, I could read again. April and I only spoke every couple of weeks, and we didn't even bother to ask if we'd heard anything. Obviously, if I had, I would've said something. Instead, she told me about her new boyfriend, and then about problems she was having with her boyfriend, and then about how she'd broken up with her boyfriend. "Offers practical advice to the lovelorn" was not among my skill sets, but I did successfully make sounds to indicate that I was listening and sympathetic to her plight.

I was starting to wonder if Ian and the others had forgotten about me.

Or, if they'd simply never come up with a favor.

Maybe, having covered up a murder, they'd decided as a group that it was safer for them not to get back in contact with me. After all, what if I refused to grant their stupid favor, and simply turned myself in? The idea that they might have simply chosen to not make me live up to my end of the deal made a lot of sense, and hopefully that's how it had all worked out.

After nine months, I was really starting to believe that this was over.

Did I have nightmares about it? Yes. But the anxiety faded to this low-level buzz, something I could stop thinking about for longer and longer periods of time. Never a full day, but eventually I could get through *most* of a day without worrying about Ian and the others returning to my life.

The constant anxiety about Luna had faded, and so did this.

One day I spoke to April, who informed me that she was doing well in school and that her new boyfriend was a total jerk, and she reminded me that the next day was the one-year anniversary of our disastrous speaking engagement.

A whole year. I'd accomplished nothing during that year except add to my number of books read, miles walked, and snack foods sold, but if we'd made it almost a full year, surely it was safe to assume that...

Well, no. Darren had waited more than a year to return.

A wait like this, long enough for me to let my guard down, was completely on brand for Darren, and quite possibly for those who were obsessed with him.

I spent the entire next day thinking that the one-year anniversary would be the perfect time for them to show back up.

They didn't.

That didn't happen until a couple of weeks later.

Tucker woke me up with a barking fit. It took a moment for my dream (I couldn't remember what it was, but it had been pleasant) to make way for the reality that my dog was going berserk as somebody pounded on my front door. I'd trained him out of this behavior when I lived in an apartment, but out here in my cabin it had been several years since my last unexpected visitor.

I glanced over at the clock. 2:02 AM.

I quickly got out of bed and hurried out of my bedroom. I'd become the kind of person who kept a shotgun by his front door, so I picked it up and peeked out the window.

It was April. I opened the door.

Her face was stained with tears and she looked terrified.

"Is everything—?" I started to ask.

"There's a gun pointed at my head," she said.

I glanced around. The porch light didn't illuminate much of the surrounding area, and somebody with a gun could've been hiding pretty much anywhere.

Tucker started to bolt from the house, but I shouted at him and he came back inside.

"I need your phone," she told me. "You have twenty seconds to hand it over or they're going to shoot me. They'll do it."

They'll do it. This wasn't good.

I ran back into my bedroom, grabbed my cell phone off my nightstand, then ran back to the front door and gave it to her. April held up the phone, showing it off to whomever was watching, then tossed it into the darkness.

"Thank you," she said, seeming to suddenly relax.

I didn't have a landline. Presumably they had already circled the cabin searching for cords to sever.

"Is it Ian and the others?" I asked.

April nodded.

I lowered my voice to a whisper. "Do you want me to pull you inside? I'll do it fast."

"No. They have three guns pointed at me."

At the edge of my yard, I saw a lighter flick on, and then a torch burst into flame, illuminating one of the guys I recognized from Detroit. Then another torch lit up. And another. And another. Soon I counted thirteen or fourteen of them. I recognized some of the people who held them, while others were strangers.

Flashlights would have worked just as well. These people were trying to be scary.

"Hello, Alex," said Ian, walking toward the cabin. "It's good to see you again."

I didn't step outside, but I pointed the shotgun at him. "Don't come any closer," I warned.

"Don't be like that. We're all friends here."

"Take one more step and I'll blow your head off."

Ian nodded and took a step backwards. "All right. I guess you're going to make this more difficult. That's fine. I completely understand. But you know why we're here, right?"

"Field trip?"

"Funny. Nobody's here to harm you, Alex."

"Of course not. Torch-wielding mobs never show up to cause problems."

"It'll be okay, I promise."

"Prove it," I said. "Let April come inside."

"No."

"You want to earn my trust? Let April go."

"I don't need to earn your trust," said Ian. "If we decide to get aggressive, you will lose. You can't fight off all of us. You owe us a favor, and we're here to collect."

"Fine. What's the favor?"

"Put down the shotgun first. I'm trying to keep this cordial, but I've got limits. How do you think this ends if you don't cooperate? Are you going to strap on a jetpack and rocket out of here? Do you have a secret tunnel that you're going to use to escape?"

"Tell me what the favor is and I'll lower the shotgun," I told him.

Ian shook his head. "You're not in control here, Alex. You need to recognize that."

That was, of course, Darren's whole deal. Control. And that's why simply dropping the shotgun and being agreeable about repaying the favor wasn't really an option. He was right—if they launched a siege against my cabin, I would lose. I could take out a couple of them, and maybe even a few, but not all of them. But I sure as hell wasn't going to make this easy for anybody.

Yes, impulsive action was why I was currently in this mess. Still, I wasn't going to passively accept my fate. When torch-waving people showed up in the middle of the night to demand payment for covering up a murder, it was safe to say that the favor wasn't going to be quick and easy.

The big advantage that April and I had was that they didn't want to kill us. These guys weren't local, so they hadn't traveled all the way down here just to shoot us. Which is not to say that they *wouldn't* shoot us, but it would probably be a last resort.

These weren't trained soldiers, ready to give up their lives for whatever deranged cause this was. If I demonstrated a willingness to pull the trigger, I couldn't imagine that any of them would charge me, prepared to take a shotgun blast to the face for no purpose except to ensure that I had one fewer shell to use to kill the others.

I wanted to whisper a warning to April that I was about to do something reckless, but Ian was too close. Even if he couldn't hear me, he'd see my lips move.

I pointed the shotgun over everybody's head and squeezed the trigger.

As expected, I was not met with a hailstorm of bullets pounding into my chest. The torches dropped, as if my visitors were ducking out of the way of a second shot. I switched the shotgun to one hand, grabbed April with the other, and pulled her inside the cabin. I left the door open.

"Holy shit!" said April. I couldn't tell if she was happy to be out of immediate danger or horrified that I'd made things a lot worse.

I handed her the shotgun. "Don't kill anybody unless they try to break in."

There wasn't time to explain my plan, so I hurried into my

bedroom. I opened the top drawer on my nightstand and took out a loaded pistol. Then I ran back to the front door.

"What if they try to burn down the cabin?" April asked.

"We're not gonna try to wait them out," I said. "Find somewhere to hide. I'll take care of this. I mean, I probably won't solve our problem, but at least we're not—actually, don't worry about it. Just hide."

I pressed the barrel of the revolver against the side of my head, then opened the door.

Ian was standing right there. "Jesus Christ!" he exclaimed.

"I'll do it," I warned him. I'd been suicidal before. This wasn't completely out of character.

"You don't think that's an extreme reaction?" he asked.

"Nope. I'm not playing your games."

"This isn't a game. Just put the gun down so we can talk like civilized people, all right?"

"There's nothing civilized about this. Darren put me through hell on earth. I'll blow my brains out before I let it happen again."

This was a bluff, and I kind of wished the gun weren't loaded. I didn't expect Ian to call the whole thing off; I just wanted to hold a bit of power in how this situation played out.

"Don't do something you'll regret," said Ian.

"Way too late for that."

"C'mon, Alex, this is insane."

"I totally agree. You're talking to a madman right now."

Ian sighed. "Okay, then. Keep a gun to your head. Try not to accidentally pull the trigger."

"I'll try. What's the favor?"

"A pledge of loyalty."

"To what?"

"To the Disciples of Rust."

154

"Are you serious? That's what you're calling yourselves? The Disciples of Rust? That's the best you could come up with?"

"Do you have a better idea?"

"I don't know," I said. "How about Darren's Dipshits?"

"We'll consider that."

"No, wait, what's a good K-word? Klan? No. Knights? Disciples of Rust Knights? It would have to be something better than that, but if you find a good K-word your acronym will be DORK."

"It's cute how you think you can stand there and insult me," said Ian. "Let's see what happens when you take it too far."

"I'd feel terrible if my words caused you distress."

Ian gave me an ugly smile. "Maybe you should go ahead and pull that trigger."

"Maybe I should."

"Do you want to meet our special guest first?"

"Is it Luna?"

"I'm impressed. It sure is."

"Well, shit, bring her on up then."

Ian whistled. Somebody, not carrying a torch, walked toward us. When she passed somebody who did have a torch, I saw in the firelight that it was indeed Luna. She walked up next to Ian and blew me a kiss. "Hello, lover."

"You look good," I said.

"Thank you."

I'd expected that when I saw her again, she'd look like a fugitive. Instead, she looked almost exactly the same as four years ago. She even had the same hairstyle. Wherever she'd been hiding, it wasn't off in a cave somewhere.

"Being in a cult has worked out well for you," I said.

"We don't like to call it a cult. It's more of an admiration society."

"That's too bad. Darren would love to know that he had a cult."

"He knows," said Luna.

"Well, I'm not going to pledge loyalty to your admiration society, so you can all just fuck right off. Go on. Just fuck right back off to Detroit or wherever you've been lurking for the past year."

"Why don't you lower the gun?"

"I like it where it is."

Luna smiled. "Remember when we were out of the woods, and I'd slashed open Jeremy's feet, and you told me that Darren wouldn't be impressed?"

"Yep. Sure do."

"I agree with you. I was angry and I hadn't thought it out well enough. But Darren *almost* drove you to suicide. You didn't actually do it. If we can take you to an even darker place, one where you finish the job, he'd be impressed, don't you think?"

She had a point. I didn't like that. "Maybe."

"We're not here to make you kill yourself. We'll be disappointed if you do. But if you think that this would be a victory for you… well, I guess you're the kind of deranged lunatic who'd fire a bullet into his brain, huh?"

"I'm not the one who worships a psychopath."

"It's not worship. Like I said, we admire him. Nobody pushes him around. He lives by his own rules."

"Not so much anymore," I said. "You don't really get to live by your own rules when you're in a maximum-security prison. It's kind of the opposite. If you want the true Darren Rust experience, you need somebody to tell you when to wake up, when to eat, and when to shit."

"Things worked out horribly for him," Luna admitted. "That's why we need to enjoy life on his terms in his honor, since right now he's trapped."

"'Right now' is understating it. He'll be locked away for the rest of his life."

"We'll see."

I lowered the gun. "Living life on Darren's terms would probably mean shooting you."

"Would it?"

"I think so."

"Then why don't you do it?"

"Because I don't want to live like Darren. I hate that fucking guy."

"Okay, Alex," said Luna. "It was a long bus ride for everybody, and we didn't come all this way to stand here and chat. You are in debt to us. You murdered somebody, my friends protected you, and now it's time for you to pay up."

"Fine," I said. "What's the favor?"

Luna extended her hand to Ian. He walked over to her and placed a knife into it.

"You've got some cutting to do," she said.

CHAPTER SIXTEEN

Luna handed me the knife, apparently not concerned that I'd try to stab her to death with it. It was a hunting knife with a brown handle and a serrated blade.

"I'm surprised it's not a red pocketknife," I said. Darren had used a red pocketknife to cut up Peter's dead dog. Later he'd given that same knife, or one just like it, to my daughter.

"I think it's time to start looking to the future," Luna said.

"What am I supposed to do?"

"Cut the word *Rust* into your flesh."

"Where?"

"Anywhere."

"I already cut my forehead open for you guys."

"That was to fool the paramedics. It was about self-preservation, not a pledge of loyalty. Looks like it healed up nicely."

"Yeah," I said. "I didn't even get stitches."

"Just pick a spot and start cutting. You can use straight lines to make it easier—you don't have to do a curved S or anything like that."

"How deep do I have to go?"

"It has to bleed," said Luna. "Not some little scrape with a couple dots of blood. It has to drip. If there's no blood on the floor, it doesn't count."

"And that's it?" I asked. "Cut four letters into my arm or leg and I'm done?"

Luna shook her head. "Then you have to cut April."

"What happened wasn't her fault."

"So? Did you already forget that we were going to shoot her if you didn't give her your phone? What made you think this was going to be fair?"

I glanced back. I wasn't sure where April was hiding.

"What if she refuses?" I asked.

"I don't know, Alex. What do you *think* happens if she refuses? Do you think something very bad will happen to her, or do you think we'll just laugh and send her on her way?"

April stepped out of my bedroom. "I won't refuse."

"Oh, look, somebody who's reasonable," said Luna. "All of it should be working out this way. You do what we tell you, get it over with, and we'll get back on the bus. I don't understand why you're trying to drag it out." She gestured to April. "Come over here, sweetie."

April slowly walked over and stood next to me.

"Where do you want him to cut you? Don't pick a spot where I'll get jealous. I don't know if he told you, but he and I used to be a thing."

"He never talked about you at all," said April.

"Ow. That hurts. But it was a pretty nasty breakup. Hey, you two didn't hook up before the event last year, did you? No, of course you didn't. That would've been gross. Sorry—now I'm the one dragging this out. Where would you like him to mutilate you, April?"

160

"My leg."

Luna nodded. "So it can't be seen. That's reasonable. Well, sit down and pull up your pant leg."

April hesitated for just a moment, then sat down on the floor. Her pants were tight and it wasn't easy to pull up the left pant leg, but she finally managed.

"I've been a rude host," I said. "You brought all of your friends and I haven't even offered anybody a drink. Where are my manners? Can I get you some lemonade? I could make some chocolate chip cookies if you want."

"Trying to pretend you aren't scared would work better if your voice wasn't trembling," said Luna.

"I'm sure you're right."

"Cut her."

"She'll probably scream. Are you okay with that?"

"If she screams, I'll make her stop. My recommendation is that she doesn't scream."

"Should I get her a gag or something?" I asked.

Luna shook her head. "She's a big girl. I'm sure she can keep from making too much noise."

I crouched down next to April. "What exactly is this supposed to accomplish?" I asked.

"Stop delaying. Cut her."

I looked at April's leg, trying to figure out where to cut that would hurt the least. She had firm, toned legs, and I didn't want to slice into muscle. Her thigh would've been a better choice, but she'd have to take off her pants and I didn't want to ask her to do that.

I touched the tip of the blade to her calf.

"No, wait," April said. She stood up. As if she'd read my mind, she quickly pulled off her shoes and then tugged down her pants. She was wearing the kind of panties a woman would wear when she had no expectation of anybody seeing them. Not quite granny panties, but certainly nothing intended for seduction purposes.

She sat back down and tapped her left thigh. "Do it quick."

I cut into her leg, making a line about half an inch long. April winced.

"Deeper," said Luna. "Bigger."

I extended the cut by another half inch, then finished the "R" using all straight lines. It wasn't spurting blood but it definitely wasn't a dry cut. I could tell that the pain was incredible, but April gritted her teeth and didn't scream.

I made the "U" look like a "V," which would require one fewer cut. A tear trickled down April's cheek.

"Halfway done," said Luna. "That's not so bad, is it?"

April gave her the finger. Luna giggled. I'd never heard her giggle.

I cut the "S" into her thigh, then the "T." The "R" was bleeding badly enough that the actual letter was obscured, but I'd done it.

Luna applauded. "Good job. It's like you've done this before."

I had no witty retort.

April was getting blood all over my floor, so I guess I'd done it correctly. She stood up and limped a bit as she stepped away.

"I'm gonna get myself cleaned up," she said.

"Oh, no," said Luna. "Keep bleeding until we're all done." She looked at me. "Your turn, lover."

"How did I miss that you were a complete psychopath?" I asked.

Luna shrugged. "Thinking with your dick, I guess."

I wasn't sure where to cut myself. If she'd been making me do this with a soldering iron, I might have gone for my legs to make sure I could hide it more easily, but if I put some ointment on the cuts right away they might heal without leaving a scar. As April put her pants back on, I decided to cut my left arm.

I'd do it quick. Not think about it.

I pressed the tip of the knife against my upper arm.

"Whoa, whoa, whoa," said Luna. "What are you doing?"

"What do you think I'm doing?"

"That's not sterilized." She extended her hand to me. "Give me the knife."

I gave it to her. She turned around and whistled to somebody in the mob. I recognized the person who stepped forward. It was the woman who'd been at the Detroit event. Wendy? No, Wanda.

"Let me borrow your torch," said Luna. She took it from Wanda, then held the blade in the fire. "I wouldn't want you to catch any diseases."

She didn't hold it in the flames very long. She gave Wanda her torch, and the woman stepped back out of the way. Luna extended the knife to me. "Now you can cut yourself safely."

I took the knife from her and wondered what would happen if I slammed it into her face. Would everybody attack? Would they keep coming if I fired a few shots into the crowd?

Unfortunately, I had no intention of finding out. I didn't want to die, and I certainly didn't want to get April killed.

I stood there for a moment.

"What are you waiting for?" Luna asked.

"The blade to cool."

"Screw that. It was only in the fire a few seconds. I can do it for you if you're too squeamish, but I'll scrape bone."

"I'll do it," I told her.

I did it quickly. There was a soft hiss as the knife touched my skin but I ignored it. Four slashes for the "R." Two slashes for the "U" that was actually a "V." Three slashes for the "S." Two for the "T." I cut deeper than necessary, making sure it would pass Luna's inspection the first time. My blood dripped onto the floor as I held up my arm.

Luna nodded her approval. "Nice work."

"Thank you. Now take your mob and get the hell off my property."

"Oh, no, no, no, sweetie. Did you think you were done? We all want to be marked by Darren Rust's best friend. All of us."

She couldn't possibly be serious. I just stared at her.

Luna turned around. "Everybody line up."

I could stab her in the back. Or try to get the knife against her neck, take her hostage, tell the others that if they didn't leave immediately, I'd slash her throat.

Luna spun back around, taking the option away from me.

"It won't be so bad," Luna told me. "If you can cut yourself and your little friend, you can cut a bunch of strangers, right?

This was completely batshit insane. But, to be fair to my completely batshit insane ex-girlfriend, she did have a point. If I could slash up my own arm, I could certainly slice people I didn't even like.

"Do you understand how deranged this is?" I asked.

"What's deranged to one person is beautiful to another. Just think of how happy you're going to make all of these people. When was the last time you made somebody truly happy, Alex?"

I decided not to argue with her. "I guess I don't have a choice."

"Oh, you always have a choice," said Luna. "It's not a *good* choice, but you can find out whether you can fight off all of us."

"Do you want to go first?"

"No, Ian called dibs on that. I'll go last. Ian?"

Ian stepped back onto the porch. He'd already pulled up his sleeve.

Luna took Wanda's torch again, and held the blade in the flames. My blood on the knife sizzled.

And then I quickly cut *Rust* into Ian's arm. It didn't even seem to hurt him. He didn't quite look orgasmic, but I got the impression that it felt really good. When I finished, his eyes were closed and he was smiling.

"You're done, asshole," I told him.

Ian opened his eyes and checked out my work. He seemed very satisfied. He left, and Wanda took his place. After Luna sterilized the blade, I sliced Darren's last name into her arm as well. Unlike Ian, she winced in pain, which was a relief.

When I was finished, she left the porch, and some guy I didn't know stepped forward. He frowned as I was halfway through. "That's not a U. That's a V."

"Sorry."

"Well, you did it wrong."

I held up my bleeding arm. "I'm doing it the same for everybody."

"Learn how to write." He glared and me and left. An unsatisfied customer. Oh well.

I kept cutting. The next two wanted their arms cut. Then a woman lifted her sweater to show that she wasn't wearing a bra. "You know what to do," she said.

Instead of protesting, I cut *Rust* onto her right breast, just under the nipple. She tugged down her sweater, thanked me, and left.

A girl who looked no older than sixteen held out her arm. I reluctantly cut her. She stared at her arm for a moment. "What the hell?"

"What's wrong?"

"You barely cut me."

"What are you talking about? You're bleeding."

"Barely. It's, like, a scratch. What, did your knife get dull?" She held up her arm to show Luna. "Do you see this?"

Luna nodded. "I agree. Not acceptable. Do it again."

"Your other arm?" I asked the girl.

She looked at me as if I were a drooling imbecile. "No. Same arm. Same cuts. Just make them deeper."

I retraced my cuts. She grimaced in pain, which is good because I'm not sure I could've handled her making any kind of sounds of pleasure. When I finished, she was bleeding as much as the others.

"Thank you," she said, voice filled with sarcasm.

"Do your parents know you're here?"

"Why do you care? Do you want my life story?"

I'd assumed that they held me in high esteem because of my proximity to Darren, but apparently that wasn't the case. The girl left, keeping the line moving.

I recognized the next man. He was the one who looked like a gas station attendant.

"Good to see you again," he said. "I'm Harvey, in case you didn't remember."

"I remembered," I lied.

"Let's do it," he said, holding out his arm.

I slashed the first line of the "R."

"Fuck!" he shouted. "Are you trying to cut my arm off?"

He was right to shout. I'd overcorrected from the young girl and cut him way too deep. Blood was gushing.

"Go see Gretchen," Luna told him. "She'll take care of you."

Harvey pressed his hand over the wound and gave me a look of pure hatred. "Fuckin' psychopath."

For a second, I felt weirdly bad about what I'd done. Then I got over it and gave him an insincere apology. Harvey left.

"Don't do that again," said Luna.

"It was an accident."

"I'm sure it was. But I'm serious—don't do that again."

There were still several people in line. Luna held the blade in the torch flames again, and I resumed my task.

CHAPTER SEVENTEEN

W ith the next woman, I got it right—not too shallow and not too deep. She seemed satisfied with the results.

I worked quickly and efficiently. The pool of blood on my floor was now a safety hazard. I needed one of those yellow signs that custodians used.

Finally the last person in line stepped through my doorway. It was Harvey, with his arm bandaged up. I cut his other arm, being more careful this time, and he left without thanking me.

That left only Luna. "Give me your arm," I said.

She smiled and shook her head. "I want it someplace more...intimate."

Intimate. Uncharacteristically discreet for her. "Am I supposed to guess?"

"You can figure it out."

"Should we go someplace more private?"

Luna grinned. "Nah. Not necessary. It's nothing any of them haven't seen up close and personal."

"Oh, so this whole thing is a sex cult?" I asked.

"That's not how I'd define it, but I do know how to keep everybody happy."

"I'm glad you haven't been lonely."

She unzipped her jeans, tugged them down, and kicked them aside. And then, with no hint of modesty, she pulled off her panties. "Got a pillow or something for me to sit on?"

I grabbed a pillow from the couch and tossed it to her. She dropped it on the floor and sat down on it. Then she spread her legs.

"You actually want me to cut your...?" I trailed off, also being far more discreet than I had been when we were together.

"No. Inner thigh right up next to it."

"Then you could have kept your panties on," I noted.

Luna shrugged. "Maybe."

I cut the "R," being sure to start far enough to the left that I wouldn't run out of room, like somebody making a poorly planned sign. Luna shivered with pleasure—actually shivered. It didn't feel completely natural, as if she was exaggerating her reaction just to make me uncomfortable, but she was definitely enjoying the experience.

I hated that she had so much power over me that she knew I wouldn't take advantage of having a knife right next to her vagina. I could *really* make her regret this whole thing, but I didn't want the others to storm the cabin and murder April and me.

When I finished the "S," Luna let out an unmistakably sexual squeal. "This is making me horny," she said. "Maybe when you're done, we can play a little bit for old time's sake. Give everybody a fun show."

"Probably not."

I finished the "T." Luna traced her index finger through the blood and touched it to her lips. She stood up and took the knife from me, then turned to face the rest of the mob.

"This is a beautiful thing!" she shouted. "We've all been marked by the best friend of Darren Rust!"

Everybody cheered. I didn't have any neighbors nearby, but there were people who lived close enough that they'd probably hear it. Unfortunately, nobody was going to call the police simply because they heard fifteen people cheering for a few seconds.

"We're all closer to him now," said Luna. "Closer to his teachings!"

Teachings. For fuck's sake. How could these people be so impressed by that guy?

"I've brought you to this place, and now it is time for me to turn things over to our new leader."

I desperately hoped that she didn't mean me.

"Ian, come on up here for your ceremony. Wanda, bring the bag for the ritual."

Ian and Wanda stepped up onto my front porch. Ian shook Luna's hand, then turned to face the others. "I am honored that you have entrusted me with this role. Luna has done an incredible job of taking us this far, and I'm disappointed that she's chosen to step down, but I promise to do my best to live up to her high standards!"

Wanda held a small black satin bag. She reached inside and took out a roll of duct tape.

Ian glanced over at her. I didn't have a clear view of his face but he looked a bit confused.

Wanda unspooled a few inches of tape and tore it off.

"Where's the necklace?" Ian asked, quietly.

Luna slammed the knife into his back. As he let out a grunt of pain, Wanda slapped the duct tape over his mouth.

I stepped out of the way.

Luna wrenched the knife out of Ian's back. "I changed my mind," she said, speaking loudly enough for everybody to hear her. "We are all here because of our admiration of Darren Rust. You, Ian, are here for profit. You were stealing from the group."

Ian shook his head and offered a muffled denial.

"We've known about it since the beginning. Because you were only skimming, we voted to let you get away with it until now, because this seemed like the most satisfying place and time to punish you. The Darren Rust way is to do what you want, when you want. And we're going to embrace that right now. Disciples of Rust...do whatever you want!"

She gave Ian a violent shove. He stumbled forward and then fell to the ground.

The crowd surged forward.

Ian screamed underneath the duct tape.

I didn't want to see this, but I couldn't help but watch.

They all had torches, so everything was illuminated. They also all had knives of their own, apparently.

No, wait. They weren't all knives. I saw a pair of pliers. Scissors. A claw hammer. The crowd had known where this was all headed, and they'd come prepared.

They started with Ian's extremities. This wasn't a violent mob getting carried away—these people were taking care to keep him alive.

Wanda went over to join the fun. Luna stood in place, still completely naked from the waist down. She didn't look like she was gloating or getting some depraved sexual satisfaction out of the grisly sight. She just seemed to be watching with interest and enjoying the show, like it was a pretty good television program.

I wanted to look back to see how April was reacting to this, but I couldn't tear my gaze away from the carnage.

One guy had a hacksaw.

Since they all had torches, somebody cauterized the hacksaw wound in his upper left arm as it was being made. When they got his arm off, it wasn't bleeding at all. Ian was still conscious, though he wasn't thrashing around much.

The guy with the hacksaw switched to Ian's left leg, which was already in bad shape. This was more difficult than the arm and he appeared to be struggling. Finally, a couple of people grabbed Ian's leg and pulled on it until it came free. Somebody cauterized the wound again, though Ian was no longer moving of his own accord and it probably didn't matter at this point.

I obviously was too far away to check for a pulse, but I was positive he was dead by the time they got his other arm off. That didn't stop them from continuing to take him apart. And after he'd been dismembered, they started on the head and torso.

I stood there, watching in horror. I had no sympathy for Ian, but this was almost incomprehensible. These weren't just a bunch of weirdos attracted to Darren's infamy. They were killers themselves.

It was difficult for me to accurately gauge the passage of time. It felt like the massacre took hours, but it was probably only fifteen minutes. *Only.* But it finally ended, and the maniacs stood in front of my cabin, covered in blood and gore, lit by torches.

One, to his credit, turned and vomited. The others looked happy about what they'd done. Ecstatic.

"Pretty messy, huh?" asked Luna. "That's how we like it."

"Are you ever going to put your pants back on?"

"Eventually. Alex, you've been a gracious host, and I hate to keep bothering you, but we obviously can't go around looking like this. You have a shower in there, right?"

"Yeah."

"Then I'm afraid we're going to use up all of your hot water."

"You're all going to use my shower?"

Luna nodded. "We'll try not to track too much blood in."

She lied. They tracked blood all over my floor. They came in one at a time and each took a quick shower, keeping their clothes on. This obviously wasn't meant to hide all evidence of the slaughter, but rather to rinse away the worst of it. While they did this, the ones who were still waiting gathered up the remains of Ian and put them in garbage bags they'd apparently brought along just for this occasion.

Meanwhile, April sat on the couch, looking comatose, while I stood there, watching these assholes parade through my cabin. And I was starting to think that this wouldn't be over even when they were done taking cold showers.

When it was Luna's turn, I half-expected her to force me to join her, but instead she had one of her fellow lunatics hold me at gunpoint. She emerged from my bathroom a minute later and then put her underwear back on.

"I was wondering what kind of meds you might be on," she told me, "but I don't go through people's private belongings, unlike others I could name."

"After what just happened, are you seriously trying to make me feel guilty about snooping?"

"Nope. Trying to lighten the mood. Look, I know you and April were hoping that we'd head off and let you tidy up the place, but that's not what's going to happen. You're both coming with us."

"Where are we going?"

"You'll find out when we get there. C'mon, let's get on the bus."

PART III
HUNTERS

CHAPTER EIGHTEEN

I was allowed to grab a change of clothes from my bedroom, under Luna's close supervision. I wasn't sure what kind of outfit was appropriate when being kidnapped by a group of homicidal maniacs, so I picked jeans and a plain gray T-shirt. Luna told me not to bother with a toothbrush, razor, or anything like that—she had a spare toiletries kit for me on the bus.

"You can bring Tucker if you want," she said. "If he shits on the bus, you're cleaning it up."

Since these people worshipped a guy who'd hacked up a dog, even if it was dead already, I decided that this would not be a safe environment for Tucker. I left out lots of food and water and hoped for the best.

Then we all walked away from my cabin. If the police investigated, they'd find plenty of traces of Ian scattered in my front yard, and blood from more than a dozen people on my floor, but Luna didn't seem worried about that. Either I'd be back before anybody noticed I was gone, or I was never coming back.

We all filed onto the bus. I half-expected the side to feature a fancy "Disciples of Rust" logo, but it was a regular charter bus that would draw no attention. A middle-aged bearded guy got behind the driver's seat. I wondered if he'd been recruited because he knew how to drive a bus, or if it was a skill that coincidentally proved to be useful.

April sat in the front seat and slid all the way over to the window. I sat down next to her. Luna sat across from us, then patted the spot next to her. "Over here, Alex. Don't be shy."

I didn't bother protesting and moved across the aisle.

After everybody was seated, the bus drove off.

"How long is the trip?" I asked.

"A while," said Luna. "Settle in."

I looked back and saw several people drying their hair with towels. They'd known they'd be taking showers at my cabin. Still, they were in wet clothes, and I hoped they were all extremely uncomfortable during the bus ride.

I hoped nobody tried to start a goddamn sing-along.

"So where does this infatuation with Darren come from?" I asked.

Luna smiled. "Infatuation? You make it sound like a schoolgirl crush."

"We can call it whatever you want. Where did it come from?"

"Just his charisma, at first. He's hot, but lots of guys are hot. I can get a hot boyfriend anytime I want, that's not an issue. But I watched an interview with him, and I thought, my God, I could listen to him talk about anything. He could talk about algorithms or macros and I'd come along for the ride. I researched everything I could find about him, and I found out that he has a lot of really great things to say. I know you don't agree with that."

"You're right. I don't."

"His approach to life isn't for everyone."

"So he turned a sweet innocent young lady into a murderer?"

"He…" Luna hesitated, as if trying to figure out how to explain it. "He helped bring out what was already there. I'll admit it. He didn't turn a hardcore vegan into a carnivore—he helped me realize that I could embrace my inner nature and be happier. Think how happy you might be right now if you'd gone along with it instead of trying to fight it every step of the way."

"I'd probably be in prison, like him. How happy do you think Darren is right now?"

Luna ignored the question. "I sent him a letter, and he sent me one back that…I can't even describe what it did to me. You know those women who marry prison inmates they've never met in person? I always thought they were out of their minds, but if Darren had asked, I honestly think I would have married him. He affected me that much. He didn't ask, though."

"Sorry to hear it."

She glared at me with genuine anger. "Don't be sarcastic about that."

"Sorry."

"I mean it. I'll fuck you up. You're allowed to be a smartass but you need to know where to draw the line. Do you understand me?"

"Sure."

Luna relaxed. "We kept exchanging letters, and I had no reason to stay in Austin, so I moved to be closer to him. Which brought me closer to you."

"I wish you'd stayed in Austin. No offense."

"Until it went bad, I really enjoyed our time together. I didn't *have* to have that much sex with you. I could've controlled you with a lot less."

"The sex was good, I'll give you that."

"Maybe we'll get to try again sometime."

"I doubt it."

"We could try it right now."

"Yeah, right."

"I'm serious. Nobody on this bus would mind. Well, we'd make April move back a couple of seats, but otherwise, my friends would be all for it."

"Not a chance in hell," I told her.

"Not even at gunpoint?"

"I couldn't get hard at gunpoint."

"Suit yourself. It's not like I'm lacking in attention. In case you didn't notice, the girls-to-guys ratio is very much in my favor. Although I didn't mind helping Wanda do some exploring."

"I'm not at all interested."

"You asked," she said.

"Not about that."

"Anyway, by the time I was sleeping with you, I'd started talking to Jax online—you know, the guy you killed."

"I remember Jax."

"He felt the same way I did. I mean, he didn't want to fuck Darren, at least not that he confessed to, but he was fascinated by him. And he had access to resources. I knew that if I pulled off my plan to impress Darren, Jax would be able to keep me safely hidden away."

"And you would've gotten away with it, too, if not for—"

"Enough."

"Well, thanks for sharing," I said. "Everything makes perfect sense now."

"I mean it, Alex. It's time for the sarcasm to stop."

"Darren's sarcastic."

"You're not Darren."

"That's true. I'm not."

"I'm kind of sleepy," said Luna. "Are you sleepy?"

"Yeah. You guys woke me up."

"You have two choices. I can cuff your hands and feet together so that you don't cause any problems, or I can give you a shot to help you sleep. Which do you prefer?"

"You can cuff me."

"It'll be hard for you to get any sleep like that. The shot would be a lot easier."

"I prefer the cuffs."

"We're going to be on this bus for a long time. You'll wish you'd gotten some rest."

"I'm not going to let you give me a shot."

"Well, Alex, I have some bad news for you," said Luna. "Because you've rejected Darren's teachings, you don't have control over your own fate. So I have decided that you're getting the shot."

"And if I refuse?"

"I guess I'll have to stab you in the back a couple of times and let everybody tear you apart. Did what happened to Ian look like fun to you? I don't think he enjoyed it very much, but your mileage may vary." She stood up. "Hey, who has the shots?"

The teenage girl, who was seated near the back of the bus, also stood up. "Right here."

"Bring them over."

"I'm not going to let you do this," I said.

Luna grinned. "You're adorable."

The girl handed Luna a hypodermic needle. Luna removed the plastic cap.

"I mean it," I warned her.

"You mean it, huh? What are you going to do? Grab it out of my hand and inject me with it first? Try to take me hostage? Trust me, whatever plan you have in mind is a terrible one, and unless you want your body parts scattered all over the road, I'd strongly advise you to let me give you this shot so you can get some sleep."

"How do I know I'll wake up?"

"Is that what you're worried about? You think we went through all of this just so I could painlessly kill you with a shot? For God's sake, Alex, use your brain. Give me your arm."

I shook my head.

"Okay. You've made your decision." She raised her voice. "Everybody take your tools back out. Alex is ready to die."

"Fine," I said. "You win."

"Of course I win. And the next time you put on a show like this to pretend that I'm not in charge, I'm going to get really, really mad. You may think you're an essential element to our plan going forward, but you're not. We can do it without you. Remember that."

I turned so that she had easy access to my shoulder.

"You're going to feel a little pinch," she said. "There you go. That wasn't so bad. What a brave little boy. You deserve a lollipop. Now just count backwards from ten."

Before I made it to eight, everything went black.

WHEN I WOKE UP, it was daylight and the bus wasn't moving. We were parked at a campground.

I sat up. April was sleeping on the seat across from me. I turned around and saw Luna a couple of seats behind me, but everybody else had gotten off the bus and were just sitting around outside.

I couldn't believe they'd managed to bring so many people into this cult, or whatever it was. If you didn't count Ian anymore, they had Harvey, Wanda, Mark, David, and Cliff from the Detroit talk. The teenaged girl. The bus driver. The guy who'd bitched that the "U" looked like a "V." The woman who'd asked me to cut her breast. Gretchen, who'd patched up Harvey's cuts. The man with the hacksaw. The woman who hadn't really distinguished herself except that she was pleased with the cutting job I did. I supposed this wasn't such a big group by cult standards, but it was impossible for me to imagine that this many people wanted to be like Darren.

"Oh, hey, you're up!" said Luna. She got up and sat down next to me. She handed me a brown paper bag. "Lunchtime!"

"Where are we?"

"It's not important. Eat up."

I ate the peanut butter and jelly sandwich, potato chips, and apple that were in the bag. I washed it down with a juice box.

"Good boy," said Luna. "Are you ready for another shot?"

"Are you serious?"

"I sure am. Our next step can't really be done in broad daylight, so we have to wait. I'll wake you up around midnight, okay?"

Could I somehow take her hostage? April was the only other person on the bus. What would the others do if I had a knife to Luna's neck?

The big problem with that plan was that I didn't have a knife, or any other weapon.

There were probably weapons on the bus, unless the others took everything with them when they got off. If I could knock Luna unconscious, I could hurry down the aisle and find something to threaten to kill her with.

Of course, these were people who'd gleefully ripped apart one of their own.

Luna was right. This was a terrible plan.

I let her give me the shot.

C—.

WHEN I AWOKE, it was dark. We were still in the campground, but everybody was back on the bus. April was awake in her same seat. Luna, again, was sitting next to me.

"Hi," she said. "Still feeling kind of woozy?"

"Yeah."

"That's okay. You don't actually have to do anything."

The bus drove away from the campsite.

"Where are we?" I asked.

"Guess."

"I have no idea."

"You don't want to guess?"

"No, I don't want to play any games. It's not cute."

"I'm *very* cute," said Luna, "but that's beside the point. We're in Oregon."

"Okay." That didn't really mean anything to me.

"Want to know where in Oregon?"

I suddenly realized where she might be going with this, and my stomach filled with acid. "Where?"

"Guess."

"Eugene?"

"Hey, good guess! Did you cheat?"

Peter lived in Eugene, Oregon. If they'd kidnapped April and me, it made sense that their next stop was to go after him. Unlike Jeremy and me, he hadn't really been involved in the effort to take Darren down. He had a wife and five children. Too much to lose. We had let him sit it out.

"Leave him alone," I said.

"Why? He's part of this."

"Not since he was twelve."

"He can't escape his past," said Luna. "Technically, he's the one who started this all."

"What are you talking about?"

"After Christmas break, he brought his dog along for the ride back to Branford Academy. If he hadn't done that, Killer Fang wouldn't have run away, and he wouldn't have gotten hit by a car or whatever happened to him. If the dog hadn't died, Darren wouldn't have found the body. If Darren hadn't found the dead dog, you wouldn't have found Darren cutting it up. If you hadn't found Darren cutting it up, you wouldn't have tried to hang him."

"We didn't really try to hang him."

"But you know what I mean. You can make a case that the chain of events began with Peter losing his dog. Maybe it would've all turned out the same. Maybe it wouldn't have. Either way, Peter is part of this history, and we'd like him to join us."

"He's a minister," I said. "You're really going to kidnap a minister?"

"What, you think we're worried about burning in hell? That's the funniest thing you've said since I've known you."

"Seriously, Luna, you don't need him. I'll do whatever it is you need."

"That's very sweet of you. But, no, we've been looking forward to this part. Peter's the one who came up with the idea for how to lure Darren out of hiding, isn't he?"

"I don't remember."

"Don't go faking amnesia now. Yes, the way you told it, and the way I've read about it, Peter had the brilliant scheme. So he doesn't qualify as an innocent bystander." Luna glanced back. "Wanda. I'll take the gun now."

Wanda handed Luna a pistol. It seemed like Luna was always asking people to hand her things. Having people carry her shit was probably some sort of power play.

I wasn't a gun expert, but it looked like the pistol had a silencer.

"This next part is going to upset you, so I'm going to keep you at gunpoint," said Luna. "If I have to, I'll shoot you in the stomach, and we'll try to patch you up later if we can. Do we both agree that you don't want to be shot in the gut?"

I nodded.

"We are going to take a lot away from your friend Peter. No, let me rephrase that. We're going to take *everything* away from him. We're going to slaughter all five of his children, and his lovely wife. Hopefully he'll get to watch all six of them die, but we'll have to wait and see how that part works out. It may not be practical. He may have to just see the aftermath."

Luna was right. She needed to keep a gun pointed at me right now. Even that might not be enough.

CHAPTER NINETEEN

"Luna, please don't do this. He's never hurt anybody. He's a good man." As I said that, I realized what a ridiculous tactic it was. Peter's inherent goodness wasn't going to change her mind. Somebody who would massacre five innocent children didn't care if their dad was a decent guy.

"Sorry," said Luna. "There's going to be so much blood on his walls, carpet, and ceiling that he'll never be able to clean it up. He might as well just burn his house down."

"What can I do to stop this?" I asked.

"Not a thing."

"Do you want me to beg?"

"Nope. Believe it or not, begging isn't a turn-on for me. There's absolutely nothing you can do to change what's about to happen. We did a lot of the prep work earlier while you were asleep. It turns out that when you're a minister with five kids, you don't have money for a state-of-the-art alarm system. Oh, he has an alarm, but we've already taken care of it. The two younger boys and the two older boys share rooms, and they're right across the upstairs hall from each other, so that will make things easier. He does have neighbors, so we'll have to make sure there's no screaming. Clear plastic bags over Peter and Debra's head should do it, don't you think?"

"Luna, please, you don't have to do this. Let me talk to him. I'll convince him to come with us. He'll do it willingly."

"I don't want him to do it willingly."

"Luna—"

"I get that you somehow think you're going to talk me out of this, but there's not a chance in hell that it will work. Not a chance in hell."

"What about Darren?" I asked.

"What about him?"

"What if Darren asked you not to do it?"

Luna looked at me as if I were a babbling idiot, perhaps correctly. "One, Darren would approve of our mission, and two, you have no way of making that happen."

"Not right this second, no. But postpone this for twenty-four hours. I'll go visit him. I'll talk to him. You can keep April with you so that you know I'll come back. That's fair, right?"

"I can't believe you think I'd actually go along with that. No, Alex, we are not going to set you free so that you can ask Darren to politely request that we not slaughter Peter's family. I get that you're desperate, but that's just flat-out insulting. Jesus."

"What can I do?"

"I already told you. Nothing."

There was one thing I could do. It might get me shot in the stomach but it was worth the risk. I grabbed for the pistol.

Luna pulled it away in time, and then bashed me in the forehead with it. Pretty much the same spot where I'd cut myself to fool the paramedics. She hadn't held back, and I groaned in pain and slumped back in my seat.

"You want another one?" Luna asked. "Want me to see if I can crack your skull?"

I tried to answer, but couldn't form the words, so I shook my head instead.

"Instead of trying to stop me, you should think about how you're going to console your buddy when he gets on the bus. He's going to be pretty upset."

I decided to quit trying to talk her out of it. That was a waste of time. Instead, I needed to come up with some sort of a plan to save Peter's family.

When the bus stopped about ten minutes later, I hadn't come up with a damn thing.

We were in a wooded area that I didn't recognize. I guess I should have known that they weren't going to pull the bus right up in front of Peter's house, but I wasn't thinking very well right now. It seemed to be the beginning of somebody's driveway, but it wound around some trees, and in the dark I couldn't tell where it led.

The bus driver opened the door. Harvey, Mark, the guy with the hacksaw, and the teenaged girl stood up and walked down the aisle. They were all wearing backpacks.

"Wait," said Luna. "Harvey, sit back down. We've already been through this."

"And I said that I'm fine."

"Let me see your arm."

Harvey held up the arm that I'd cut too deep. Spots of red were visible through the thick layer of gauze.

"No. You're staying behind."

"This is bullshit."

"I'm sorry you're upset. But you're a liability now."

"It doesn't even hurt."

"I don't care."

"Everybody else got cut up, too," said Harvey, almost pouting.

"Are you still arguing with me? Go back to your seat. You're not going."

Harvey looked at me with almost homicidal rage. "This is your fault," he said, as if I was going to feel remorse for him not getting to murder any children.

"You heard the boss," I told him. "Sit your ass back down."

Harvey spat at me but missed. Then he went back to his seat.

The other three got off the bus, and then got into a black car that was parked next to it. They drove off.

"And now we wait," said Luna. "They're going to send pictures as it happens, so we can follow along." She took a step back, so she was right next to the bus driver.

I looked over at April. She was slumped forward in her seat, almost in plane crash position.

"I'm going to kill you for doing this," I informed Luna.

"Are you?"

"I may be powerless right now, but it's not going to last forever."

"Well, damn, maybe I should just shoot you in the head right now."

"Maybe you should."

"Do you even know his kids' names?"

"Eric, Kaitlyn, Bobby, Pascal, and Shrader. Eric is fifteen, Kaitlyn is thirteen, Bobby is eleven, Pascal is—"

"—nine and Shrader is seven. Apparently Peter the minister likes to fuck his wife every two years. What are you trying to do, humanize them for me? By the way, you're wrong. Bobby just turned twelve. Should we talk about their hobbies? Their favorite foods? Their beloved stuffed animals? Anything else you can think of that will make me feel really heartbroken about what's about to happen?"

Peter also had a few dogs. I wondered how they figured into Luna's slaughter. I decided not to ask.

"What's your endgame?" I asked. "Let's say it works. You murder Peter's wife and kids. Are you going to tell Darren it was you? You don't think that could come back to bite you in the ass?"

"He'll know."

"How?"

"I'm not going to tell you all of my secrets. You think I don't know what I'm doing, but I promise you that I do. I know *exactly* what I'm doing."

"Okay, well, if your whole plan is to impress Darren, why aren't you out there trying to kill Peter's kids yourself? Why let those other three get the credit?"

"Sometimes I think you don't even know him."

"I think the same thing about you."

"It's too bad he's not here to settle it. Maybe he will be someday."

"He's never getting out of prison."

"You don't think so?"

"Do you know something I don't?"

"Maybe it's another one of my secrets."

Luna's phone buzzed. She glanced down at the screen. "They made it there."

"Please, call it off," I told her. Consciously, I knew that this wasn't going to do any good, but I couldn't stop myself from making one last plea. "I'll do anything you want."

"You'll already do anything I want."

"They'll get caught. Peter's a fighter. He's not going to let anything happen to his family."

"So he can deflect bullets? Are you saying that if we chop off his hand he'll stick it right back on? Is he, like, able to create a magical force field to protect them?"

189

"He's a lot more fearsome than you think."

Luna shrugged. "If I'm placing a bet on a minister woken out of a sound sleep versus three heavily armed intruders, I'm afraid my money's going on the intruders."

I clapped a hand over my mouth.

"What's wrong?" Luna asked. "Are you going to throw up? Is the panic really getting to you?"

I kept my hand over my mouth for a few more seconds, until the urge to vomit subsided. Yes, the panic was getting to me. Sitting here helplessly while Luna's goons were on their way to massacre Peter's family was driving me to the brink of insanity, if I wasn't past the brink already. But there was nothing I could do. Even if I broke Luna's neck and escaped from the bus, there was nothing I could do.

Luna glanced down at her phone. "No update yet, but I bet they're inside the house right now. Sneaking up the stairs, slowly and quietly. Step, step, step."

"Hey!" Harvey called out. "We at least get to know what the fuck is going on, right?"

"Yes, yes, sorry." Luna slid out of the seat and stood up in the aisle. "They're at his house."

What I wanted to do right now was cover my ears and squeeze my eyes shut and block out everything in the world. But even though I couldn't save Peter's family, I couldn't pretend this nightmare wasn't happening.

"Anything?" Harvey asked.

"Do you think I forgot to tell you something? Chill out, Harvey, or you can wait outside."

"You're being a real bitch, you know that?"

"I want you to start thinking of an apology. A sincere one. When this is over and we're back on the road, you can stand up in front of everyone and share it. Does that sound okay to you, or do we need to have a really detailed discussion about your attitude?"

Harvey was quiet for a moment. "I'm sorry."

"No, the apology comes later, and it's going to be way better than that. Until then, you can just—crap, you distracted me." She looked at her phone and grinned. "*Nice*."

"What?" I asked.

She held it up for me. It was a picture of somebody on a bed, covered in blood. Before I could get a good look at it, Luna pointed the screen toward the others on the bus.

"Everybody move up closer," she said. "It's starting to get good." She showed the bus driver, who nodded his approval.

As the other psychopaths moved to the front, I reached for the phone. "Let me see."

"Yeah, right."

"You hold it, then."

She held the phone up, and I slid over to get a closer look. It was Eric, Peter's oldest. His throat had been slashed open so wide that it looked like they might have been trying to decapitate him.

I wanted to scream with fury. I wanted to rip chunks out of Luna's face.

I settled for the scream.

"Enough," said Luna. "Don't make me gag you." She pointed the phone away from me and looked at it again. "Wow. They really aren't playing around. What kind of sound do you think Peter will make when he sees that, if he hasn't already?"

I wasn't going to be able to handle the rest of these pictures.

Eric hadn't yet decided if he wanted to be the drummer in a heavy metal (but emphatically not satanic) band or a veterinarian. Peter was trying to gently sway him toward the veterinarian option.

I tried to distract myself by thinking about what I was going to do to Luna and the rest of these monsters when I was no longer helpless and pathetic. Maybe I'd manage to get a hold of a gun and finish them off in the next few minutes. Maybe I'd have to devote the next twenty or thirty years to hunting them down. Either way, they were all going to die.

I couldn't stop trembling.

"Just got another update," said Luna. She touched the screen, then frowned. She looked more closely. "I can't tell if this is Bobby or not. I've only ever seen him in pictures." She held the phone up to me. "What do you think?"

It was indeed Bobby. I could tell by his red hair. His natural red hair—not his newly red hair. I wasn't sure if I'd have been able to recognize him by his face, which looked like it had been stabbed at least a dozen times.

"Only twelve years old," said Luna, holding up the phone for everybody else to see. "So sad. Who knows what he might have done with his life?"

I threw up all over my seat.

"That's okay," Luna told me. "Don't be embarrassed. I'd be puking all over the place if I were you."

I wiped my mouth and began to cry.

"We should have these blown up to poster-size. What does everybody else think? We could hang them up in the recreation area."

"No," said Harvey.

"No?"

"That's fucked up."

"I can't tell if you're being serious or not," said Luna.

"I'm being serious. I'm all on board with this. I wish I was there right now. But turning those pictures into posters and hanging them on the wall is next-level depravity. I'm not okay with that." Harvey gave her a half-hearted shrug. "Sorry. Just my opinion."

"Obviously, I was kidding. I said it for Alex's benefit."

"Do you think he really needs you to do a super-villain monologue while he's seeing those pictures?"

"Well, I don't know, Harvey. What would Darren do?"

Harvey was silent for a moment. "I just don't like the poster idea."

"Noted. Now stop trying to ruin this for everybody else." Luna looked over at April. "Hey! Participate!"

April didn't move.

"April! I'm talking to you! You don't get to sit this out."

April very slowly lifted her head.

"You're one of us now," said Luna. "You've got the marking to prove it. So take a look at what your soulmates have done."

She held up the phone. April turned away in horror.

"Have you ever seen *A Clockwork Orange*? I can make you look at these pictures, but I'd rather you do it on your own."

April turned back toward her. She looked at Luna's phone, lips quivering, and kept looking for the full ten or fifteen seconds that Luna pointed the screen at her.

"There's just something about knowing it's real," said Luna. "I can watch the goriest movies ever made and eat a big plate of lasagna, but these pictures on a tiny little screen are so much different."

I wondered what was happening in Peter's house right now. I was able to envision his horrified, agonized expression as he saw what they'd done to Eric and Bobby, right before they put the plastic bag over his head.

Luna lowered the phone and continued standing in the aisle, looking very pleased with how things were going.

A moment later, she checked the phone again.

Lowered it.

Checked it.

Frowned.

"What's wrong?" asked Harvey.

"Should've had another update by now. No big deal. They've got a lot going on."

She lowered the phone and stood there silently for almost a full minute. Then she tapped at the phone, apparently sending a text message. When she was done, she lowered the phone again.

We all waited.

Kept waiting.

Luna checked her phone and sighed with frustration.

It suddenly seemed to make her uncomfortable that everybody on the bus was staring at her. She typed another text message.

We waited some more.

"What the hell is going on?" she wondered aloud.

CHAPTER TWENTY

"W hat's wrong?" asked the bus driver.

"What do you think is wrong? They haven't sent another picture." Luna began to type on her phone again.

I wanted to take this as a sign of hope. But I wasn't convinced that this was good news. Regardless of how upset Luna was becoming, it made perfect sense that people who broke into a house to slaughter five children and a mother, sleeping or not, might find it difficult to respond to text messages. They probably had more pictures that they simply hadn't had a chance to send yet.

Hopefully Luna's texts were distracting them.

I wanted to say something that would get Luna even more flustered, but I couldn't speak.

"Calm down," said the bus driver. "I'm sure it's all going fine."

Luna looked like she wanted to shout at him, but instead she took a deep breath and then nodded. "Yeah. Yeah, you're right."

She stood there while we all waited for the next update. Peter had already experienced unimaginable losses, but maybe he'd been able to stop further ones.

We kept waiting.

Luna cursed under her breath. She clenched her fist and glanced around as if trying to find something or somebody to punch.

"For real, you need to calm down," said the bus driver. "There's nothing we can do. They know that we're leaving their asses behind if it takes too long."

"Maybe they chickened out," said Harvey.

"What the hell are you talking about?" Luna asked him. "They wouldn't chicken out after murdering two kids."

"We don't know who did what."

"Shut up," Luna said. "Shut the fuck up. Don't say another word."

She glanced at her phone again.

"Goddamn it," she muttered.

I wondered if this might be a good opportunity to try something. If Luna was angry and frantic she might not be prepared if I suddenly dove out of my seat and tried to subdue her. But, again, I had no idea what the others would do if she was a hostage. Would they let April and me go, or would they come after us all at once, without much concern for what I might do to Luna?

Maybe I should take the risk.

Luna's phone rang. She immediately put it to her ear. "Yeah?" She nodded, even though the person on the other end couldn't see her. "How did it go?"

I could tell that the answer was not good news. Her face contorted with fury.

"We'll be here," she said.

Luna disconnected the call, then shoved the phone into her pocket.

"What'd they say?" asked Harvey.

"What do you think they said?"

"I don't know. That's why I'm asking."

"Everything is fucked, okay?"

"What happened?"

"Harvey, if you say one more word, I swear to God I will shoot you in the head. I don't want to hear your shitty voice again until I give you permission to talk. Do you understand me?"

I didn't look back to see Harvey's expression, but he didn't say anything else.

Though Luna didn't actually pace around, she kept anxiously stepping back and forth, and scratched at her arms, neck, and stomach as if she had several itches at once.

Several minutes later, the black car pulled up alongside the bus. Only two people got out, both of them wearing facemasks. One was the teenaged girl. I wasn't sure if it was Mark or the hacksaw guy who'd been left behind—I'm not good at remembering what people are wearing.

Peter was not with them, although I supposed he could be in the trunk.

They hurried to the open door of the bus. Luna stepped out of the way as they got inside. Both of them had a lot of blood on their clothes.

"Go!" said the man. I recognized his voice. It was Mark.

The bus driver shut the door and began to back out of the long driveway.

"What happened?" Luna demanded. "Where's Benjamin?"

Mark tore off his facemask and tossed it on April's seat. He tried to answer but was completely out of breath. He plopped down next to April. The girl sat down next to me, leaving her mask on. She sounded like she was hyperventilating.

"You assholes have thirty seconds to get yourselves under control," said Luna. "Then I want answers." Then she smacked the bus driver on the shoulder. "Don't drive over the speed limit! Are you insane? What was the point of all our planning if you can't even remember to follow goddamn traffic laws?"

"Again, I need you to calm down," the bus driver told her. "I need everybody to calm down. I'm not going to drive this thing while all of you are having meltdowns."

"Is that a threat?" Luna asked. "You're not the only one who can drive a bus. Don't go acting like you're not expendable."

"It wasn't a threat. I'm just saying that everybody in this bus needs to take a deep breath and chill the hell out."

Luna turned to Mark. "Is Benjamin dead?"

Mark nodded.

"You're sure?"

"He got shot right in the throat. From three feet away."

"By who?"

"Peter's wife. Debra."

"Did you kill her?"

"No."

"Did you kill Peter?"

"No."

"Did you kill *anybody*?"

"I sent you pictures."

"You killed the two oldest boys. That leaves three other children. So I'm guessing they're all alive and well? Ready to live long, healthy lives?"

"It wasn't as easy as we thought!" said Mark. "We were as quiet as we could possibly be, but Peter woke up."

"There were three of you. You all had guns."

"I don't know what to tell you. I didn't see you in there, putting your ass on the line."

"Because I was giving you the honor! This was supposed to be a great moment, and you fucked it all up!"

"Not all of it," said the teenaged girl. "We still hacked up two of his kids."

"Answer me this, Gloria. Is Peter on the bus with us right now?" Luna asked.

"No."

"Then it's all fucked up."

"Peter has two dead kids. You think he's happy right now?"

"This wasn't about making him sad. This was about taking *everything* from him, and then making him discover that it could be even worse."

"Still…"

"No. Not 'still.' This was a complete disaster. And now they can identify you."

"No, they can't," said Mark. "We never took off our masks."

"You weren't supposed to leave any witnesses. How many of the other kids saw you?"

"None. They never came out of their bedrooms."

"How can I believe you?"

"He's telling the truth," said Gloria.

"Take us back," Luna told the bus driver.

"Where?"

"Where do you think? To where we were just parked. Stop questioning everything I say."

"What are we doing?" asked Mark.

"Tying up some loose ends."

"You mean killing the rest of them?"

Luna didn't answer. The bus driver found a place to turn around, and before too long we were parked next to the black car again.

"C'mon," said Luna to Mark and Gloria. "Let's go."

"Where?"

"Get off the bus."

The bus driver opened the door, and Luna stepped off. Mark and Gloria reluctantly followed. I slid over to the window so I could watch what was going to happen.

"Take out your gun," Luna told Gloria.

"Why?"

"If you question me again, I'll nail you to a tree. Take out your gun."

Gloria reached into her inside jacket pocket and took out her pistol.

Luna pointed to Mark. "Shoot him."

"Luna, don't," said Mark. "This isn't necessary."

"You're a liability."

"You're taking it too far."

"Gloria, I told you to shoot him. Just how proud do you think Darren will be of us if we all go to prison? Shoot him. Every second counts right now, so shoot him."

"He's—he's one of us."

"Not anymore."

Mark, apparently realizing that he wasn't going to be able to talk his way out of this, turned and sprinted away.

With her silenced pistol, Gloria shot him in the back. Mark fell to the ground, and desperately tried to get up.

"Finish him off," said Luna.

Crying, Gloria walked over to Mark and shot him in the back of the head.

"Good girl," said Luna. "You're helping the cause. Now kill yourself."

"What?"

"I think I was pretty clear."

"No."

"Gloria, you messed up. You messed up bad. And all of this reflects on Darren. If you kill yourself, that ties up the loose end, and then we can all move on. That's what he'd want you to do. It's pretty fucking noble."

Gloria frantically shook her head as she sobbed. "I don't want to do it!"

"And I don't want to make you do it. But everything is out of our control now. It won't hurt. If you do it, you won't even realize what happened. If you force me to help you, I can't promise that."

"*Please*," Gloria wailed. "I'll just run away. Nobody will ever see me again."

"Put the gun to your head and pull the trigger."

"No!"

"Imagine that Darren is standing right here. What would he tell you to do?"

"I don't know!"

"He would tell you to put the gun to your head and pull the trigger. Look at your arm, Gloria. Do you think that having the word *Rust* cut into it is meaningless? That you can just run away from it all? Kill yourself."

"No!"

"We're running out of time."

"I won't do it!"

"Then you're going to make me help you. And it'll be awful."

"There's another way! I know it!"

"I'll banish you from the Disciples of Rust. And then I'll kill you. All of this will have been for nothing."

Right now I didn't care what Luna did to me. I wanted to make things worse for her.

"Don't do it, Gloria!" I shouted. "Darren would never want you to do it!"

Gloria and Luna both looked back at me. Gloria with confusion, Luna with rage.

"She's lying to you! Luna is trying to protect herself!"

"Ignore him," said Luna. "He's our prisoner. He's not doing any of this willingly. Which of us do you trust more?"

"Gloria!" I shouted. "Don't do it!" I could tell that somebody behind me was walking up the aisle, almost certainly to get me to shut the hell up. "Darren will be disgusted with you if you do it!"

I turned around just as Harvey punched me in the face. I slammed against the window, hitting my head hard enough to put a spiderweb pattern in the glass.

"I'm done," I whispered to him. He didn't hit me again.

"We're out of time," Luna told Gloria. "This is going to be horrible for you."

Gloria placed the barrel of the pistol against the side of her head. Then she apparently changed her mind and shoved the barrel into her mouth instead. She let out one last choked sob and then pulled the trigger.

To me, it sounded like a stick of dynamite exploding, even though the pistol had a silencer.

Luna was headed back for the bus before Gloria even dropped to the ground.

She got in and sat down next to me, trembling with anger.

The bus driver shut the door and once again backed out of the driveway.

"How did that make you feel?" I asked. "Strong and powerful? Totally in control?"

"I'll kill you," Luna told me. "Don't think I won't."

"Do you think everybody's still on your side? What's to stop any of them from becoming the next victim?"

"Was Peter a good friend, Alex?"

"Yes."

"Then how about you sit there and think about the fact that your good friend right now is mourning two of his children? Maybe focus on that instead of worrying about me."

"This isn't going to have a happy ending," I said.

"You may be right." Luna stood up.

They'd lost four of their members since showing up at my cabin, but there were still ten of them on the bus. April and I remained pretty much helpless.

I turned around to face the others. "You might not die, but you're all going to prison. You can't get away with this."

"Shut up," said Luna. "Not another word. I murdered your buddy Jeremy *years* ago. Do you really think I don't know how to hide?"

She did have a point. She'd been a fugitive all this time, so clearly she had a secure place to hide from the law. I wondered how long she was planning to keep April and me there.

CHAPTER TWENTY-ONE

The driver went the speed limit, obeying all traffic laws. I was waiting for us to encounter a police barricade, or at least see red and blue flashing lights, but thus far it didn't seem as if there was an all-points bulletin out for a chartered bus.

I kept looking back to gauge the mood. None of the cultists seemed to be very happy. They all just sat there, looking worried. I would have preferred that they all be sobbing and vomiting and tearing at their hair, but if they were quietly afraid, I'd take it.

The bus took the Highway 5-South exit. We'd made it out of the city.

About five minutes later, I heard a siren.

Everybody immediately looked out their window. I couldn't tell where it was coming from. I wasn't sure whether to be relieved or not. I welcomed the arrival of the police, but if Luna and the others had a "You'll never take us alive!" attitude, April and I might be a couple of the bodies on the way to the morgue.

Then I saw it. A police car. Lights flashing.

It sped past us.

I kept watching until it was out of sight.

Luna stood up. "All right," she said. "We don't know what's going to happen for the next few hours, but I'm going to be a ray of sunshine and say that we're clear."

A couple of people half-heartedly applauded.

"I'm devastated about the way the last part played out, but let's focus on the positive." She pointed to April. "April is now our very special guest." She pointed to me. "And so is Alex. He marked us all. That's two big things we wanted to accomplish on this trip, and they went without a hitch. Give yourselves a round of applause."

Now everybody on the bus applauded, though I wasn't sure all of their hearts were in it.

"Ian got what was coming to him. I know we all appreciate everything he did for us, but we're family, and you don't steal from family. I watched you. You can't tell me it didn't feel *good* to do that. A lot of you probably still have him underneath your fingernails." Luna, who had not participated in Ian's massacre, pretended to check her fingernails for specks of him.

"The siege on Peter's home didn't go the way we planned," she continued. "Yes, that's an understatement. Three people we trusted to get the job done let us down, and that's a tragedy. But it wasn't a complete failure. They spilled some blood. I promise you, right now Peter is feeling worse than we are. Darren will be proud of us."

"No, he won't," said Harvey. "Why would he be?"

"Have you been sleeping all this time? We murdered two of Peter's children."

"But that wasn't the plan. The plan was to kill all five, plus his wife, and then to take Peter with us when we were done. We didn't even come close to that. Why would Darren look at this as anything but a colossal botch job?"

"Maybe he doesn't have to know everything," said Luna. "Maybe what happened was the plan all along. We were going to murder Peter's two oldest children, or oldest boys I guess, and then leave him terrified that we might come back to finish the job. Maybe this will destroy his marriage. Maybe this worked out exactly the way it was supposed to."

"Bullshit," said Harvey. "You can't put a positive spin on this."

Luna was starting to look a bit flustered. "I disagree."

"I don't even want to be part of this anymore. Alex cut me too deep, I didn't get to go to Peter's house, which is why it all went to hell, and now we're probably all going to prison."

"I promise you, we're not going to prison."

"You can't promise that! You don't know! This has all been a waste of time!"

"Are you renouncing your vow? Is that what's happening here, Harvey?"

"No. I'm just...this isn't what I thought it was going to be."

"Life is full of disappointment. Stand up."

"Why?"

"Because if you're trying to take over as leader, I want you to do it face-to-face. Come on up here and take control. Apparently we'd be so much better off if you were in charge. Stand up."

"I'm sorry I said anything."

Luna pointed her gun at him. "Stand up."

"I said I was sorry!"

"Stand up."

Harvey stood up. "I was upset, okay? I wasn't trying to take your place. I'm sure it will all be fine."

Luna shot him in the chest. Harvey tumbled out into the aisle. A few people screamed.

"What the hell are you doing?" shouted the bus driver.

Luna pointed the pistol at him. "Do you want to be next?"

For an instant I legitimately believed that she was going to shoot the bus driver while we were doing sixty miles an hour on the interstate. She seemed to realize that this wasn't a good plan and lowered the gun.

"He's still alive," said Gretchen. "Do you want me to do something?"

Luna shook her head. "Just let him bleed out."

"I mean it," said the bus driver. "You have to get yourself under control. We're fleeing the scene of a double murder and you're killing people right here on the bus. I can't have you acting like a crazy person while I'm trying to drive!"

Luna let out a scream of frustration. There was a *lot* of bottled-up madness being released in that scream, and it scared the hell out of me.

And I realized that I might not get a better chance to turn things around.

I jumped up and lunged at her. My plan was to get her gun, twist her around, and threaten to shoot her if the bus driver didn't immediately slam on the brakes and let April and me out. Maybe he'd do it to save her life, and maybe he'd be relieved to have her dead, but I was almost positive that they had no intention of ever letting us go, so I might as well attack while Luna was in the midst of her screaming fit.

April sprung to action just as I did, as if her defeated nature had merely been an act while she waited for the right moment to strike.

I was, of course, not able to simply pluck the gun out of Luna's grasp. I managed to grab her by the wrist, which kept her from pointing the gun in my face and pulling the trigger, but she was surprisingly strong and I couldn't get her weapon away from her.

Several people on the bus jumped up.

"Don't shoot! Don't shoot!" shouted the bus driver.

I didn't think they'd listen to him. I needed to make sure Luna was in the way.

April punched her in the stomach.

"Let her go!" Wanda shouted. I didn't know if she was pointing a gun at me or not. I didn't look back to check. Instead, Luna and I continued our violent struggle, as I tried to simultaneously wrench the gun out of her hand and twist our bodies around so that she was in the line of fire. Even if I couldn't get Luna in front of me, I hoped I could keep us flailing around enough that the other cultists would be reluctant to shoot for fear of hitting the wrong person.

Luna bashed me on the side of the head with the gun. I lost my balance and tumbled down the single stair in front of the door. I crashed against the door, realizing to my horror that if the bus driver pulled the lever to open it, I might very well spill out and hit the pavement. I wanted to exit the bus, but not at this speed.

April was attacking as if she'd gone feral. Maybe she legitimately had.

As I moved away from the door, I saw that almost all of the others were on their feet. And I saw a lot of guns. They seemed unsure of how aggressive to be in this moment, but I kind of suspected that if one of them took the initiative to fire the first shot, there'd be a hailstorm of bullets headed our way.

The safest place I could be was right next to Luna.

I had desperation and the will to survive on my side. She had insane fury. In theory, the two-against-one fight should've been over quickly, but it was like trying to subdue a wild animal. Her grip on the pistol couldn't have been stronger if it had been surgically grafted to her hand.

"Stop it!" the bus driver shouted. "Stop this shit!" He sounded like an angry driver hollering at a bus full of misbehaving schoolchildren.

Luna punched April in the face. Blood sprayed from April's nostrils and her legs gave out beneath her. She fell. She looked enraged rather than frightened, but before she could get back up, somebody grabbed her arm and dragged her down the aisle away from us.

Though they might not want to shoot, they had plenty of other weapons to use on her at close distance.

I was fighting as hard as I could. There was no reserve left.

I got a handful of Luna's hair and yanked as hard as I could, hoping to break her neck. Her hair would probably tear out before her neck snapped, but at least it would hurt.

She pulled her arm back, preparing for a devastating punch.

In doing so, she smacked the bus driver in the head.

The bus abruptly swerved to the left.

Several of the cultists lost their balance, tumbling into the seat across from them.

The driver jerked the steering wheel to the right. The bus swerved back, overcorrecting.

We smashed into another vehicle.

As cultists cried out, the driver slammed on the brakes, and then swerved again. Instead of worrying about trying to win the fight against Luna, I focused on finding something to hold on to as the bus went out of control.

I couldn't tell what was happening outside of the bus, but it didn't appear that the driver was handling it properly.

The bus began to tilt to the right.

Oh shit...

The tilt continued. Luna tumbled against me.

I prayed for the bus to steady itself.

And I realized that this wasn't going to happen. The bus was going to topple over and there was absolutely nothing we could do to stop it.

I joined in the screaming as the bus fell over on its side.

Shards of broken glass flew everywhere. I fell against the bus door, which was now just its metal frame.

Slamming on the brakes had slowed it somewhat, yet not entirely. It continued to slide along the pavement, shooting sparks up into my face.

I didn't know what was happening to Luna, April, or the others. For right now, all I could think about was trying to keep myself from touching the pavement and shredding whatever body part came into contact with it.

Finally, the bus stopped moving.

And then the bus driver landed on me. I thought I heard something crack, but I was in so much pain I wasn't sure who it came from.

Luna lowered herself into the seat behind me.

"Everybody stay calm!" she shouted. "We need to move fast! Separation protocol!"

The bus passengers weren't staying particularly calm. I enjoyed the sounds of their dismay, though the fact that they were screaming meant they weren't all dead.

Luna reached over and poked me in the shoulder, which hurt way more than a normal poke to the shoulder should have. "Get out of the bus. If you try anything, I'll shoot you dead." I was almost positive she was telling the truth.

The bus driver had bashed his head against something when he fell. He was unconscious and bleeding from a scalp wound. Some of his blood smeared on my shirt as I tried to get out from underneath him.

April seemed to be okay. At least by the standards of somebody who'd been on a fast-moving bus when it toppled over.

Fortunately for us, the entire front windshield had shattered, giving us an exit. Luna climbed out first. She didn't actually point her gun at me while I followed, but she made sure I knew it was right there. Kudos to her for managing to hold on to it during the accident.

I reached back to help April out. Though my whole body hurt, the fact that I could climb out of the bus meant that I at least wasn't filled with shattered bones.

Others began to climb out.

"Hurry, damn it!" Luna told them.

One by one they quickly exited the bus. David. Cliff. Wanda. The woman who'd made me cut her breast. The guy who was angry about my knife handwriting.

Luna peered inside. Gretchen was trying to help the last woman, whose name I didn't know. She was barely conscious and they were near the back of the bus.

"Gretchen! There's no time for her! Finish her off and get the hell out of there!"

Gretchen nodded and then, with no hesitation or any apparent qualms, took out a knife and stabbed the woman in the back of the neck, five or six times. As she crawled over the seats, Luna shot the bus driver in the head.

Now there were nine of us. Me, April, and seven cultists.

There wasn't much traffic in the middle of the night, but a couple of cars had pulled over to help. Luna hurried over to them.

I realized what was about to happen and shouted out a warning.

I was prepared for Luna to turn around and shoot me in the face, but she stuck to her mission. The woman in the first car had already gotten out of her vehicle, and she only had about a second to realize that she was in danger before Luna shot her in the chest. Luna hurried past her to the second car.

The cultists ran over there, one of them putting a bullet in the woman's head as they passed her body.

The second driver hadn't gotten out of his or her car. Luna fired a shot through the driver's side window. Then she ran around the front of the vehicle, as the passenger door flew open. She shot the passenger as well.

I felt something jab me in the back. It was David, using the barrel of his gun to silently warn me not to try to run away. Gretchen took ownership of April.

Luna pulled the dead driver out of the car, while Cliff pulled out the dead passenger.

"Let's go! Let's go!" Luna shouted. She pointed at me. "I want both of them with me! Let's go! Separation protocol!"

April and I didn't resist. Every second counted in their efforts to escape, and Luna had demonstrated no real reluctance to kill her own people, so I had absolutely no reason to doubt that Luna wouldn't simply cut her losses and execute us.

April and I got into the back seat with Gretchen. Luna got into the driver's seat. David took the front passenger seat, but immediately turned around to keep a gun on April and me. The four others got into the other car.

We sped off.

CHAPTER TWENTY-TWO

Once again, I wasn't sure if I wanted us to get caught or not.

Crashing a bus, murdering three people, and speeding off in stolen cars seemed like the kind of activity that would get criminals apprehended in a very quick and efficient manner. There wasn't much traffic, but surely somebody had called 911 as soon as the bus tipped over, and emergency vehicles would've been on their way while Luna was adding to her body count. I didn't see how we could escape.

And I also didn't see any way I'd survive if the police stopped us. Luna was not going to say, "Oh, okay, I guess I have no choice but to let my hostages go." As soon as she found herself in a no-win situation, April and I were dead.

Luna was no longer concerned about traffic laws. She was rocketing down the interstate. The car with the other cultists was right behind us.

Then she slowed down and took the next exit. The other car

didn't follow us. Luna didn't seem bothered by this, so apparently that was part of the plan.

She drove for a few blocks, then turned into a residential neighborhood. She turned off the headlights and we drove with only streetlamps for illumination.

"What about that one?" Luna asked, pointing ahead.

"Too new," said David. He glanced back and forth as we drove. "This area may be too wealthy. No, wait, right there. Stop."

Luna pulled up behind a blue sedan. David got out and hurried over to it. He tested the door handle. Locked. But he reached into his pocket, took out something, and in less than a minute he'd opened the door. He got into the driver's seat and ducked down out of sight.

Less than another minute later, the car's engine started.

"Let's go," said Luna.

We all got into the other car and drove off. Not only were these unfortunate people going to wake up to find that their automobile had been stolen, they'd discover it had been swapped for a vehicle that had blood and pieces of brain in the front.

Luna drove for about fifteen minutes. I didn't know if she knew where she was going or not.

"There!" said Gretchen. "Twenty-four-hour diner!"

Luna pulled into the parking lot of the diner and then shut off the engine.

Everybody just sat there.

"What next?" I asked.

"We wait," said Luna.

"For what?"

"Nothing that you need to worry about. If you want to get some sleep, go right ahead. We're going to be here for a couple of hours."

We just sat outside the diner, with nobody speaking. I'm sure

Luna had a lot of anger and frustration that she wanted to vent, but I guess the plan was that we would simply sit quietly so that nobody at the diner really even noticed we were here.

Obviously, I didn't sleep.

Darren, as scary and psychotic as he was, hadn't really killed that many people. Luna had started by murdering Jeremy, even if it wasn't entirely intentional. And though she hadn't killed them all herself, seven of the cultists were dead. As were three innocent people who'd stopped to help. For all I knew, the driver of the car the bus had crashed into was also dead, or dying at this very moment.

And Peter's children. Eric and Bobby. A fifteen-year-old and a twelve-year-old, gruesomely murdered in their own beds. So much had happened since their deaths that I hadn't had the opportunity yet to have a complete mental breakdown over it.

I couldn't even imagine what things were like for Peter at this moment. He probably didn't even know that it was intended to be so much worse. He might count his blessings later, but he sure wasn't doing that right now.

I hoped Tucker would be okay. I didn't think they were ever going to let me go home.

He'd be fine. I'd fail to show up for work, and somebody would come out to check on me. Nothing bad was going to happen to my dog.

I wondered how foolproof Luna's "separation protocol" plan was. These people were not criminal geniuses. Maybe the other four were in the back of a police car right now.

Something buzzed. Luna took out her phone.

"They're okay," she said. "Waiting just like we are."

Shit.

I tried not to think about Peter's children, but that was like being devoured by a giant worm and trying to focus my attention elsewhere. There were no tears, though. Apparently my subconscious mind knew that if I started crying, thus creating a suspicious sight inside of this car, I might get shot.

We sat in the car until sunrise. Then Luna backed out of the parking space and drove away from the diner.

A few blocks later, she stopped in front of a used car dealership. The gate was still closed.

"I don't think this one will work," said Luna.

"Nope," said David. "We need something a lot sleazier."

We kept driving. It didn't take long to find another used car lot. This one was already open, and though it didn't look any sleazier than the other one to me, Luna and David seemed satisfied.

Gretchen removed a fanny pack she'd been wearing and passed it up to David. He thanked her and got out of the car. He walked toward the small building, but a man came out and greeted him before he got there. David spoke to him a moment, and then they went inside.

David emerged a few minutes later. He smiled as he returned to our stolen car. He opened the door but didn't get back inside. "We came to the right place. He gave us a shitty deal on two cars, no questions asked, and he's going to make this one go away."

"Perfect," said Luna, opening her door. The rest of us got out as well. "You and Gretchen take April. I'll take Alex."

"All right." David tossed Luna a car key. "You're that one." He pointed to a white car. As Luna and I went over to our new ride, I noticed that David, Gretchen, and April went to a much nicer car.

"Should I sit up front?" I asked.

"For now."

Luna and I got in the car. She took a moment to familiarize herself with the new vehicle, then started the engine. She had the gun on her lap. There was a chance that I could grab it from her, but not a *good* chance, and she'd be on high alert right now. Better to wait, especially if we parted ways with the others.

We drove away from the used car dealership. And then, less than a minute later, Luna pulled into the parking lot of a Mexican restaurant that wasn't open yet. She drove around the building, put the car in park, and pointed the gun at me. "Get out."

As I got out, the other car pulled up right behind us. Luna reached down and tugged the lever to pop open the trunk. The trunk of the other car popped open as well.

"You know what to do," Luna told me, gesturing with her pistol.

I walked around to the back of the car. "Seriously?" I asked.

"Did you think you got to ride up front? After the shit you pulled on the bus?"

That was, I had to admit, a fair point.

"Behave while you're in there," Luna told me. "Right now I don't feel like I have to shoot you in the kneecaps. Don't make me change my mind."

I climbed into the trunk. She slammed the lid shut.

A moment later, the car was moving again. I wondered if there was anything I could have done to keep myself from being locked in the trunk of this car on my way to an unknown destination. Possibly. Too late now.

I hoped April would be okay.

Now that I didn't have a gun pointed at me, I could focus more on my pain. Nothing seemed to be broken, but I was covered in bruises and cuts, and there simply wasn't going to be any position in which I could lie and not be in agony. I almost wished she'd given me another shot with the hypodermic needle, so I could sleep through the trip.

After ten or fifteen or twenty minutes, the car stopped for longer than we'd be waiting at a traffic light. I heard muffled voices.

Was she talking to a cop?

I wanted to start pounding on the lid and calling for help. But I was pretty sure I knew how that would turn out. I'd hear something that sounded like it might have been a body falling to the ground, and we'd drive off. The chances of me being rescued were far less than the chances that she'd shoot a cop and speed off, and I didn't want to be responsible for another death. The three people who'd been murdered after the bus crash would still be alive if I hadn't attacked Luna.

Also, she might have been talking to Gretchen and David, and my attempt to draw attention to being locked in the trunk would just piss her off.

She resumed driving.

Her speed picked up significantly, as if she was back on the interstate. My thoughts alternated between terror and guilt, with frequent detours to think about how much pain I was in. At least it was a relatively smooth ride.

It was a couple of hours before the car stopped again.

As far as I could tell, Luna was pumping gas.

Then silence for a few minutes. Had she gone in to pay? Surely she would've just paid at the pump, unless she didn't have a safe credit card. But again, pounding on the lid and shouting for help might just end with her shooting several innocent people.

The car began moving again. Stopped about ten minutes later.

The trunk lid opened. I had to hold up my hand to shield my eyes from the sun.

Luna held a bottle of water. She unscrewed it and poured it out. I thought she was just being a bitch and mocking me by pouring out the water I so desperately wanted, but instead she tossed the empty bottle into the trunk. "That's your piss bottle," she informed me.

"Thanks."

"Got you a couple of waters and some snacks," she said, tossing a plastic bag into the trunk, next to my piss bottle.

"Can I get out and stretch?" I asked.

"Yeah, right."

"If I don't walk around, just for a minute, I won't be able to move for days. Please, Luna. You can keep me at gunpoint."

Almost none of this was a ruse to attempt to get the upper hand. Yes, if I found that we were isolated from any potential innocent victims, I *might* try something, but my whole body was cramped up and I had virtually no chance of succeeding.

She slammed the lid shut without saying anything.

I opened up one of the bottles of water and drank half of it. I couldn't see the snacks, but it seemed to be a couple of bags of chips and a candy bar. I tore open one of the bags and could smell that they were vinegar and salt flavored. I hated vinegar and salt flavored potato chips. Luna knew this. It did not appear that she was making an effort to reconcile our differences.

I ate the bag of chips anyway, of course, and then tore open the second bag, which was the same flavor. I saw no reason to ration my chips, so I ate them all. I'd save the candy bar for later. As far as I could remember, we'd never discussed our least favorite brands of candy bars, so I wondered what nasty thing she'd chosen for me.

I finished off the rest of the bottle of water and then resumed laying there in agony.

Trying to fall asleep seemed like an impossible task, but eventually I did.

I woke up to another blast of the blinding light. I had no idea how long I'd been asleep. My entire body was numb.

"Get out," said Luna.

I tried. My body refused to cooperate in any way. "I can't move," I said.

I expected Luna to be very angry about this. Instead she just nodded. Cliff stepped into view next to her, and the two of them pulled me out of the trunk. They set me upright, but as soon as they released their grip I collapsed to the ground.

It looked like we were at another campground. It was night. The four cultists from whom we'd separated right after the bus crash were there. I didn't see April, David, or Gretchen.

"You can just crawl around while you wait for the feeling to come back," said Luna. "We've got a while to wait."

"Where are we?"

"None of your business."

"Where's April?"

"Are you asking if she's dead?"

"I'm asking where she is."

"How upset would you be if she was dead?"

"I'm not in the mood to play games," I said.

"Oh, I'm sorry, do you think *you* get to decide when the games are over? Sorry to throw some harsh reality in your face."

Since I was currently writhing around on the ground like a baby who hadn't yet figured out how to control its arms or legs, I decided not to say anything else.

"When I talked to David, he didn't specifically say that April was dead," Luna told me. "I'm sure he would have told me if she was, so it's probably safe enough to assume that she's still alive. I don't know how often they checked on her in the trunk, though."

She was clearly just trying to mess with me, so I ignored her. This was very easy, since I was now getting the pins and needles sensation in my extremities and I couldn't focus on anything else.

Finally, the agony subsided. I probably could have sat up, but I decided to remain lying on the ground. Might as well let Luna think I was helpless.

"You're probably wondering what the fugitive situation is," said Luna. "Thus far they haven't identified any of us. They will—we left lots of DNA on the bus—but the plan was never to do this completely anonymously. Two of Peter's children were murdered, and there are dead bodies with *Rust* carved into them, so the FBI will have connected this to Darren right away."

"And that's a good thing?" I asked.

"Of course. We want Darren to know we did this for him. Otherwise, what's the point?"

"Do they know I'm involved?"

"Not yet. At least not that's been publicly released. But they'll figure it out, and you'll be famous again. Way more famous than if you'd just talked to that lady for her documentary."

"So where does this end?"

Luna smiled. "It doesn't end. Why would I want it to end?"

"Then what's your goal? When Darren finds out that you slaughtered Peter's boys and kidnapped me and April, what's next?"

"Plenty. So much great stuff. Some of it we still have to figure out, because it's going to be too dangerous to go after Peter and his family again, at least for a while. We had this thing set up that was a hell of a lot of work, but without Peter I don't know if we're going to throw it all out or figure out a different way to use it."

"Sorry for the inconvenience."

Luna crouched down next to me. She leaned so close to my face that I might have been able to bite her if I moved quickly enough.

"I bet the question on your mind right now is whether our plans are to ever let you and April go," she said. "As you've probably guessed, the answer is no. We are never letting you go. Once you've been marked, you're with us forever and ever and ever. Will that be a long time? A short time? You'll find out. But you're never going home."

CHAPTER TWENTY-THREE

The other car arrived about an hour later. When they pulled April out of the trunk, she looked terrible, but at least she wasn't comatose. Her recovery period was a lot shorter than mine; her trunk had quite a bit more room to stretch.

They fed us, taunted us, let us each have a gun-covered bathroom break, and then we went right back into our respective trunks while everybody else slept.

When I woke up, the car was moving again.

I tried to go back to sleep. I couldn't manage that, so I sang quietly to try to distract myself from whatever awaited me when we reached our destination. I tried to think of the best earworm tunes that I wouldn't be able to get out of my head, but none of them stuck.

A couple of hours later, the car stopped. Nobody opened the trunk. A few minutes later, it resumed moving.

A couple of hours after that, the road suddenly became far bumpier, and I could tell we were no longer on pavement. This lasted for ten or fifteen minutes, until the car stopped once more. I just lay there, hoping the ride was finally over. Though I wasn't looking forward to whatever nightmare awaited me, at this point I simply wanted to know what was going to happen.

The lid of the trunk opened. Again I had to shield my eyes from the blast of sunlight.

"We're home," Luna informed me.

My body wasn't as cramped up this time, so Luna was able to help me out by herself. I collapsed onto the dirt and waited for my eyes to adjust to the light well enough to figure out where I was.

It looked like another campground, deep in the woods. There were a few small cabins. I could hear a river, or maybe it was just a stream. We were parked in front of a larger wooden building, with a sign over the door that read "*Peace. Calm. Serenity.*"

The other car arrived a moment later. Now we had everybody: Luna, David, Cliff, Wanda, Gretchen, the woman I still only knew as "the woman whose breast I'd cut," and the man I still only knew as "the man who was mad that the U looked like a V." They opened the trunk and pulled April out.

Luna took a long, deep breath. "Love that fresh air."

The other cultists took deep breaths of their own. I had to admit that this place was weirdly peaceful, though after what I'd been through I'd probably feel the same about being at an overcrowded day care center.

The door to the building opened. A plump woman wearing an apron stepped outside and gave everybody a wide smile. "I'm so glad you're all back!" she said. Her smile faded only slightly. "And I'm so sorry about our losses. Heartbreaking."

"But we gained two," said Luna.

"You sure did." The woman walked over and extended her hand to me. "I am so happy to meet you."

I wasn't sure if she was offering a greeting or if she meant to help me to my feet. I just shook her hand. She moved over to April and shook her hand as well.

"You must all be hungry!"

"Oh, hell yeah!" said David. "Starving!"

"Well, come on in!"

April and I stood up, and everybody walked into the building.

On the inside, it had almost a nursing home vibe. The walls were covered with art that looked like it had been done by grandchildren. Four people sat around a table playing cards, while a couple of others sat on a couch, reading magazines. Signs like the one above the door said things like *Love, Happiness, Kindness, Friendship*, and *Family*.

Everybody got up as we entered.

"No hugs until we get cleaned up," said Luna. "Just wanted you to know we were back."

"Welcome back," they all said, but not in creepy unison. A few others walked in from another room. Surely these weren't all Darren worshippers, were they? How many utterly deluded people could there be? How the hell had they all found each other?

They all seemed friendly and cheerful.

"I'm going to give Alex and April a tour of their new home, and then we'll do introductions." She turned to the others who'd gone on the field trip. "Go get showered up. Take a nap. Whatever you want. We all deserve it."

Wanda and the others left. A man who looked about sixty walked up to me. "I'd just like to say what an honor it is to meet you."

"Enough, Charlie," said Luna, sounding amused as she waved him away. "Give them some space."

Charlie nodded sheepishly and went back to the card table. Luna gestured to April and me, and we followed her into a large room that was mostly taken up by a long wooden table.

"This is where we have our meals," Luna told us. "We take turns cooking. Some of us are better than others, but we eat pretty well. Except when it's Cliff's turn. You do *not* want to try his meatloaf. Oh my goodness, no."

"Cut the bullshit," I said. "Is this where you've been living all this time?"

"Yes. You don't like it?"

"It's kind of weird."

"I'll agree with that, but let's say you showed up here as some sort of investigator. Feels like a commune, right? Sort of a new age hippie feel?"

"I guess."

"I like this place. It's cozy. But the best part is that we have plenty of notice from the time that somebody pulls onto the road that leads here to when they actually show up. I can tell that you don't care about this part of the tour, so let's go back outside and I'll show you where you'll be living."

Luna led us out of the building. She didn't actually keep her gun pointed at us, but she waved it around enough to make it clear that we should not attempt to escape. We walked around the side of the building, and then to a trail behind it. We didn't walk through the woods very far, not even a quarter of a mile, until we reached a point where the trail split off. The branch to the right led to an outhouse.

"Go on," Luna said, giving me a gentle shove toward the outhouse. "Your new home awaits."

April and I walked up to the outhouse, a rickety structure with a moon carved into the door. I wanted to believe that she was kidding, but it was also entirely possible that our fate was to live in the bottom of a well-trafficked outhouse until our demise.

"Open the door," Luna told me.

I opened the door. It looked like a normal outhouse inside: a circle cut into some wood with a roll of toilet paper resting next to it.

"Notice anything?"

"The spiderweb?"

"Take a whiff," Luna said.

"No, thank you."

"Just smell it."

I did as I was told. "Nothing."

"Correct. It doesn't stink. Doesn't that seem unusual for an outhouse?"

"Yes, Luna, it's very odd and unusual that the outhouse doesn't smell like shit. Should April and I be amazed at how tidy you keep this place? Do you scrub it yourself every day?" Actually, I knew where this was headed, but as long as she didn't get angry enough to shoot me, I felt like it was best to keep her annoyed.

"This land was owned by a survivalist. He made himself a very nice underground bomb shelter. It's not luxurious, but it's a pretty good place to hide. Go ahead and lift the bench."

I stepped into the outhouse and lifted the bench. A ladder led down into the darkness.

"The hatch should be already open for you. Climb on down. Don't be shy."

Protesting would do absolutely no good, so I climbed down the ladder. I didn't climb down very far, maybe six feet, before I passed through the open hatch. From there it was about ten feet until I reached the bottom.

There was low level lighting, so though I couldn't see very well, it looked pretty much like I was standing in somebody's living room. I stepped out of the way as April climbed down the ladder after me, followed immediately by Luna, who did it one-handed, using the other to make sure we knew she'd shoot us if we did anything stupid.

Luna turned on a switch, and the whole room lit up. Yep, it was a spacious, comfortable living room. "Not bad, huh?" she asked.

"Lovely," I said.

"April, go take a nice hot shower. It's right through that door. There are some clothes on the sink, and a toothbrush and toothpaste. I know that you're going to look in the mirror and think about how maybe you should try to discreetly break it and take a shard of glass, but don't do that, please. Keep the door open. I won't let Alex peek."

April went into the bathroom.

"She'll probably use up all the hot water," said Luna. "But you need a cold shower after spending so much time around me, right?"

"Sure."

"Damn, you're morose. C'mon, how many people get to live in a bomb shelter? It's an adventure. Admit it, it's a lot nicer than you were expecting, right? You thought we were going to chain you down in a basement or something."

"It's better than living in the bottom of an outhouse, yes."

I heard the shower turn on. I was covered in grime and sweat and blood and, to be honest, a shower sounded absolutely wonderful. I hoped April didn't really use up all the hot water.

"So this is where I've been living. Not down here the whole time, but this area. You'd think I'd have gone stir crazy, but I've got everything I need."

"Where's the shrine to Darren?"

"I think you were just trying to be a smartass, but we do indeed have a very nice shrine to Darren. Would you like to see it?"

"No."

Luna shrugged. "That's fine. It's kind of a sacred place for all of us, and it would piss me off to hear you talk bad about it. Go ahead and have a seat. Not on the couch, on the floor, since your clothes are all grungy."

I sat on the carpeted floor.

I hated that Luna had shown me the secret entrance to this place. If she didn't care that we knew, then she truly did have no intention of ever letting us go. And what did this mean? Were we going to live here until we died of natural causes? Were we going to be executed soon?

A few minutes later, David climbed down the ladder, wearing clean clothes. "I'll take over," he told Luna. She thanked him, handed him the gun, and told me that she'd be back soon.

David held the gun on me while April finished her shower. Neither of us tried to make conversation.

April emerged in plain but clean clothes. "There was still hot water," she said.

"Thanks." I went into the bathroom, stripped out of my dirty clothes, and stepped into the shower. The bathroom didn't have the cozy feeling of the living room—it felt more like the kind of bathroom one might find in an underground bomb shelter—but when the hot water hit I had no complaints.

I lathered up and stayed under the water until it had gone from hot to warm to room temperature. I dried off and put on the jeans and white T-shirt that rested on the sink. I didn't feel like I wanted to dance or sing, but I felt better than I had before.

I walked out of the bathroom. April was seated on the couch. David gestured for me to join her. We waited silently for a while, until Luna returned, wearing a black outfit. She'd put on makeup and fixed her hair.

"Recognize this?" she asked.

"Should I?"

"It's what I was wearing the night I met you."

"You mean the night you stalked me?"

"Yeah. That night."

I wasn't sure what to say. It was a very nice outfit, but I wasn't feeling nostalgic for the first time I'd seen her wearing it.

"I'm starving," said David. "Is everybody else starving?"

"Oh, yeah," said Luna. "We'll go upstairs, get some food, and let them meet everybody."

"Do I have to cut them?" I asked.

"No. That honor is reserved for those who volunteered to go on a dangerous mission. The others will have to earn it. Come on, let's go meet your new family!"

CHAPTER TWENTY-FOUR

There were lots of handshakes and hugs. Nobody seemed to acknowledge that I hated their guts, or that I'd murdered Jax. It was almost as if I was there to meet my girlfriend's extended family. None of them mentioned Darren. I wondered if they'd been warned that I'd respond in an extremely negative manner.

We had chili for dinner. It was bland and too watery, but I was ravenous and asked for a second bowl. Halfway through the second bowl I thought about Peter and his family and completely lost my appetite.

After dinner, Luna explained that she and the others had a lot to talk about, so she took April and me back to the bomb shelter. "I'll be honest," Luna told us. "You'll never get to walk around freely outside. But someday you may get to treat the shelter like it's your own apartment. It's going to require you to build a lot of trust with us. Until we're confident that you'll behave yourself, we have to assume that if you're left alone down here, you'll try to find weapons or set traps or do something else that we don't like."

"So who's going to be our babysitter?" I asked.

"Nobody," said Luna. "We're just going to lock you up."

I envisioned being chained to a wall, so I was pleasantly surprised when April and I were locked in a room together. It was a pretty small room, maybe six feet square. I could stand up straight, but if I tried to stand on my tiptoes I would've bumped my head on the fluorescent lights on the ceiling. Apart from a steel door with a slot near the bottom, presumably to be used to deliver meals, there was absolutely nothing else in the room, just concrete floors and walls.

April and I sat down against opposite walls.

"I'm going to apologize to you one last time, and then I'm going to stop, because it won't do any good," she said. "I am so, so sorry that I dragged you into this. I can't even describe how sick I feel about it."

"I would love to say that this is all your fault," I told her. "It would make me feel way better about my own life choices. But the truth is that my history with Luna goes back three years before you convinced me to go to Detroit. It wouldn't have played out *exactly* the same if you hadn't asked me to give the speech, but in the end I still would've had those Disciples of Rust maniacs showing up at my cabin. So you have nothing to feel guilty for."

"Thank you," said April. "So I'll cross 'guilt' off the list of negative emotions I'm feeling right now."

"How many does that leave?"

"Five or six hundred. Though 'fear' pretty much overwhelms the rest of them."

"I hear you."

"What do you think they're going to do to us?"

"I don't know. I mean…I don't know."

"They don't know themselves. They're discussing it right now. I wasn't asking if you knew and were keeping it from me. I was asking what you *think* they're going to do."

"Well, they aren't just going to take us somewhere and shoot us. So that's good, at least."

"Good in theory," said April. "We might find ourselves wishing that they'd take us somewhere to be shot."

"We might. I'm really not sure what to say here, because I feel like it's my job to be reassuring, but if I try to tell you that it's going to be all right I'd be lying. I want to believe that we'll figure out a way to get out of this. We might. We've both survived some pretty awful shit. But whatever they come up with in their little discussion, well, it's going to be bad."

April nodded. "Yeah."

"But we'll stick together. We'll never give up."

April nodded and said "yeah" again, but with less conviction.

C—

THE DOOR OPENED about an hour later. Luna was there, and a crowd of the other cultists were in the shelter behind her.

"Thank you for your patience," she said. "Like I said before, we had a great plan for you that got spoiled when we weren't able to bring Peter along for the ride. So we had to come up with Plan B. We wanted something that Darren himself might suggest if he was part of the discussion."

"He'd probably—" I began, intending to make a smartass comment.

"Nope, stop," said Luna. "It's not your turn to talk. This is the time for you to listen. We came up with something simple and elegant. There's almost nothing to it. So here's the deal. You two will live in that tiny room. You'll each have your own bucket. Once a day, we'll slide a meal under the door—maybe rice, maybe bread, just enough to keep you alive. You'll also get water. You won't thrive by any stretch of the imagination, but you won't die. Do you follow me so far?"

"Yes," I said.

"April?"

"Yes."

"Only one of you is ever going to leave that room. No. I take that back. Only one of you is ever going to leave that room *alive*." She held up a small knife. "There are two ways it can happen. Option one: you can kill your roommate with this knife, and with this knife only. No bashing their brains out against the floor. Use anything but the knife, and we'll leave you in the room to rot. Option two, if you're feeling selfless: you can sacrifice yourself for them. Sound simple enough?"

Neither April nor I answered.

"There's a camera in there to record everything, so we can keep an eye on you and replay the most dramatic parts whenever we want. But let me be very clear. Whoever wins is still a prisoner. You'll get better food, but you're staying down in this shelter for a long, long time. Maybe forever. So if one of you does kill the other one, it's not a free pass, it's just slightly less hellish conditions. Any questions?"

Again, we said nothing.

"Good," said Luna. "Oh, there's one thing I didn't tell you. The knife won't be there in the room with you. You have to knock on the door and ask for it when you're ready. I think this will be fun. Bye."

She closed the door.

Then she opened it, tossed in two wooden buckets, and closed it again.

April and I just stared at the door for a few moments. When I finally looked over at her, she was quietly weeping.

I wished I could be noble enough to say, "You're younger, you have more to live for, so I shall kill myself so that you might survive!" But no. I would not be dying willingly. But I also wouldn't be trying to murder April. There had to be another way out of this.

I scooted over to her, getting very close. She flinched. I leaned and whispered very quietly into her ear. "Let's whisper everything. No matter what we're talking about. Every single word a whisper."

April whispered into my ear, "Okay."

"We'll wait this out," I whispered. "They killed a bunch of people. The FBI will track them down. We'll be rescued."

April didn't whisper anything back.

COMPARED to the trunk of a car, this room felt like it *should* be pure luxury, but having space to move around was offset by having to sit on concrete. Though I had experience as a long-term prisoner, that hadn't really toughened me up for a repeat. If anything, I wasn't sure I could go through that again.

The authorities would be looking for us. Even if my boss at the convenience store assumed that I'd simply quit without notice and didn't bother to report me as a missing person, the murder of Peter's children and the disappearance of April would be linked before too long, especially with corpses on the overturned bus that had *Rust* cut into them. Law enforcement had probably already shown up at my cabin, and Tucker was being cared for. If they hadn't connected the dots already, they would very soon.

That didn't mean they had any clue where to find us.

The fact that Luna and the others were willing to bleed all over my floor meant they weren't concerned about a DNA trace leading them here. David had bought a couple of used cars from somebody who saw his face. They must have anticipated the risk that the dealer would realize that he'd sold a car to murderers and rat them out. So either Luna and the cultists were stupid and reckless, or they were extremely confident that this place was secure.

April and I might have a very long time to wait.

I couldn't quite gauge where April was, mentally. Clearly she was terrified and frantic and the countless other negative emotions she'd mentioned, but was she ready to slash my throat to earn her own release from this room? I didn't think so. But I'd also proven myself to be a catastrophically poor judge of character.

I wondered if she was worried that I'd try to kill her?

He's done it before, when he had no choice...

Not having a solid grasp of April's mental state created a challenge for trying to make a plan to escape. Because, clearly, having the knife in the room would be a good thing for somebody who wanted to attempt to overpower their captors at some point. But having the knife in the room would be problematic if, say, one was uncertain if their fellow prisoner would try to kill them while they slept.

I understood what Luna was going for. She didn't want this to end on the first day. She didn't want me to wake up with blood spurting from my throat because April had decided, why wait? One of us would have to commit. Let the other know that we were prepared to do this.

For now, we'd leave the knife outside the room.

C—

"Fuck," said April.

"What?" I didn't bother to remind her of our whispering-only policy.

"I can't hold it anymore. I have to use the bucket."

"All right." I moved the buckets to the far corner of the room, then stood in the opposite corner like a kid being punished. I put my hands over my ears.

"Don't do that," she said.

"Just giving you extra privacy."

"I know. But I don't want you to worry that I'm going to sneak up on you."

I lowered my hands. "You're not allowed to kill me without the knife."

"Still…"

"Okay. Whatever you want."

"Those perverts are going to watch me on video anyway, so what difference does it make?"

I had no choice but to listen as she unzipped and lowered her pants, then peed into the bucket. Considering all the bloodshed and death I'd witnessed recently, listening to a woman urinate was a minor inconvenience, but it still felt kind of creepy.

"I'm done," she said. "No toilet paper, of course. This is gonna get gross."

C⸺

WE SAT THERE for a few hours. I'd expected somebody to check in on us, even if it was just Luna opening the door to say something evil. But nobody did. Finally we laid down on the miserably hard floor in the fully lit room and tried to go to sleep.

When I woke up, I had absolutely no idea how long I'd been asleep. One hour? Twelve hours? I definitely didn't feel rested.

I had a desperate need to pee, so I tried to do it quietly without waking April.

"Hello," said Luna, startling me in mid-stream.

I spun around, having the foresight not to pee on the floor and thus my bed. Luna wasn't actually in the room. She was speaking to me through the slot at the bottom of the door. Her timing probably wasn't coincidental, since they were watching the room.

April sat up. There was a big red mark on her face where it had been pressed against the concrete.

I turned back around, finished, and zipped up.

A tray slid through the slot. It had two plates of rice, and two bowls of water. Presumably cups would've been too tall.

"We're ready for you to empty the buckets," I said.

"Oh? Are they full already? What have you been drinking?"

"Do they have to be full?"

"It's adorable that you think we're going to empty your buckets. What do you think this is, a hotel? Do you want a mint on your pillow? Enjoy your meal."

She hadn't said if it was breakfast, lunch, or dinner. I suspected that not letting us know if it was day or night was part of the game.

April and I ate our rice in silence. It was overcooked. I wondered if we simply had a bad chef, or if it had been prepared that way on purpose, as a bonus element of our torture.

"It's going to be all right," I said.

C—.

"YOUR ARM LOOKS BAD," April told me.

I'd been trying to ignore it. *Rust* was infected. Not crusty or oozing pus, but red and painful. My other cuts and gashes were also suffering similarly from their lack of treatment.

"How's your leg?" I asked.

"About the same as your arm."

I knocked on the door. It took about ten minutes for anybody to acknowledge me, but finally Luna spoke. "Yes?"

"Can you open the door?"

"No. Are you ready for the knife?"

"We don't want the knife."

"Well, Alex, the only reason you should be knocking on that door is if you want the knife. That's it. I already made it clear that there's no room service here."

"Our cuts are infected," I said.

"All right."

"So we need some antiseptic."

"I'm afraid I have to say, tough shit."

"Then how about some soap and water?"

"Here's what I can do for you," said Luna. "If it gets really bad, ask for the knife, and maybe you can use it to amputate. Beyond that, I don't give a fuck if you get gangrene."

"Luna, please."

"Let me stop you right there. If you beg, all it's going to do is entertain us. If you're okay with that, go ahead and beg away, but it won't get you any medical treatment. I'll be more than happy to take care of your wounds—hell, I'll even kiss the boo-boos to make them all better—but to make that happen you have to use the knife. Until then, just try to keep your limbs from rotting."

"I think I like you even less than Darren," I said.

"I'll take that as a compliment."

BY THE THIRD MEAL, which may or may not have also been the third day, I was losing hope that gun-toting FBI agents would fling open the door and tell us that we were safe now.

They didn't give us a change of clothes. Nobody emptied the buckets, so the smell was stomach-churning. My infected wounds never stopped hurting.

It was unbearable. It was hell on earth.

I didn't want to die. But I was ready to do almost anything to escape.

CHAPTER TWENTY-FIVE

I'd already lost track of meals. Ten? Eleven? I was pretty sure it was one of those.

We alternated between overcooked rice and stale bread. For the first few meals, we'd had our own bowls of rice. After that, they'd started giving us a larger single bowl, and our bread was torn into pieces as if we were going to feed it to birds. I assumed that this was to create conflict over portion sizes; the better with which to get one of us to ask for the knife.

April and I didn't speak much. Conversation might have helped keep us sane, but it was also difficult to summon the energy, and it was impossible to think of anything to talk about except our nightmare. My infected wounds got a little worse every day. *Rust* was swollen to the point where it was hard to read the word.

We shared a bucket, putting the empty one over it in an unsuccessful attempt to block the stench. When it came perilously close to overflowing, it occurred to me that we had a way to get rid of it, one that might enrage Luna but was worth the risk. After we finished eating our rice, I poured the contents out onto the tray.

Somebody pulled the tray through the slot, and I expected the door to open and for Luna to fling it back at us. That didn't happen. Apparently they were going to allow us this very minor victory.

I wasn't sure if we'd had twelve meals or fifteen.

Instead of going to sleep, I began to black out for unknown amounts of time. I was feverish. A little delirious, but never to the point where I was granted the gift of not realizing where I was. I had a distinct memory of April cradling me in her lap, using some of her drinking water to moisten a torn strip of her shirt, which she placed on my forehead. I was pretty sure it had actually happened.

What if I killed her?

How bad would that really be?

Nobody was going to save us. Maybe they'd investigated the area above, never discovering that we were prisoners underground, or maybe their search hadn't even extended to whatever state this was. Were we back in Michigan? I had no idea. It didn't matter.

Only one of us was getting out of this room alive.

Why were we letting it go on this long? My infected wounds were just going to keep getting worse and worse. What good would it be to win my freedom if the cultists then had to perform amateur surgery, leaving me an armless, legless torso? Would Luna feed me, or would they simply jam a feeding tube into my stomach?

April was in hell. I'd be granting her mercy if I killed her. I'd be ending her misery.

The true cruelty was in *not* killing her.

She might welcome it. She might close her eyes and tilt her head back, to make it easier for me to slash her throat.

She might.

She just might.

Why were we letting this go on and on and on and on and on? Why weren't we ending it?

April was stroking my hair like I was a child or a pet.

244

Maybe I should be the one to die.

No. I didn't want to die.

She had more to live for.

Did she? I didn't know. Maybe she had nothing to live for. Being younger didn't mean she had more to live for. Maybe this experience had left her irreparably broken. Maybe if she got out of this concrete room she'd do nothing but scream and scream and scream. What would be the point of that? Why let her out if she was going to squander her freedom by being completely insane? Right? Right?

"What?" April asked.

"Huh?"

"What's right?"

"What?"

"You said 'right.'"

"No, I didn't."

"Okay."

My life started to happen in flashes. A quick flash of eating stale bread with spots of mold on some of the pieces. Urinating into a bucket and not quite hitting the target. Pacing back and forth, back and forth, back and forth, back and forth, back and forth, until April asked me to stop. No, that wasn't a flash. I remembered all of the pacing. But other stuff happened in flashes. Scratching at my arm until a sobbing April pulled my hand away was a flash. Trying to push myself all the way into the corner, and being upset that my head wasn't shaped properly to fit—that was a flash.

The lights went out.

They stayed out.

At some point I had a moment of clarity, realizing that an impatient Luna was trying to speed up the process. It would be scarier in the dark. Demons could find us more easily. We'd be more likely to succumb to the temptation to beg for the knife.

Back to the flashes.

Somebody was knocking. Who was knocking? What did they want?

Had I heard it right? The knock wasn't very loud. Maybe it was my head pounding.

Maybe it was my heart beating like in that Edgar Allan Poe story.

Was it Edgar Allan Poe or Edgar *Allen* Poe? I knew it wasn't Edgar Alan Poe, but I wasn't sure if it was Allan or Allen. That was horrible. I should know that. He was famous.

I did know the story, though. "The Telltale Heart." Telltale? Tell-Tale? Tell Tale? It was the one where the guy felt so guilty about the murder he'd committed that he thought the sound of his infernal beating heart was the corpse under the floorboards taunting him with the evidence of his ghastly crime. No, he thought it was the corpse's heart, still beating. He didn't like the guy's eye. April's eyes were fine.

Had I killed April? Was this the beating of my heart? Or her heart?

I didn't want to have killed April. But if I had killed April, it would be nice that I couldn't remember it. Fewer nightmares that way. I remembered every detail of murdering Andrea Keener.

April. Andrea. They both started with A. Did that mean anything?

I started with A, too. Did that mean anything?

Had I killed April?

Had I?

Yes.

Wait, no.

If I'd killed her, I wouldn't still be in the room. They would have let me out. I would have won the game. I'd knocked on the door and asked for the knife, but I hadn't used it yet.

I didn't remember knocking on the door or asking for the knife. Who was caressing my hair?

It was April. It had to be April. It was definitely her. I knew what she smelled like.

She was whispering to me.

I liked it.

She was telling me that everything was going to be all right.

I believed her.

She was comforting me like she was my mother. My mother had never really comforted me. Was this what it felt like? It was nice. I was safe.

She kept stroking my hair in the dark. I wanted to purr like a kitten.

If I had to die, this was the way to go.

April was softly crying, and I felt like I should reach up and wipe away her tears, but I was so comfortable right now, except for all the pain, that I didn't want to move.

She kept apologizing to me. I'd told her already that she had nothing to apologize for. This wasn't her fault. She just kept whispering, *"I'm sorry...I'm so sorry..."*

It wasn't her fault. When would she understand that?

Suddenly everything seemed wrong.

I wasn't comfortable anymore.

I'd been in pain the entire time we were locked in this room, pain that often became absolute agony, but this new pain was different. A sharp pain. Like a...

Oh my fucking God suddenly everything was in complete crystal-clear sharp focus April was working up the courage to stick a knife blade into my neck and I had to stop her.

I twisted away from her.

Grabbed for the knife.

Cut my hand in the darkness.

Punched her.

Grabbed for the knife again.

Got a hold of her wrist.

Wanted to break it. Didn't.

April dropped the knife. I heard it clatter on the concrete.

We both fumbled around trying to find it.

I found it first.

April lunged at me.

We struggled on the floor.

The lights came on, burning my eyes so badly that I cried out.

I heard the door open.

"No!" said Luna. "Stop it!"

She yanked the knife out of my hand. I spun around but couldn't see her. It was like I was inches from the sun. I thought my eyeballs were going to melt and pour out of their sockets.

"Both of you, stop."

She stood there for a few moments, giving April and me a chance to calm down.

"That's not how this works," Luna informed me. "You don't get to kill her in self-defense. The game was that one of you had to make a conscious attempt to murder the other."

April began to sob.

"Technically, I guess April won," said Luna. "She was driven to the edge."

"I wasn't going to do it," April insisted.

"Oh, bullshit. You had the knife in his neck. There's nothing to be ashamed of. I would have done it a hell of a lot sooner."

"What next?" I asked.

"The game wasn't that you had to *try* to kill the other. You had to succeed. So by the rules of this game, I need to shut off the lights, close the door, and wait until one of you snaps again."

She paused. The lights stayed on and the door stayed open.

"Lucky for you, we have a very special guest. He's been watching for the past couple of days, and he approves. Says he would've done the same thing himself."

It was still hard to see, and I thought I was hallucinating. This could be a fever dream. Or maybe April really had slashed my throat, and my mind was conjuring up this horrifying image right before I bled out.

Then I heard his voice, and knew that this was completely real.

"Hey, Alex, how's it going?" asked Darren.

PART IV
WORSHIPPED

CHAPTER TWENTY-SIX

My reaction was to pass out.

I don't think this counts as "fainting." It's not as if my mouth dropped open and I toppled over in shock. I was already weak and delirious and my body responded to the sight of Darren by simply shutting down.

Things happened in flashes again, but this time the flashes were less hellish. Ointment being rubbed on my wounds. Sitting in a shower. Somebody feeding me soup. Sleeping on a bed that, though far from comfortable, was better than lying on concrete.

Finally I opened my eyes for more than a few seconds at a time. I was in a very small room. Darren was seated in a wooden chair next to the foot of my bed, tapping at the screen of a cell phone as if playing a video game. He hadn't noticed that I was awake yet.

He'd put on quite a bit of weight. Not enough to make him obese, but enough that it was jarring to see. His hair, which had even more gray in it than mine, was short and unevenly cut. I wasn't sure if it was a prison haircut or one that somebody here had given him. Though he was still a handsome guy, he had the overall appearance of a man who had not fared well behind bars.

Darren saw me, put down the phone, and smiled. Ian had been right—they'd done an awful job replacing the teeth I knocked out. They were the wrong size, crooked, and the shade of white didn't match his real teeth.

"Well, look who's awake," he said.

"Go to hell," I told him.

"Whoa, hostile already? We're not gonna exchange a single cordial word before we start acting like mortal enemies? You can't be polite long enough for me to offer you a sandwich and something to drink?"

I didn't want to be civil to Darren Rust. But I did very much want something to eat and drink. "Sorry," I said.

"It's okay. You've been through a lot." Darren stood up. "I'll be right back. Just as an FYI, we're locked in an underground bunker and everybody down here has easy access to guns, so if you try to escape it'll be pathetic and embarrassing. Stay in bed."

"Where's April?"

"Why?"

"Because I want to know if she's okay."

"She tried to kill you."

"I didn't ask you for a recap. I asked where she is."

"Wow. I don't remember you being this unpleasant. April is fine. I mean, she's not *fine*, but she's alive. She's still in the cell you guys were sharing, but they dragged a mattress in there, and they patched her up like they did you. Three meals a day. They let her out every once in a while so she doesn't have to shit in a bucket. She does have this haunted look, and she doesn't really talk, and I suspect that her mind is a very scary place these days…but she's fine."

Darren left the room.

I pulled aside the blanket. I was in boxer shorts and a T-shirt that didn't belong to me. I wasn't chained to the bed, but Darren was almost certainly right that an escape attempt right now would be laughably unsuccessful. Honestly, if I leapt out of bed I'd probably just lose my balance and knock myself unconscious against the floor.

Darren returned a moment later. Apparently my lunch had already been made. He handed me a paper plate with a sandwich, some chips, and a chocolate chip cookie, along with a bottled water.

"Thanks," I said, by reflex, not because I'd decided to be polite.

Darren sat back down in the chair.

I took a bite of the sandwich. Bologna with way too much mustard, but I was too ravenous to care about the condiments.

"How did you escape?" I asked.

"I had a court hearing for the search warrant thing."

"What search warrant thing?"

Darren looked surprised by the question. "You didn't watch the documentary?"

"No."

"Oh. Well, there was a search warrant thing. Nothing that could get my whole sentence thrown out, but maybe it could knock a bit off it. Get me out of prison when I'm ninety-eight. I was sitting there on the bus, minding my own business, and suddenly all these gunshots started firing and the bus went off the road. I thought, oh shit, somebody on the outside is trying to kill me. So I ducked down as well as I could, and I heard somebody get on the bus, and there was another shot, and I thought, no, wait, they're killing the guards. A minute later I was in the back of a van. A few minutes after that I was in the back of a different van, and they'd set out a whole feast for me. After the feast I got laid. I got laid a couple more times during the ride, and then we arrived here. Nice place."

"Who'd you have sex with?" I asked without thinking.

"I forget her name. You know her. You cut my last name into her tit."

"Okay."

"It's mostly healed. You can barely see it now."

"Okay."

"I bet you were wondering if I fucked Luna."

"I don't care who you were with."

"I did. First night I got here. God*damn*. She's got some energy, doesn't she?"

"I'm not interested in talking about this," I said.

"You're the one who asked. She spoke highly of your talents. Said that you couldn't get it up a couple of times, but overall she was very satisfied."

I was too hungry for this conversation to kill my appetite, and took another bite of my sandwich.

"Would you like some good news?" he asked.

"Sure."

"Your dog's fine. One of the other employees at your convenience store has him."

"Thanks." This was a huge relief. "Any news about Peter?"

"From what I understand, our roomie is going through a rough patch right now. He'll be fine, though. He had five kids. He can afford to lose a couple." He chuckled. "Damn, Alex."

"What?"

"You're looking at me like you want to rip my head off."

"How do you want me to look at you?"

Darren's smile disappeared. "I'm trying to be friendly here.

What I hope you understand is that, like always, you're not in the power position. I can have them throw you right back in that cell and let you starve to death. If I snap my fingers, somebody will bring me a hacksaw and hold you down while I cut off your legs. So what I'd like you to do, Alex, is recognize how much danger you're in."

"Fine."

"No, not *fine*. Fine is when the teacher tells you to knock it off or you'll get detention. I'm all that's standing between you and hell on earth. They only care about you because of your history with me. I can make things really bad for you, or I can make them…not so bad."

"I'm listening."

Darren smiled again. "We've got a good thing going here. I have no idea how long it will last. At some point, I figure this place will be surrounded by helicopters and tanks and the fun will end. For now, we get to live like cult leaders. All the sex we want. People catering to our every whim. Why not embrace it?"

"Because they're a bunch of psychopaths."

"Yeah, well, so am I."

"I'm not."

"I know, I know. Mr. Alex Fletcher. So superior to the rest of us because he's not a psycho killer. Pretty low bar you've set for yourself. When we were in college, did you ever think you'd be in your thirties and working at a convenience store? Not even a good one. I'm told that you work at the kind of place where the employees warn teenagers not to go to the abandoned summer camp."

"Considering where I am right now, do you really think you're going to make me feel bad about my job situation?" I asked.

Darren shrugged. "An honest day's work is an honest day's

work. I'm just saying, if we set you free, it's not like you're returning to a life of privilege. This could be an amazing experience. We'll get you a little golden bell. Ring it whenever you want a blowjob. Can you imagine that? You could be thirty seconds away from a blowjob, day or night. That's an ultimate fantasy, and I'm offering it to you."

"And what do I have to do?"

"Nothing. Not be a sullen asshole. Act like this place isn't so bad. Pretend that I was right all along. I think that swallowing your pride in exchange for full use of the blowjob bell is a pretty sweet deal."

"How do you think I'm going to respond to this, Darren?"

"Well, I hope you'll respond in a way that doesn't make me think you're a suicidal idiot. Here's the deal. I told them I needed time to process what had happened, so they've pretty much left me alone, except for the sex. That wasn't true. I've processed it all just fine. I wanted a chance to talk to you. Y'know, when you were coherent and not hallucinating. Because what I say to everybody next is going to set the tone for how the rest of your life plays out, and I wanted to give you the opportunity to listen to reason."

"Like I said, I'm listening."

"I like these people. They're ambitious. They're obsessed with me, so we know they have great taste. Yes, I was in prison, so anything is a step up, but if you can get over your hatred of me, I think you'd agree that we're in a good place here."

"It's not just you that I hate," I said. "Luna murdered Jeremy."

Darren nodded. "She did. That's true."

"She killed a bunch of innocent people. I watched a bunch of your new friends butcher one of their own. You're acting like I just need to overlook some minor character flaws."

"I'm acting like you need to weigh the pros and cons. If you go along with me, you're going to have a great life. I can't emphasize enough how wonderful the blowjob bell will be. I don't mean this metaphorically—I'm talking about a literal bell that you'll have on you at all times, and when you ring it, a woman will be there in half a minute to service your needs. And it doesn't just have to be oral. You can do whatever you want to her. I've only just scratched the surface of what Luna will let me do to her, and I've gotta say, you squandered a lot of opportunities."

"I'm not—"

"I know, I know, you're not interested. That's all right. Even if you don't want the bell, isn't it better to *not* be tortured to death? Like, if you reviewed the two options. Option one: get tortured to death. Option two: not get tortured to death. Regardless of whatever other factors are involved, wouldn't you choose option two every time?"

"Maybe I'd rather be tortured to death than join you."

"Maybe you would. And while I was listening to you scream as they sliced off the top layer of your skin with a potato peeler, I'd think, 'Wow, he really showed me.' Because that is one hell of a diss. If I asked a girl out on a date and she said 'I'd rather be tortured to death,' and she meant it *literally*, I'd definitely have self-esteem issues."

"I have to admit that the bell sounds great," I said. "Overall, you've presented me with plenty of evidence and given me more than enough information to make my—"

"Don't do that," Darren told me.

"What?"

"You're being a smartass right before you tell me to go fuck myself."

"How'd you guess?"

Darren leaned forward in his chair. "You should be more scared of me."

"I promise you, I'm terrified," I said, and I was being honest. It was taking every bit of self-control to pretend I was feeling calm. "But I'm not going along with you."

"Then you're a moron."

"We already knew that."

"How's your sandwich, Alex?"

"It sucks."

"That's too bad. Because it may be your last meal." He sighed. "When I walk out of this room, they're going to ask how our conversation went. If I give them the honest answer, I know exactly what the next step is, and you're not going to enjoy it. Don't you even want to pretend to play along so that you can wait for an opportunity to escape?"

I shook my head. "Nope."

"You're insane."

"You've defined my life since I was twelve," I told him. "Even when I've gone years without seeing you, the shadow of Darren Fucking Rust is always there. Because of you, I'm *happy* to be making minimum wage at a gross convenience store way out in the middle of nowhere. Every time I think I might be moving on, you're back in my life, even if you're in prison. I'm done with it. I'm not doing this anymore. This cycle is over. I don't care what happens to me anymore—I'm not going along with your bullshit. Fuck you, Darren."

Darren just stared at me for a while.

"All right," he said. "Point taken."

He stood up.

"You're going to make some people here very happy. They put a lot of work into the next part, and now it won't be wasted. I'm the one who was hoping you'd cooperate. I assumed that you would, but I'm pretty much always wrong about you, aren't I?"

"Yep," I said, suddenly having very intense second thoughts. Maybe I *should* play along and try to find an opportunity to escape.

"You've made your choice, and I'm not going to try to change your mind," Darren said. "I did what I could to help you."

"Thanks. Much appreciated."

"Oh, by the way, I made the same offer to April, and she didn't even hesitate."

Darren winked at me and left the room.

CHAPTER TWENTY-SEVEN

Gretchen came to get me a couple of minutes later. She informed me that she would shoot me in the stomach if I tried anything, and I confirmed that I completely understood. She led me out of the room at gunpoint, and over to the ladder. As I climbed up, it occurred to me that she couldn't actually shoot me in the stomach from this angle, but I didn't want to get shot in the ass, either, so I didn't do anything that would cause her to pull the trigger.

I emerged into the fake outhouse, where the woman whose breast I'd cut was waiting for me with a gun of her own. I still had no idea what her name was.

"What's your name?" I asked.

"None of your business," she told me.

Yeah, they definitely were no longer enamored with me.

We waited for Gretchen to climb out of the shelter. She closed the hatch and locked it, then they led me at gunpoint down the trail. I'd assumed we'd be heading back toward the other building, but instead they led me in the opposite direction. I was less at peace with the idea of dying than I would've hoped.

We didn't walk very far, maybe a quarter of a mile, before emerging into a clearing. The cultists were standing in a group. David, Cliff, and the others from the bus were there, along with the others I'd only met right before being locked away.

Luna was also there. I couldn't deny that she looked absolutely stunning, like she was ready to walk the red carpet at the Academy Awards. Darren stood next to her, with his arm around her waist.

The only seats were two folding chairs, side by side. April sat on one, wearing handcuffs and a blindfold. Whatever was in the chair next to her was covered with a brown blanket.

The rest of the clearing, which was a circle a few hundred feet in diameter, was filled with cacti. They were mostly waist-high and in pots.

"Let's hear it for our special guest!" said Darren. Everybody applauded. Gretchen stayed next to the chairs while the other woman walked over and joined the others.

"What is all this?" I asked. It was a stupid question. Obviously they were going to tell me.

"You haven't figured it out?" Darren asked. "Don't worry, you will." He pulled his arm away from Luna and took a few steps forward.

I clenched my fists and braced myself, even though I couldn't imagine that he was walking over to kick my ass. He turned to face the group.

"As you know, Alex and I go back a long time. I've known him since he was my nosy roommate, getting into things that weren't his business. He tried to lynch me. Can you believe that? He put a noose around my neck and kicked away the box I was standing on."

That wasn't accurate—he'd accidentally knocked over the box

264

when he wouldn't stop struggling—but there was no reason to point out the error.

"Alex and my other roommates got what they deserved, and when I met him again in college, I didn't hold a grudge. We were friends for a while. Hell, we might've been lifelong friends, but the poor guy was in denial about what he truly was. I don't blame him. I'm sure plenty of you struggled with it at first. But you're all happier now, right?"

Everybody applauded. I noticed that whatever was under the brown blanket was moving.

"I'd like to thank each and every one of you for your part in this. I never thought I'd see Alex again, but here he is, completely helpless. It would never have even occurred to me to bring April back into the game, so kudos to the genius who came up with that."

Luna smiled as David patted her on the shoulder.

"I thought I'd be in prison for the rest of my life. Never in my wildest dreams would I have thought that amazing people like you would put yourselves at risk to save me from that fate. That was courageous and selfless and, dammit, give yourselves a round of applause!"

Everybody applauded.

"And I haven't forgotten about the slaughter at Peter's place. I'm a brave son of a bitch, but even I wouldn't have the balls to just break into his home and start killing his kids! I mean, holy shit! What do you think he's doing right now? Sobbing into his wife's chest? Forcing the family to sleep in the same bed because he's scared you'll come back? Maybe Peter the Minister lost his faith in God. Wouldn't that be something? Because of you, a man who has devoted his whole life to the supreme being probably thinks it was all a big fat fucking waste of time. Now *that* is power! Congratulations to everybody who was part of that!"

More applause. I couldn't take my eyes off the blanket.

"Everybody here contributed to my triumphant return," said Darren. "But I do have to single out one person in particular. My prison pen pal...Luna!"

Luna beamed as everybody clapped for her.

"What a host she has been. Tight, firm...if you haven't had the pleasure, I highly recommend it. I may never leave!"

Darren applauded and the others joined in again. Luna's smile faltered a bit. She'd clearly expected to hear more substantial praise than "tight" and "firm."

Then Darren turned back to me. "Okay, let's get to the reason we're here today. This is a 'greatest hits' moment. Alex, you've had time to think about it. Do these cactuses—cacti, whatever—bring back any memories?"

Suddenly they did. My stomach sank.

"The setup's a little bit different, as you can see. These had to be brought in special, which is why they're in pots instead of growing out of the ground. And they're shorter, because we wanted everybody to have a good view. But it's a nice, fun, cactus maze. Alex, do you want to remind them of the significance?"

"Don't they already know?"

"You're just not going to help me out with *anything*, are you?"

I didn't answer.

"You played this game in college. I gave you a hatchet. Your opponent had a head start, and you had ten minutes to bring me back her head. You won. You did indeed bring back Andrea Keener's severed head, so congratulations on your victory. At the five-minute mark, I began to inflict pain on six-year-old April. I still remember her screaming about how much it hurt. Do you remember that, April? Of course you do. Hey, somebody take off her blindfold."

Gretchen pulled off April's blindfold. April kept her eyes closed.

"*It hurts! It hurts!*" said Darren. He chuckled. "Gretchen, while you're there, do you want to reveal our special guest?"

Gretchen nodded and removed the blanket. A little girl sat in the chair, looking absolutely terrified.

"Alex, meet Stacie. I think she's eight. It would've been nice to have a six-year-old with the same hair color, but it's not that easy to kidnap little kids without getting caught, so let's be grateful for what we've got. At the five-minute mark, I will start cutting into her with a great big knife. If a severed head doesn't get dropped at my feet at the ten-minute mark, say goodbye to little Stacie."

"I'm not doing this," I said.

"Oh, shut the hell up, Alex. Last time, we had a fence. This time, we have a lot of spectators with guns. So why don't you all get in place now, to just sort of cover the perimeter?"

The cultists walked away, moving to various spots around the edge of the clearing.

"If you go out of bounds, you will be shot and dragged right back inside. Obviously, there's a strategic disadvantage to getting shot, so I'd try to stay in bounds if I were you. Luna, sweetie, would you be a dear and get rid of April's handcuffs?"

Luna took a small key out of her pocket, then went over and unlocked the cuffs. She dropped them onto the ground. April barely seemed to realize that this had happened.

Darren walked over to join them. "April?"

She opened her eyes.

"Are you ready?" Darren asked.

April nodded.

"Then stand up."

April hesitated for a moment, then stood up.

"Do you want to get me the bag?" Darren asked Luna.

Luna picked up a paper bag that was close enough that Darren could have easily retrieved it himself. She handed it to him. Darren reached inside and took out a hatchet.

"Recognize this?" Darren asked me, holding it up.

"It's not the same hatchet," I said.

"Nobody said it was the same one. Pretty damn close, though."

"You acted like it was the same hatchet. I think that if I'd gasped or something, you would have let me go on believing that it was the same one. It's too small. The handle on the other one was darker." Though I was only saying this to piss him off, my observations were accurate. I had a *very* clear memory of that hatchet.

Darren held up the hatchet and looked at it more closely. "Yeah, I guess you're right." He did a test swing. "Still a perfectly fine hatchet, though. A few good whacks and you could take somebody's head off with it."

He gave the hatchet to April.

"All right, Alex," he said. "Step into the maze."

Even then, it took me a few seconds to realize that we'd been given new roles, that it would be my severed head dropped at Darren's feet to win the game.

I suddenly wondered if it was too late to be Darren's best buddy again.

"Get in the maze," Luna told me. "Do it now if you want your head start."

"What if I changed my mind?" I asked. I wasn't really hoping to join them, but some extra time to figure this out would be nice.

"Way too late for that," said Darren. "You knew it was going to be something like this, right? You knew you were basically committing suicide by not listening to reason. I'm not sure why you'd think things have changed now."

I wasn't sure, either. I guess it felt more real actually seeing the maze of cacti, and April with a hatchet that I was pretty confident she was willing to use. I wasn't as brave—or nihilistic—as I thought.

I glanced around.

"Don't do it," Darren warned me.

It was only a twenty-foot sprint, but there was almost no chance in hell that I could make it to the woods before somebody shot me. Still, "almost no chance in hell" wasn't the same as "no chance in hell," so I turned and ran.

Somebody shot at me.

I cried out and fell to the ground as searing pain tore through my left leg. I started to drag myself toward the woods, but realized that it was a completely ridiculous and embarrassing effort that would never succeed.

Darren and Luna walked over to me.

The wound wasn't *that* bad. A bullet had grazed my thigh. I wasn't going to bleed out while they stood and watched.

"You've just disappointed a lot of people," said Darren.

"They were—" Luna began.

"They were looking forward to a good show," Darren interrupted. "They didn't think you were a complete dumbass. Now what are you going to do, just crawl through the maze? They won't even be able to see you. Jesus, Alex, did your brain go all soft while I was locked away? What's the matter with you?"

I stood up. My leg hurt as if a red-hot poker were pressed against it, but I thought I could still walk.

I fell back to the ground.

"Well, shit," said Darren. "This is a great big bummer." He raised his voice, calling out to the others. "What do you think, everybody? Should we shoot him in the head and put him out of his misery?"

There were a couple of cheers, but the response was far from unanimous. I wasn't sure if I should take that as a compliment or not.

"Don't do that," Luna said.

"Why not?"

"We didn't go through all this with Alex just to shoot him in the head while he's lying there on the ground."

Darren chuckled. "Well, we'd prop him up."

"We shouldn't shoot him."

"Oh, I'm sorry. I didn't realize you had such a strong opinion on the matter."

"It's not that I have a strong opinion, it's just that—"

"I know, I know, I get it." Darren patted her arm. "You're right. It would be a waste to shoot him. We said we were going to drag him into the maze, and that's what we'll do. Luna, Gwendolyn, do you want to do the honors?"

Gretchen didn't correct him. The ladies pulled me back up to my feet and dragged me toward the maze. I made no attempt to make it easier for them. They dropped me at the entrance.

"This is going to be kind of pathetic, but oh well," said Darren. "Alex, your thirty-second head start begins now."

I stood up. If I tried to run, I'd end up right back on the ground, but I could probably do a fast walk if I forced myself to ignore the pain. I walked forward, almost losing my balance immediately. There was nothing to break my fall but cactus, so I kept my arms at my sides and walked as quickly as I could without falling.

Clearly, I was not going to be able to outrun April for ten minutes. I needed the head start to give me a bit of time to figure out a plan.

"And…*go!*" Darren shouted.

I glanced back and saw April enter the maze. It hadn't been

thirty seconds already, had it? If he wanted to give the cultists a more exciting show, why not cheat in my favor?

Behind April, I saw Stacie, still sitting in her chair. And I realized how poor my mental state was right now—it hadn't even occurred to me that if I successfully fended off April for the ten minutes, the little girl would die.

CHAPTER TWENTY-EIGHT

For a moment, I considered simply letting April win. I could drop to my knees and lower my head like somebody ready to accept the executioner's axe. I was sure April would make it as quick and painless as possible, though she certainly wouldn't be able to lop off my head with one swing. It might take several attempts to chop all the way through the flesh and bone. I'd be better off tilting my head back and letting her rip open my throat with the hatchet blade. She could finish decapitating me after I was dead.

The moment passed.

I didn't want to die. That didn't mean I'd stand in the middle of the maze and listen to the little girl shriek as Darren or a giddy volunteer cut her up, but game had just begun. There was still time to figure out a way to turn this around.

Trying to flee would be a waste of effort. Even if I hadn't just been shot, April was younger and more athletic. I'd either have to rely on my wits—though April was probably smarter than me, too —or brute strength.

She walked toward me, hatchet held in what was definitely an "I'm preparing to chop off your head" position. April didn't look as if she relished this task. If anything, she looked like she was simultaneously trying to hold in a scream and struggling against the urge to vomit. But she also had a look of determination, like somebody who knew that the only way to live another day was to finish me off.

"April," I said, "you can fight this."

You can fight this? She wasn't possessed! What the hell was I babbling about?

I backed away from her, trying to be aware enough of my surroundings not to walk into a cactus. Trying to secretly convey a message to her would squander time we didn't have, but if we were a little further away from the spectators, it would be more difficult for Darren and the others to overhear what we were saying.

I had no idea what secret message I wanted to share with her. I had no plan. No clue how we'd get out of this except for April to win the game.

I wondered what they'd do with my head when the game was over.

Why not share that thought with them? Distract them a bit.

"Hey!" I called out to Darren and Luna. "What are you going to do with my head when we're done?"

They both glanced at each other, surprised by the question.

"I guess we'll have your head professionally mounted and put on display," said Darren. "Maybe on the wall in the main room. So when you die, think about what facial expression you want immortalized." He didn't turn to Luna for her feedback.

"Thanks," I said.

"No problem."

April swung the hatchet back and forth in front of her as she slowly walked toward me. Tears streamed down her cheeks. Not much space separated us.

"April, you don't have to do this," I told her. That was almost as lame as "you can fight this," but there was no way I was actually going to be able to talk my way out of this. I was only talking to buy myself some extra time.

"Why would you even say that?" she asked. "You know I do."

"No, you don't."

"You were in my exact situation. How did it play out?"

"I chopped off Andrea Keener's head with a hatchet."

April nodded. "So what do you want me to do? Magically teleport us out of here?"

"Can you?"

She swung again. This time the blade came unnervingly close to slicing open my belly. That would be the last swing where I was out of range.

I still didn't have a plan. But I wasn't yet ready to stand there and let April kill me.

"You have ten minutes," I told her, not caring if Darren and Luna overheard. "I can't outrun you. Give me some more time. We'll figure something out."

April swung the hatchet at me again. Like an idiot, I put up my hands to deflect the blow. Fortunately, the blade slashed across my left palm instead of lopping off my entire hand at the wrist.

"Aw, *fuck!*" I screamed. Though it did indeed hurt like hell, I was purposely overreacting, hoping to startle her.

Then I screamed with feigned rage and lunged at her.

The scream did just enough. It didn't paralyze her, but she hesitated for a fraction of a second.

I grabbed for the hatchet.

She yanked it away.

I shoved her with both hands. Intense pain shot through my

slashed-open palm, and it left a splotch of blood on her shirt as she stumbled backwards.

The back of her legs struck one of the cacti. She yelped in pain and lost her balance. The cactus toppled over in its pot, and April landed on top of it.

She lay there, mouth wide open but not making any noise.

Though I couldn't tell how badly she was hurt, she didn't look like she was going to spring back up and resume the battle.

I took the hatchet away from her. She resisted, but not much.

I stepped away from her and held the hatchet high up in the air. "Now what?" I shouted at Darren and Luna. "She can't bring you my head without the hatchet! What happens next?"

"What happens next, dear buddy, is that we shoot you," Darren informed me.

"No," said Luna. "The game is still going on. At five minutes, we start cutting Stacie. At ten minutes, we kill her. Those are the rules. Why would we just shoot him?"

Darren smiled. "I'm starting to feel a little less godlike all of a sudden."

"This is all for you," said Luna. "But we had it all worked out, so I'm not sure why you're changing things. Saying the game is over and shooting Alex—that's not satisfying, is it?"

"Depends who gets to shoot him."

"Okay, that's fair, I guess, but still..."

I glanced over to check on April. She was trying to get up but couldn't.

"If this is all for me, shouldn't I be able to change the rules whenever I want?" Darren asked. "Shouldn't I have total control? Isn't that what I've tried to teach you?"

"You've taught me about the thrill of having control, yes," said Luna. "But you've kind of..."

"Kind of what?"

"Kind of taken it away from *me*, right?"

"Sweetie, there has to be a ranking system. We can't all have total control. It doesn't work that way and you know it. Second in command is a pretty impressive accomplishment. But right now you're making me look bad in front of my followers, and we can't have that, can we?"

Luna looked at the ground. "No. I'm sorry."

"You've done some amazing stuff here, and you should be very proud," Darren told her. "Look at this maze you all set up. I didn't do anything like this. I just built a fence. You far exceeded anything I could ever have expected, and when we're done here I am gonna take you back to my room and fuck you senseless. Like, you won't be able to walk for a week. How does that sound?"

"It sounds great."

"Look at me."

Luna did. "It sounds great," she repeated, smiling, though her smile looked a bit forced.

"April has lost!" Darren shouted to the others. "So we're going to leave her there to die."

"Unless—" said Luna, but she stopped herself.

"Unless?" Darren asked.

"Nothing."

"Unless what?"

"Unless we have to go back inside, but that went without saying. I spoke without thinking. I'm sorry."

"You did speak without thinking. But that's okay. You're trainable." He raised his voice again. "Yes, as each and every one of us knew, if we have to hide away in the shelter, we obviously will not be leaving April behind. I know, shock and surprise, right? But I'm not sure she has all that much time left, so it's probably a moot point anyway."

Darren wasn't that far away. If I threw the hatchet, I might be able to hit him. It was extremely unlikely—maybe a one or two percent chance—and then I'd immediately be riddled with bullets, so I'd never even know how badly I injured him. It was something to consider when I was completely screwed and entirely lacking in options, which probably wouldn't be too long from now.

"Alex," said Darren, "like you said, your whole life has been in my shadow. And now we're going to set you free. So take a deep breath of the fresh air and try to be at peace. Though if you want to beg, you can do that too. Totally up to you."

"Which do you prefer?"

"I'd rather you take it like a man."

"I wasn't asking you," I told Darren. "Luna, which do you prefer? How do you want me to handle this?"

Darren looked mildly annoyed. I didn't expect him to fly into a fury. Mild annoyance was enough.

"I'd rather see you finish off April," said Luna.

"All right."

I did not try to finish off April. Nor did I take a deep breath of fresh air, or beg for mercy. Instead, I jumped up and down, flapped my arms wildly, and shouted "Hey! Hey! Down here!"

There wasn't a rescue helicopter overhead, and it would only take a few seconds for the cultists to realize this. But as I pretended to try to signal to a chopper, I was hopeful that they'd at least *look*.

I didn't check to see if they did. No time for that.

My biggest advantage in this nightmare—perhaps my only one —was that I was not determined to survive at all costs. Which meant that I could spring into action without being sure that all of the cultists were distracted, to enact an insane plan that would most likely get me killed.

I ran at Darren.

This abysmal plan required me to leap over a cactus that was blocking my way out of the maze. Without a bullet wound in my leg, I could probably manage leaping over a waist-high cactus with a running start. I didn't have time for a running start, and my left pantleg was soaked with blood, but what I had was adrenaline and the desperation of knowing I could die any second now.

I leapt over the cactus.

Almost.

I didn't quite clear it, and crashed to the ground as I knocked it over. Ironically, my mostly failed effort possibly saved my life, as a bullet flew over me.

Keeping my tight grip on the hatchet, I got up and scrambled toward Darren.

Somebody else fired.

Gretchen cried out in pain.

"Jesus Christ, be careful!" somebody shouted.

If the cultists all opened fire, that was it for me, but I was now close enough to Darren and Luna that the others couldn't shoot me without risking accidentally hitting one of them. The big question, upon which my life depended, was whether Luna would endanger herself trying to protect Darren.

Earlier today, I would've assumed that she'd happily sacrifice herself for him. Now I wasn't so sure.

Luna stepped out of the way.

Darren raised his four-fingered hand, as if momentarily forgetting that he didn't have a gun. He was surprised by my recklessness but he wasn't afraid of me. He rushed at me, colliding with me before I had a chance to raise the hatchet to strike.

I tried to twist around and slam the heavy blade right into his face, but couldn't make it happen, and he pulled the weapon away from me. I pressed myself against him, both to prevent him from swinging the hatchet at me and to keep the cultists from taking the risk of trying to shoot me.

The cultists ran toward us. David hurried over to help Gretchen, who was lying on the ground.

They might not shoot at me, but they'd have no concerns about pulling me away from Darren, so I had to end this immediately. I grabbed for the hatchet and missed. Darren got a hold of my injured hand and squeezed. I cried out in excruciating pain as blood dribbled between my fingers.

"Stop!" Luna shouted.

It took me a moment to realize she wasn't shouting at me. She was shouting at the other cultists.

"Let this play out," she said.

Darren continued to squeeze, and the agony was so intense that I dropped to my knees. It felt like he was literally going to crush my hand in his grip.

He bashed me in the face with his knee. My vision went black for a second.

Then he spat in my hair and raised the hatchet over my head. "I'll show you how this is gonna play out."

CHAPTER TWENTY-NINE

I didn't close my eyes. Didn't accept my fate. If Darren was about to deliver a fatal blow, I was going to stare directly at him as he did it.

"*What?*" he asked, sounding annoyed as hell.

Nobody answered.

"Luna! I'm talking to you!"

"I didn't say anything."

"It's the way you're looking at me."

"Why wouldn't I look at you? Should I avert my eyes?"

"You know what I mean. What's your fucking problem?"

Luna was silent for a moment. "I'm disappointed."

"In what?"

"In all of this."

"This was all your idea," Darren insisted.

"But you messed it up."

"Oh, I messed it up. It was all me, huh? It's not my fault Alex is so stupid that he tried to run away and got shot. It's not my fault that April underperformed. I'm disappointed, too, but you can't blame me for it."

"I'm just saying."

"I hear what you're saying, and *I'm* saying that you're wrong!"

"You're the one about to slam a hatchet into Alex's head."

"Do you want me *not* to?"

"I don't care."

Darren glanced down and gave me a *can you believe this shit* look.

"I'll let him go if you want," said Darren. "We'll send him merrily off to go tell the cops about this place. Hell, one of you can give him a ride. Whose car is the comfiest?"

"That's not what I meant," said Luna.

"Then, again, what's your fucking passive aggressive problem?"

"Do you really want me to say it?"

"Sure."

"I'm not impressed with you."

Darren chuckled and rolled his eyes. "Okay. Whatever."

"We put in all this work, took all of these risks. I've spent the past few years hiding away, fleeing into a bomb shelter whenever a plane flies overhead, all for you. We'll all be fugitives for the rest of our lives. And, honestly, it doesn't seem to be worth it. We worshipped you. We devoted our lives to you. And…you're just a guy."

"Just a guy, huh?"

"For God's sake, Darren, I shouldn't have had to fake an orgasm."

Darren's smiled vanished.

"I mean, I was with *Darren Rust*. He was inside of me! And I had to fake it!"

"It's time for you to stop talking," Darren told her.

"I know you're only human. I lowered my expectations. I knew you weren't going to be a sex god. But it just wasn't that much fun."

"I said, shut the fuck up."

"I'm done talking," said Luna. "All I'm saying is that we put a lot of time and expense into your return, and we took serious risks, and a bunch of us died, and I feel a little bit like maybe we wasted our time."

"Duly noted," said Darren.

"I…I kind of agree with Luna," said the woman whose breast I'd cut. "It wasn't terrible, I've had worse, but it wasn't anything special."

A couple of the cultists snickered.

"Why are you being so disrespectful?" Wanda demanded. "Darren Rust is standing right here, and *that's* the way you're treating him? He was in prison for several years! Cliff, how well do you think you'd perform after a few years of a dry spell?"

"Hey, I didn't say anything!" said Cliff. "I have no problem with Mr. Rust. I'm not let down at all."

"Because you didn't have to screw him," said Luna. Now she was purposely trying to be hurtful. I liked it.

Darren twitched with anger, and I worried that he might take it out on me. But he took a long deep breath, and then spoke. "I would like to apologize. They say, don't meet your heroes, and I guess sometimes that's true. We jumped into this too quickly. We should have left Alex and April locked up while I recovered from my ordeal in prison, and played this game after I'd had the time to get to know each and every one of you better. This was my mistake. Like Luna said, I'm only human, and as much as I try to be, I'm not perfect."

I wished he would lower the hatchet, but he kept it raised above my head.

"We need to realize that we're stuck here together, like a family.

A great big dysfunctional family. I don't know about the rest of you, but I don't want to be trapped in an underground shelter with people I'm fighting with, so we're going to work this out. You're all here because of me. You did all of the work, and for that I'm eternally grateful, but we're all together because of my teachings."

Teachings. What a douchebag. Obviously, I didn't say anything.

"Do we all agree?" Darren asked.

Most of the cultists seemed to indicate that they did.

"And do you agree that we need to work this out, right now?"

Further agreement.

Darren's smile returned. "Then I'm going to need you to kill Luna."

In his mind, I think he believed that they were going to immediately drag a screaming Luna off to her doom. Tear her apart like they did Ian. Let her serve as a warning to anybody who would dare cross Darren Rust.

Nobody said anything. Nobody moved.

"Kill her," Darren said. "I don't care how."

Still, nobody moved. The whole vibe was remarkably awkward.

"They like me more than they like you," said Luna. "When they're having sex with me, they don't have to pretend to get off."

Darren's face contorted into the ugliest mask of rage I'd ever seen. And I realized that though this experience might very well still end with a hatchet chopping deep into my skull, this might be my best opportunity to act.

I punched him in the knee as hard as I possibly could.

I knew this was going to hurt my fist, and it did. Oh, God, it did. But his leg buckled, and though he tried to slam the hatchet down on me, it was a surprised self-defense move instead of an execution, and I was able to grab his arm before he could murder me.

I stood up and kneed him in the groin.

It was convenient and effective. Most importantly, it was an embarrassing injury for somebody who was desperately trying to retain the respect of followers who'd become disillusioned with him. Though he let out a grunt instead of a high-pitched shriek, he doubled over and dropped the hatchet.

I didn't try to pick it up. Instead, I grabbed Darren by the back of the neck with my good hand and dragged him away from the group. Somebody might shoot me. They might not. I didn't care.

"Wait!" Darren said, apparently realizing my intention. I ignored him.

He struggled and almost got away as I violently led him over to the edge of the maze. He should have struggled harder.

I slammed him face-first into a cactus.

This time he let out a high-pitched shriek.

I yanked him back up, then slammed him down again.

Nobody shot me.

I did it again.

And again.

And again.

Darren pulled free. He staggered a couple of steps away, then turned toward me. His entire face was red and filled with cactus needles. I couldn't tell if his eyes were open; not with all the blood and the dozen needles protruding from each of them.

He howled in misery.

Darren did a blind lunge at me. I easily redirected him, then slammed him into a different cactus. He fell to the ground, whimpering.

Still nobody shot me.

He started to get up. I kicked him in the ass so hard that it felt like I might have injured my foot.

His head struck the pot.

The cactus toppled over.

As it landed on him, Darren's body twitched as if he were being electrocuted.

A moment later, he was still.

I wanted to slam my foot down on the cactus and drive it deeper into his body, just to be sure, but fortunately I resisted the urge and spared myself a foot full of needles.

I kept waiting for the sound of a gunshot followed by a black void. Nothing happened.

I turned around. Luna and the others were all just standing there, staring at me.

"Okay," I said. "I'll join you fuckers."

It was hard for me to process how I was feeling. Darren was dead—or would be soon—and I should be feeling euphoric, but of course I was still in some very, very deep shit.

"Should we kill him?" Wanda asked.

"No," said Luna. "Not yet."

"Can I check on April?" I asked.

Luna shrugged. She looked over at David. "How's Gretchen?"

"She'll make it."

"Good."

"I honestly think we can work this out," I said. "I don't want any part of this. You know that. Let me go. I won't say a word. I'll tell them that there was a burlap sack over my head the whole time—that I don't know who kidnapped me. I don't want to help the police. I don't want to be involved in any way. All I want to do is get home to my dog."

"You know we're not going to just let you walk out of here, right?" Luna asked.

"Why not? Seriously, why not? Why can't it be this easy? We all go our separate ways."

"It's cute that you're living in a fantasy world. We'll figure something out, but I meant it when I said that you're here forever, either alive or buried somewhere."

"To hell with this." I didn't know the guy's name who said that. He was the one who'd been mad that my carved "U" looked like a "V." He dropped his gun on the ground. "Nothing has worked out right. It's been one screwup after another after another, and quite frankly I don't even know that I can trust our early warning system. The FBI could be watching us through binoculars this very minute."

"Nobody is watching us," said Luna.

"Either way, I'm done. I'm going back home."

"You can't show your face at home."

"Then I will hide someplace else. I've got deep pockets. I don't need any of you." He turned and began to head back toward the trail.

"Don't you walk away from me!" Luna shouted.

Without looking back, he gave her the finger.

Everybody just sort of watched him go. By the time he reached the trail, a few others had followed.

Stacie still sat in her chair, not looking at anybody.

"Looks like your cult's falling apart," I told Luna.

"It was never a cult."

"Whatever it was, I think it's time to give it up."

"Let me be very clear, Alex," said Luna. "You seem to think you have the upper hand right now, but you most definitely do not. There are a million things I can do to you that are infinitely worse than having somebody chop your head off. Get too comfortable and you'll find out what they are."

I shrugged.

A couple of the others, including Wanda, started to walk away.

"Where the hell are you going?" Luna demanded. "You can't just abandon us!"

"I don't know where I'm going," said Wanda. "I think I'm going back to the shelter. I can't be here right now. I can't…" She gestured to Darren's corpse. "I can't look at that."

I cleared my throat. "Luna, I think your whole problem is that your cult-thing never had a good name. It's hard for people to be loyal to the Disciples of Rust. It's stupid. It's a very stupid name. Disciples of Rust. If people are self-conscious about saying the name of the cult, you're not doing yourself any favors."

"You need to watch your mouth."

"Why? You said I was never leaving. If I'm trapped here forever and ever and ever, why do I need to be polite? Kiss my ass."

On the ground, Gretchen coughed.

Luna and I both looked over at her. Her face was flecked with blood.

"Is she coughing up blood?" Luna asked. "I thought you said she was fine!"

"I didn't say she was fine," David insisted. "I said she was going to make it."

"Well, do something for her!"

"I'm trying!"

Luna walked over to her. I figured this meant it was okay to go check on April. When I looked over there, I saw that she was already up.

There was a lot of blood on April's shirt, and she was walking with a minor limp. Her face had no expression. She reached down, picked up the gun the other guy had dropped, and pointed it at Luna.

Though the situation was far from being resolved, this had the potential to make it a lot worse.

"No!" I shouted.

Luna spun around, as did the few remaining others.

"April, no," I said. "You don't want to do that."

April, looking like a zombie, kept walking toward Luna, gun extended. "She destroyed my life."

"This won't fix it," I said. "You're not a murderer. You haven't killed anybody. You can still come back from this."

"I was going to kill you."

"But you didn't."

"I'm ruined."

"No, you're not. Please, April. Give me the gun. They might let us leave. You and me and Stacie can get in a car and drive home. Don't kill her. Just give me the gun. It'll be all right, I promise."

"She deserves to die."

"Yes, she does. But you'll hate yourself if you do it."

"I already hate myself."

"Give me the gun, April."

"No."

"April, if you pull the trigger, you'll die right after that."

"Good."

"No, it's not good. Give me the gun and we'll get out of this, I swear to you."

April began to sob.

She lowered the gun and let me take it from her.

"Thank you," I said. "You did the right thing."

I didn't know if it was actually possible for April to come back from this. She might be permanently broken. But I did know that the process would be much easier if she didn't murder Luna Booth. She didn't want that in her psyche.

My psyche was already damaged beyond repair.

I turned and shot Luna in the head.

CHAPTER THIRTY

Before Luna's body even hit the ground, I went into hardcore self-preservation mode, swinging the gun around at everybody who was left. "Do you want to die for her?" I shouted. "I'll kill as many of you as I can before you bring me down! I'll do it! But this doesn't have to be any more of a bloodbath! Don't sacrifice yourself to avenge her!"

Yes, "avenge her" was kind of corny, but this wasn't a rehearsed speech. I honestly felt lucky to be able to speak at all.

One plan for escape would be to force somebody to take us back to the building and give us a car. Then April, Stacie and I would speed away from here to freedom.

There were a lot of ways that plan could go wrong. All it would take is one person with a gun to spoil our victory. A more immediate way to get out of danger was for the three of us to head for the woods and hope for the best.

As I continued to wave the gun, I called Stacie over, praying that the little girl wasn't catatonic. She wasn't. She got right out of the chair and ran over to me.

We slowly backed away, toward the edge of the clearing. Once we entered the woods, we continued to slowly back away until we were confident that nobody could see us well enough to successfully shoot us, after which we picked up our pace as well as our injuries would allow.

My hope was that the ex-cultists would be too busy trying to get the hell out of there to bother trying to hunt us down.

After about an hour, I stopped worrying about being recaptured, and worried more about finding a way out of the woods. I was sure that April was a mess on the inside, but on the outside, she hid her mental state well. She probably knew that there'd be plenty of time for a complete breakdown after we were safe.

Considering all that we'd been through, being lost in the woods was no big deal. At first. Then it started to get dark and we had to sleep on the ground—though none of us slept—and the lack of water became a real issue. We kept walking the next day, praying that if we couldn't find a road we could at least find a stream, but we found neither. The second night we slept, but only because of our total exhaustion.

The third day, with my leg badly infected and hurting with each step, and my socks drenched with sweat and the pus of countless burst blisters, we emerged onto a paved road. About half an hour after that, a burly man and his equally burly wife gave us a ride in the back of their pickup truck.

We sat there, gulping down our bottled water and passing around a bag of black licorice they'd had in their glove compartment. I couldn't believe it was over. Oh, I'd lied before—I was most *definitely* going to cooperate with the authorities in their efforts to track down each and every surviving member of the Disciples of Rust. But Darren was dead. Luna was dead. The worst was behind me.

As far as I knew, nothing truly awful had happened to Stacie during her abduction. She talked cheerfully about seeing her mother and father again. Hopefully she'd be able to put this experience behind her.

I didn't know about April. Right now she just looked relieved. Maybe with a shitload of therapy, and very long talks with me where I assured her that she'd had no choice, she'd learn to live with herself.

"What are you going to do next?" April asked me.

"Get back my dog."

"And then?"

"Pay a visit to Peter. See if there's anything I can do. He may not be happy to see me. He may scream at me or punch me in the face or tell me to go to hell. It's his choice. I'll be there for him, whatever he needs."

"You're a good friend," said April.

"I couldn't save Jeremy."

"That wasn't your fault, but you already knew that. I guess you have a lot of healing to do, too."

I nodded. "Yeah."

"So you're going to get Tucker, and then you're going to see Peter. What are you going to do after that?"

I took a big drink of water and thought about it for a moment.

"Whatever I want."

—The End—

ACKNOWLEDGMENTS

Thanks to Jamie La Chance, Tod Clark, Donna Fitzpatrick, Lynne Hansen, Bridgett Nelson, Paul Miller, Michael McBride, Jim Morey, Rhonda Rettig, and Paul Synuria II for their assistance with this project.

ABOUT THE AUTHOR

Follow Jeff's ridiculous musings here:

- amazon.com/Jeff-Strand/e/B001K8D3F0
- facebook.com/JeffStrandAuthorFanPage
- twitter.com/JeffStrand
- instagram.com/jeffstrandauthor
- bookbub.com/authors/jeff-strand

OTHER BOOKS BY JEFF STRAND

The Writing Life: Reflections, Recollections, and a Lot of Cursing. A comedic (but entirely true) non-fiction book about surviving in a brutal business.

Candy Coated Madness. Another demented collection of gleefully macabre tales.

Autumn Bleeds Into Winter. A coming-of-age thriller set in Fairbanks, Alaska in 1979. Fourteen-year-old Curtis saw his best friend get abducted, and he's going to confront the man who did it.

The Odds. When invited to a game that offers a 99% chance of winning fifty thousand dollars, Ethan rejoices at the chance to recoup his gambling losses. But as the game continues, the odds constantly change, and the risks become progressively deadlier...

Allison. She can break your bones using her mind. And she's trying very hard not to hurt you.

Wolf Hunt 3. George, Lou, Ally, and Eugene are back in another werewolf-laden adventure.

Clowns Vs. Spiders. Choose your side!

My Pretties. A serial kidnapper may have met his match in the two young ladies who walk the city streets at night, using themselves as bait...

Five Novellas. A compilation of *Stalking You Now, An Apocalypse of Our Own, Faint of Heart, Kutter,* and *Facial.*

Ferocious. The creatures of the forest are dead...and hungry!

Bring Her Back. A tale of revenge and madness.

Sick House. A home invasion from beyond the grave.

Bang Up. A filthy comedic thriller. "You want to pay me to sleep with your wife?" is just the start of the story.

Cold Dead Hands. Ten people are trapped in a freezer during a terrorist attack on a grocery store.

How You Ruined My Life (Young Adult). Sixteen-year-old Rod has a pretty cool life until his cousin Blake moves in and slowly destroys everything he holds dear.

Everything Has Teeth. A third collection of short tales of horror and macabre comedy.

An Apocalypse of Our Own. Can the Friend Zone survive the end of the world?

Stranger Things Have Happened (Young Adult). Teenager Marcus Millian III is determined to be one of the greatest magicians who ever lived. Can he make a live shark disappear from a tank?

Cyclops Road. When newly widowed Evan Portin gives a woman named Harriett a ride out of town, she says she's on a cross-country journey to slay a Cyclops. Is she crazy, or...?

Blister. While on vacation, cartoonist Jason Tray meets the town legend, a hideously disfigured woman who lives in a shed.

The Greatest Zombie Movie Ever (Young Adult). Three best friends with more passion than talent try to make the ultimate zombie epic.

Kumquat. A road trip comedy about TV, hot dogs, death, and obscure fruit.

I Have a Bad Feeling About This (Young Adult). Geeky, non-athletic Henry Lambert is sent to survival camp, which is bad enough *before* the trio of murderous thugs show up.

Pressure. What if your best friend was a killer...and he wanted you to be just like him? Bram Stoker Award nominee for Best Novel.

Dweller. The lifetime story of a boy and his monster. Bram Stoker Award nominee for Best Novel.

A Bad Day For Voodoo. A young adult horror/comedy about why sticking pins in a voodoo doll of your history teacher isn't always the best idea. Bram Stoker Award nominee for Best Young Adult Novel.

Dead Clown Barbecue. A collection of demented stories about severed noses, ventriloquist dummies, giant-sized vampires, sibling stabbings, and lots of other messed-up stuff.

Dead Clown Barbecue Expansion Pack. A few more stories for those who couldn't get enough.

Wolf Hunt. Two thugs for hire. One beautiful woman. And one vicious frickin' werewolf.

Wolf Hunt 2. New wolf. Same George and Lou.

The Sinister Mr. Corpse. The feel-good zombie novel of the year.

Benjamin's Parasite. A rather disgusting action/horror/comedy about why getting infected with a ghastly parasite is unpleasant.

Fangboy. A dark and demented fairy tale for adults.

Facial. Greg has just killed the man he hired to kill one of his wife's many lovers. Greg's brother desperately needs a dead body. It's kind of related to the lion corpse that he found in his basement. This is the normal part of the story.

Kutter. A serial killer finds a Boston terrier, and it might just make him into a better person.

Faint of Heart. To get her kidnapped husband back, Melody has to relive her husband's nightmarish weekend, step-by-step...and survive.

Mandibles. Giant killer ants wreaking havoc in the big city!

Stalking You Now. A twisty-turny thriller soon to be the feature film *Mindy Has To Die.*

Graverobbers Wanted (No Experience Necessary). First in the Andrew Mayhem series.

Single White Psychopath Seeks Same. Second in the Andrew Mayhem series.

Casket For Sale (Only Used Once). Third in the Andrew Mayhem series.

Lost Homicidal Maniac (Answers to "Shirley"). Fourth in the Andrew Mayhem series.

Cemetery Closing (Everything Must Go). Fifth in the Andrew Mayhem series.

Suckers (with JA Konrath). Andrew Mayhem meets Harry McGlade. Which one will prove to be more incompetent?

Gleefully Macabre Tales. A collection of thirty-two demented tales. Bram Stoker Award nominee for Best Collection.

Elrod McBugle on the Loose. A comedy for kids (and adults who were warped as kids).

The Haunted Forest Tour (with Jim Moore). The greatest theme park attraction in the world! Take a completely safe ride through an actual haunted forest! Just hope that your tram doesn't break down, because this forest is PACKED with monsters...

Draculas (with JA Konrath, Blake Crouch, and F. Paul Wilson). An outbreak of feral vampires in a secluded hospital. This one isn't much like *Twilight*.

For information on all of these books, visit Jeff Strand's more-or-less official website at http://www.JeffStrand.com

Subscribe to Jeff Strand's free monthly newsletter (which includes a brand-new original short story in every issue) at http://eepurl.com/bpv5br

And remember:

Readers who leave reviews deserve great big hugs!